To Stephanie,
Best Wishes,
hope you enjoy —
don't think your uncle
crazy after you read,
Love,
Ralph
2014

AND GOD CRIED

And God Cried

The struggle

The eternal struggle between good and evil comes to an end!

Ralph Cole

authorHOUSE®

AuthorHouse™
1663 Liberty Drive
Bloomington, IN 47403
www.authorhouse.com
Phone: 1-800-839-8640

© 2011 by Ralph Cole. All rights reserved.

No part of this book may be reproduced, stored in a retrieval system, or transmitted by any means without the written permission of the author.

First published by AuthorHouse   05/24/2011

ISBN: 978-1-4634-1170-1 (sc)
ISBN: 978-1-4634-1168-8 (dj)
ISBN: 978-1-4634-1169-5 (ebk)

Library of Congress Control Number: 2011908839

Printed in the United States of America

Any people depicted in stock imagery provided by Thinkstock are models, and such images are being used for illustrative purposes only.
Certain stock imagery © Thinkstock.

This book is printed on acid-free paper.

Because of the dynamic nature of the Internet, any web addresses or links contained in this book may have changed since publication and may no longer be valid. The views expressed in this work are solely those of the author and do not necessarily reflect the views of the publisher, and the publisher hereby disclaims any responsibility for them.

Contents

About the author vii
Dedication ix
Works Cited xi
About the book - Prologue xiii

Chapter one - The decision 1
Chapter two - The arrival 8
Chapter three - The first encounter 12
Chapter four - The Decision 27
Chapter five - The arrival of Satan 34
Chapter six - The drive 47
Chapter seven - The couple 50
Chapter eight - Henry Fiddleman 56
Chapter nine - Witnessing a death 69
Chapter ten - Dinner with Sheila 80
Chapter eleven - The dam destruction 84
Chapter twelve - Smiley Rider 96
Chapter thirteen - An encounter in Rhode Island 102
Chapter fourteen - The news spreads 113
Chapter fifteen - Washington, DC 121
Chapter sixteen - The ice man 130
Chapter seventeen - Satan speaks 136
Chapter eighteen - Jesus remembers 143
Chapter nineteen - Signs of trouble 150
Chapter twenty - Jolly 153
Chapter twenty one - What next? 157
Chapter twenty two - Jesus speaks 164
Chapter twenty three - Satan reacts 177
Chapter twenty four - Separate ways 182
Chapter twenty five - Satan spreads fear 186

Chapter twenty six - The Christmas holidays 194
Chapter twenty seven - Pastor John Lincoln 198
Chapter twenty eight - Satan meets the pope 203
Chapter twenty nine - Jesus hears the news 217
Chapter thirty - Jesus attends mass 220
Chapter thirty one - Finding Jesus 227
Chapter thirty two - Talking with Satan 235
Chapter thirty three - Jesus plans 240
Chapter thirty four - The day of reckoning 242
Chapter thirty five - Jesus appears 246
Chapter thirty six - Judgment Day 249
Chapter thirty seven - The cost of redemption 254

About the author

This novel is the initial publication of Ralph Cole.

This is Ralph's first novel and has been a personal goal of his for years. Being an avid reader of mystery, adventure and horror novels (especially those of Stephen King) it has been his personal desire to someday pen a book that would bring enjoyment to others.

Although his main goal in writing this book was to provide the reader's with a suspenseful novel; he also wanted to send a message that we each can play a role in making the world a better place by driving actions that will eliminate the presence of evil in our society.

The eternal struggle between good and evil has radically affected us for centuries. Hopefully the book will, also, serve as a means for us to realize that we have the potential to make things better through our own actions.

He has a Bachelor's degree in Business Management from Johnson and Wales Business College located in Providence, Rhode Island and an Associate degree from Rhode Island Junior College.

He presently resides in Hopkinton, Massachusetts, is happily married, and has two sons (Ralph and Jason) and a granddaughter (Brandi) that he is proud of.

He sends his personal thanks to you for your interest in the story and hope you enjoy it as much as he enjoyed writing it.

Dedication

This book is dedicated to my wife, Donna, who inspired me to write this book. It was her continued initiative to encourage me to place my thoughts on paper and to complete something that I always wanted to do. Without her support this novel would not have been written.

Works Cited

Crucifixion of Jesus Christ—Bible Story Summary
By Mary Fairchild, About.com Guide

Fatalities at Hoover Dam
Bureau of Reclamation: Lower Colorado region
www.usbr.gov/lc/hooverdam/History/essays/fatal.html

Hoover Dam—frequently asked questions and answers
Bureau of Reclamation: Lower Colorado region
www.usbr.gov/lc/hooverdam/faqs/damfaqs.html

Yellowstone National Park
Yellowstone National Park.com
www.yellowstonenationalpark.com/index.html

Hoover Dam
Hoover Dam—Wikipedia, free encyclopedia
http://en.wikipedia.org/wiki/hoover_Dam

Black Death
Black Death—Wikipedia, the free encyclopedia
http://en.wikipedia.org/wiki/Black_Death

About the book - Prologue

The struggle between good and evil has haunted mankind since its very existence. Temptation has created a conflict in man since Eve enticed Adam to bite into the apple in the Garden of Eden. The encounters between Christ and Satan are well documented through the written scriptures and can be traced back centuries.

Throughout the centuries we have experienced horrific events that resulted from the constant struggle between good and evil for the domination of mankind. In each of these cases we have seen tremendous losses to both sides and, yet, we tolerate the co-existence of both forces and suffer the same negative consequences time and time again.

So it came to be that Christ and Satan forged a pact to end this madness with the winner eliminating the other forever! The presence of the loser—either good or evil—would be completely wiped away and mankind, who had so many opportunities to determine their own fate, would incur the consequences.

Their return to earth will lead each in separate directions in using their specific powers to be the victor! Jesus will cross paths with a couple in dire need of restoring their faith in god after a horrific encounter between their son and a mad man; a man who persevered through the devastating events of his childhood; an old man that personally challenges Jesus on the loss of his beloved wife and a minister that comes face to face with death and survives.

Satan's path follows one of total destruction. He chooses to instill enough terror into everyone that they will turn to him in fear of what will happen to them should Jesus lose. Along the way he creates horrific events that will inflict thousands with a disease not seen in hundreds of years; destroys a national treasure; cold bloodedly murders a world leader and utilizes the existing forces of evil to spread the word that he is walking among us.

The Struggle is a roller coaster ride of emotions. At the end there will be only one standing and the world's fate lies in the balance.

The outcome will shock you and will change the future and destiny of mankind forever.

Free preview—a preview of the book to be used on the website to give customers a sample of my work

Nathan gently removed his thumb from the grasp of his son and asked the nurse standing outside the door to have the doctor return to the room as quickly as possible. The doctor arrived within minutes expecting that he would formally pronounce the little boy dead. Instead he found him grasping his mom's finger and breathing easily without the aid of any life support equipment. Nathan told him that Will had opened his eyes for a few short minutes and smiled at them and then dozed back off. Not a word was spoken by the doctor or the nurses who had assembled at the foot of the bed as they could not believe what they were seeing. Every test conducted, every possible medical evaluation performed on the child indicated that it was a lost cause—the boy was basically gone. The only thing keeping him alive was the mechanical devices attached to his body. This was beyond the realm of possibility and was, indeed, an unexplained miracle. The doctor watched the heart monitoring equipment and the steady pulse of the heart beat signal its way across the screen. The blood pressure had climbed to an acceptable level and the child exhibited no signs of distress.

The doctor reached for the boy's wrist to feel the pulse for himself when he noticed the cross lying on the boy's chest. What caught his eye was the fact that it appeared to be slowly changing color before his very eyes as if in rhythm with Will's heart beat. He asked Nathan where he got the cross and Nathan told him that he had met a stranger during their short stay at Yellow stone Park. The man had given him the cross and told him to give it to his son and to never give up his faith regardless of what happened. The doctor picked up the cross and held it in his hand and carefully examined it. It was old, perhaps, hundreds if not thousandths of years. It was in remarkable shape for its age and the thing that stood out was that it still pulsed in color with the breathing of the little boy. The doctor laid it back on to Will's chest and asked Nathan what the man's name was and if he knew how to contact him. There was something special about the cross and the remarkable recovery of the boy and the doctor had to dig deeper to uncover some answers.

Nathan thought for a minute and said the man's name was Jesus. The doctor initially thought that he was kidding but Nathan did not even break a smile as he stared directly into the doctor's eyes. He said that his name was Jesus Nathan repeated as if taking in what was happening to him and his family. He had said he had come a long way and they were the first family that he had talked to in quite some time. Nathan told the doctor how the stranger listened so intently to him and his wife about what happened and the pending difficult decisions that they were faced with. He was a god sent as his wife managed to open up to this stranger and express herself and the difficult time she was having in coping with the potential loss of her son.

Nathan thought of what he just said—a god sent! He was a stranger coming down a deserted trail who his daughter and puppy took an immediate liking to. A man that easily consoled his wife and whose piercing brown eyes appeared to own their own share of misery and despair. A man named Jesus who asked him to keep his faith so that others would also know that there is goodness and happiness for those who believe. Nathan and his wife had no doubts about who they happened across that day in the park. He had brought their son back from death and returned Will to them with a second chance on life. The doctor sat down in the chair next to the bed and simply clasped his hands together and said a silent prayer. He had no doubt that this was indeed a miracle beyond any medical explanation on how or why. He would not think of taking any credit for the boy's recovery but, instead, issued a commitment to himself that his faith has been restored and he would be committed to doing whatever he could to help those in need whether they had the personal assets to cover his expenses. Today he witnessed a miracle and would do everything in his power to assure that the news carries forth from this day.

Chapter one

The decision

Mankind had struggled for centuries with the forces of good and evil pulling at them in an endless tug of war. The same unending conflict would continue for centuries unless there was finally an intervention by the two supreme leaders of these two, powerful, yet so different forces. It was with such an intervention that each decided to return to earth for one final showdown that would decide the fate of man. The eternal struggle for the domination of mankind would be decided in the ultimate challenge between these rivals.

In was obvious that mankind was ill prepared or decisive enough to be able to choose between the two forces. Based on historical events it was insane to think that man could gain some common ground in ending this struggle. The constant daily battles between good and evil were reflective in everything you read in the news accounts on the web, national television and satellite broadcasts. The scales were so evenly balanced that it was obvious that the struggle could continue for another 1,000 years with no clear cut winner. Even with all the scientific improvements and technological advancements in today's society we could not seriously alter the fact that mankind did not possess the ability to rid itself of evil and build a world of harmony for all. So the two arch enemies forged a pact that they would finally exercise their influence and unimaginable powers to finally determine an ultimate winner. That winner was solely dependent upon one critical factor. That key factor was how man would deal with the catastrophe events that will lead them to realize that there could be only one champion to lead them through eternity. That champion would then form and shape the entire planet into both a living hell where mankind will finally understand the consequences of their ways or a place of harmony and tranquility where man can live peacefully forever.

Evil reigned under the ultimate control of Satan. He thoroughly enjoyed the fruits of his labor with his constant bombardment of world events centering on havoc, misery and destruction wherever possible. Jesus repeatedly counter punched by striving to spread peace and harmony while also trying to salvage something good from the terrible acts caused by his rival.

It seemed that with the passing of time that man seemed to relish in the fact that they lived in a world where opposites co-existed in a carefully balanced struggle between good and evil. Throughout history there has always been a presence of the "good guy" and "bad guy" and one could easily point to example upon example of their impact on the development of countries and cultures around the world.

So the two arch enemies met in the heavens. It was difficult for each to be in the presence of the other as they despised everything that each stood for. Jesus, surrounded by his disciplines, patiently waited for the arrival of Satan. His father had tried to reason with him that compromise with his arch enemy was fruitless and Jesus should let each individual be able to determine their own fate through their life on earth. God, also, feared that he would lose his son a second time and the stakes were even set much higher. The loser of this conflict would be gone forever and it frightened God that the ultimate end of this battle could be beyond the wildest dreams of any living thing. Jesus had listened to the soft words of his father and his soul was tormented each day on whether the path he had chosen was the right one. Yet the driving factor was the absolute horrors that he witnessed each day that man was committing with growing unrest and little concern to the consequences. It was this key factor that concerned him that he must do whatever possible to stop this evil.

Jesus prayed with his disciplines and asked for their guidance and support as he prepared for the arrival of Satan. Each loved him deeply and again feared for his safety as they did thousands of years ago. The horrific memories of their inability to stop the crucifixion echoed in their minds and it frightened them beyond words that this time he would be facing evil in its purest form. Over the past months it became more and more obvious at each of their meetings that Jesus was growing more determined to offer the ultimate challenge to Satan. Now the day had arrived as Jesus received confirmation that Satan would indeed meet him and determine if such a pact could be agreed upon. As they waited together they held hands to gain the inner spiritual strength to be in the same presence as Satan. They bowed their heads and silently prayed for the total salvation of mankind and the safety of their leader.

As they prayed the generating light of heaven slowly grew dim and dark, sinister looking, clouds settled above them. There were flashes of lightning and sounds of rolling thunder moving closer and closer to where they waited. Within minutes the skies lit up as if they were a gigantic fireworks display on a 4th of July night. Instantly a band of demons numbering at least three hundred ambled towards the meeting destination. They were all shapes and sizes yet each held the same facial expression of fear and agony based on their years of torment under the domination of Satan. Their faces deformed some missing eyes, lips, noses and even limbs resembled creatures from some horror movie. Some carried wooden rods to help support their deformed bodies but each one of them seemed to make a grunting sound as if each step forward was ripping them apart inside. As they grew closer the sounds coming from their mouths were gaggled and incomprehensible. Finally the disciplines could make sense to the words being repeated over and over again—"Satan is king and he will destroy you and your pathetic Jesus". They seemed hypnotized and in a deep trance guided by the presence of evil that followed the procession as if he as a conquering hero from a recent victory!

As the demons formed a semi circle directly across from Jesus and his disciplines they turned and bowed as Satan moved slowly forward. He had waited until all the demons were in position and then in all of his majestic glory and defiance that he could mustard made his way into the meeting area. He was everything and more of what the disciples had imagined. His skin was a deep, almost blood, red and clustered with scabs that appeared to pulse all over his face. At the top of his head were two horns extending at least eighteen inches from each side. The skin on his arms, legs and chest seemed to be in constant movement as if things were alive and crawling behind the surface and the smirk on his lips showed his contempt to those standing before him. He wore a dark red robe and his image seemed to be simmering in a fog of smoke that placed a ring of shadows around his body. He stood at least six feet six inches tall and was an imposing figure of pure evil.

Jesus had taken in the grand entrance of Satan and was not truly impressed. He knew that he would have not expected anything less from his rival and actually thought it was somewhat comical that he needed to put on such a display for those in attendance. Whether it was trying to strike fear into Jesus' disciples or Jesus himself only Satan knew. It would, however, do little in the upcoming conflict to determine the one left standing when all was said and done.

Satan stood there and for a few brief seconds did not move or say a word, he simply stared directly at Jesus and then, displaying his anger and disgust in meeting his arch enemy after so many years—spit on the ground. Words of disgust spilled from his mouth as he said, "So you religious little bastard want to take me on in a winner take all battle for the total redemption and fate of mankind. I despise just being this close to you as your smell sickens me and makes me want to puke. The only pure enjoyment I could get out of winning would be the opportunities to rip your righteous heart out of your chest and feed it to these happy fellows you see standing in front of me. I will fucking destroy you but then I ask myself why? I like things just as they are since I am gaining more and more support every fucking day on earth. You are a fucking joke".

Jesus remained calm throughout the rampage and would not give Satan the personal satisfaction of showing his disgust and hatred of him at this time. There is a time and place for everything and this was not it. Jesus knew that he had to get Satan to agree to the pact and he also believed that Satan wanted it as much as he did. What just happened was just a show and an attempt by Satan to mask his true feelings. Jesus' goal was to drive an agreement without prolonging the intolerable conditions that mankind lived with each passing day. So Jesus bit his tongue and held back the fury that seemed to grow in his body with each passing moment as he negotiated with his rival on the pact. Satan on the other hand continued to openly torment Jesus throughout the negotiations and relished every moment of it. He defiantly peered at Jesus and said that you win a few and lose a few but the shear excitement of the moment when evil wins is an absolute rush and one that he would surely miss. Yet deep down inside this was the meeting that he had desired for thousandths of years. He wanted to wipe goodness from the face of the earth and then he would be in control of everything and everyone. But Satan could not miss his opportunity to further torment his arch enemy and pushed Jesus to his very limits as they neared a mutual agreement on the terms of the pact. Finally Satan peered at Jesus and told him he would take the challenge and he could not wait for him to lie defeated at his feet. He told him that you will suffer like no other man has ever suffered and he could not wait for that moment when the entire world would see him squirm and beg for mercy.

With that closing comment he told Jesus that he would accept the conditions of the pact. They each would return to earth in body form. There they would battle and the winner would eliminate the other forever and the struggle would cease. Each would use their own creative methods and means to demonstrate to the world that it was time to make a choice. With the agreement signed the heavens thundered and lightning flashed across the skies as Satan returned to the depths of hell. Jesus was satisfied with the outcome and pleased with his restraint in dealing with the outrageous insanity of Satan. He would demonstrate in his actions rather than words to Satan that he is a force to be reckoned with. He had faith in man that they would join hands and follow the path of righteousness to rid evil forever. If he was wrong he knew that he would be gone forever and mankind would be suffering ungodly consequences under the rule of Satan for eternity.

Choices—man had so many choices. They seem so easy when you think back in time and review what should have been done to prevent them. But mankind has always demonstrated an inability to act quickly and in unity against pending evil. Instead they allow it to grow until it blossoms into an uncontrollable situation that will inflict heart ache and despair to those involved.

Think back with me and look at the consequences that evolved when entire nations lead by radical fanatics caused mass chaos and the deaths of millions. Germany devastated after World War I continued to pick up the pieces throughout the following years by re-building their nation. The devastation caused by that war created a situation in Germany that led to another war twenty some odd years later. Through the constant struggles to re-build their nation they created a blame culture that persecuted the Jews for all the problems that existed in their country.

Lead by a psycho path they followed like a bunch of blood thirsty zombies and murdered and butchered millions of innocent people to satisfy their perversion. A dark society began that thrived to create a super race, a master race that would lead to world domination. It was fanatically justified in all their minds and implemented with precision in the persecution of so many people. Regardless of the consequences the masses condoned all the pain and suffering being inflicted all around them yet did nothing to stop it. They just decided to look away as millions lost their lives. This is evil at its purest form yet it was allowed to grow and flourish like a delicate flower that you nurture every day. The same situation developed in Japan when they decided to bomb Pearl Harbor on a sleepy Sunday morning in a sneak attack like nothing else ever recorded in world history. The attack dragged the United States into a world war by murdering hundreds of innocent people on that faithful day. As the war progressed, thousands more would be butchered and tortured by the Japanese to justify their superiority over other races. Rather than treat others as equals they raped, murdered, tortured and brutalized them at every opportunity. Once evil sinks its fangs into something it is like being in the grasp of a great white shark that will rip you to pieces. The sad part is that they enjoyed it. No mercy, no regrets, no pity! Only the desire to satisfy their own craving for inflicting pain and suffering on all those they come in conflict with.

Yet for every evil deed that is goodness. For each of the concentration camps that were opened there were eventually relief centers that enabled the victims to try and recover from their suffering. Cities were rebuilt and homeless children were cared for. For every soldier battling for evil there was one fighting for good and to make the world a better place. There have been religious leaders who have crusaded for the betterment of man.

Individuals as Billy Graham, a gospel preacher, who touched the hearts of millions through his words and devotion to god is just one example.

So over the centuries Jesus and Satan waited for that one opportunity to take full control. And they waited. And they waited until each one knew deep down inside that the day for mankind to choose one over the other would never come to pass. It would need their intervention to come up with a resolution. Their patience had run out and they would personally take over the course of human history or end it themselves. It would be a power struggle that has never been experienced in the annuals of history; yet it was one that was necessary to end the nonsense of what man failed to accomplish without this intervention. So the conflict begins!

Chapter two

The arrival

Jesus was the first to make his presence known. He descended from the heavens on that sun lit June Sunday morning. It was invigorating to take a deep breath of fresh air after so many years away. He had walked this earth so many years ago and it initially seemed so awkward to him to return. He had decided to arrive in a fairly isolated location that allowed him time to gather his thoughts and determine exactly how to proceed with his plan. One thing was crystal clear—he would do everything in his power to dramatically change the world forever or he would die a second time for mankind. Only this time Jesus would be gone forever in person, spirit, mind and soul—that would be the devastating consequences if he lost.

As Jesus stood there he realized how much he missed earth and the beauty of all things that were created. He shared in his father's joy of the beauty of life that was bestrode upon man and the unhappiness that it was gradually being destroyed through the selfishness and greed of those who knew better. In his limited time on earth he had relished the travels with those he loved and who had tried to protect him. Now things were very different from the sights and sounds of long ago. There will be tremendous changes that he would see with his very eyes that would surely shock and surprise him in comparison to how things were so many years ago.

Jesus had decided to start his journey in the United States which seemed to be the country in the most turmoil in the world today. Other countries were having difficulty but it paled in comparison to what was happening in the great nation that was barely three hundred years old. Jesus had watched the events transpire over the years and he was not thrilled with the results. He had truly hoped and prayed that with the technological advances implemented over the years society would become more appreciative and supportive to their fellow man but it never occurred. Instead it has lead to a further separation of the classes in society by providing those with wealth the ability to further expand their riches. It allowed huge companies to utilize their power and move their operations to low cost countries thus creating a further separation of rich and poor with thousands of jobs loss in such transitions. With the separate of wealth grew a discontent in the masses resulting in hard working people losing everything that they worked for and also created an opportunity for evil to flourish. Crime has increased and people started to fear and despise others. Those who were supposed to be role models such as religious figures, politicians, presidents, professional sports stars and celebrities were caught in despicable acts of violence, rape, bribery, adultery and cruelty. He was saddened with what he has seen and was determined to put an end to it or he would die again trying. Only this time he would not return.

Jesus had decided to arrive in one of America's most beautiful locations to start his journey. He was standing in a national park in the mid west which was an inspirational experience for those who have managed to see it, better known as Yellowstone National Park it was a thing of beauty.

It was the World's first national park and consisted of over 2 million acres—larger than the states of Rhode Island and Delaware combined. With thousands of miles of trails, 322 species of birds, 16 species of fish, 1,100 native plants and 7 species of bison, moose, elk and pronghorn it was as majestic place in the world to begin a voyage.

As he strolled slowly down the path he breathed in the clean, fresh air and was thankful to be alive again. He noticed the beauty of the trees as the birds flew gently from branch to branch and he listened to the softness of their songs. As he reached the top of the hill there were the bison and elks grazing in the open fields. He thought back hundreds of years on how the Indians must have felt as they blazed these very trails. He witnessed the majestic flight of the bald eagle as it soared overhead in search of unsuspecting prey below. As he stood there he thought to himself how could man possibly not understand and appreciate what they have around them? Beyond the beauty of the country was the fact that man also has family and friends that care and love each other deeply. Each person has the ability to grow and flourish through child hood to adult hood by gaining an educational base unlike anything in history and yet for many this is not good enough. Jesus, himself, had a very difficult time understanding these things and became disillusioned that they may never truly get it.

He had a plan, a simple plan, but one that was going to be followed come hell or high water. It was not a play on words because he knew that hell would indeed play a role in the eventual outcome of the events. Jesus truly believed that man was beginning to lose faith and that this would be the last attempt to give it back. If he failed than man would be at the mercy of the other and he would have failed. Everything was at stake and there was no turning back. It was soon to be a chess game involving two foes that despised one another. His foe would stop at nothing to come out on top and the very thought of what he would do to win actually frightened Jesus. Man had experienced all types of hardships and horror over the centuries but it would jump to a much higher level than anything that they have ever seen in this struggle. Jesus was saddened with just the thought of the pending misery that will be inflicted until a final winner is left standing.

As Jesus reached the edge of a lake he looked down to see his reflection in the cool, clear, water. He was pleasantly surprised at what he saw. Gone was the flowing robe and sandals that he was so used to wearing. They were replaced with a pair of blue jeans and a short sleeve shirt. Beneath his clothes was a pair of white boxer shorts and a v neck tee shirt while on his feet were a pair of white cotton socks and a pair of canvas hiking boots. It was then he noticed his face's reflection in the water and studied it carefully. The long flowing brown hair was cut back short over his ears and neatly combed. He had decided to shave the beard and replaced it with a small brown mustache over the top lip. He still possessed those glaring dark brown eyes that could still peer through the very soul of anyone that he encountered and quickly uncover any lie and mistruth so easily. In his back pocket was a leather wallet. This was certainty something new and different for him. Jesus opened it and checked the contents—a driver's license with the name of Jesus Christ and a photo. At first he thought it was truly ridiculous to even think of carrying his true name on the identification card. Yet he knew that this was one key element of his return to earth that he would not change. He realized that those seeing it may laugh at ridicule him, as some did thousands of years ago, but it was who he truly is. And for that he has to answer to no man. Also inside the wallet were four twenty dollar bills, six fives, seven tens, and two one hundred dollar bills; and an American Express credit card. He closed the wallet and returned it to his back pocket and proceeded to check his other pockets. There he located a set of car keys that he thought would be very interesting since he had never drove a motorized vehicle before and some loose change. As he replaced the items into his pocket a small smile came to his face when he realized that he would, hopefully, fit right in with others. On his back was a small brown canvas back pack that would help him further blend in with the sight seers. On the side of it was a bottle of spring water. Inside was the normal items packed for short walks in the country to include some energy bars, paper tissues, small cans of preserved fruit, eating utensils, and a compass and walking map.

Jesus noticed a hardened dirt path that appeared to gradually turn into an asphalt walking or bike path just ahead. He knew that if followed it that it would eventually reach a more traveled area where he would mingle with others who were visiting the national park. He strolled down the path walking like any other tourist. It was critical not to stand out from others if he wanted to implement the initial stages of his plan.

As he walked it was difficult to imagine that anyone running into him would ever believe that he was the spiritual leader of the Christian religion. Yet he knew that he would need to eventually demonstrate his presence and alert the world that he was on their side once again. This time, however, everything was at stake and each and every person needed to fully understand their role and importance in the coming events.

Chapter three

The first encounter

Approximately twenty minutes later Jesus noticed that the trail was leading to a large, asphalt paved, parking area with a combination of cars, trucks, SUV's and campers. He also noticed an array of picnic tables and fire places set beneath some large pine trees. Just as he reached the clearing he felt something hit his lower right leg and heard a small voice saying oops, sorry mister. Jesus looked down and sitting there at his feet was a young girl looking up with him and a small puppy licking the side of her face. Apparently he had fetched a small yellow tennis ball that he held in his mouth and the little girl was chasing him. Paying more attention to her small friend than her surroundings she did not see Jesus step out of the clearing and ran directly into his leg. The puppy looked up at Jesus and dropped the ball from his mouth, lowered its front body to the ground while keeping the rear portion in the air with the tail wagging a mile a minute. As the puppy peered up at him it barked for attention. The little girl had been startled by the obstacle that was in her way and looked up to say that she was sorry.

Jesus bent down and rubbed the head of the puppy and scratched it behind the ears. The puppy flopped on its back as if telling Jesus not to stop as he wanted his belly scratched too. Jesus smiled and did just that as the little girl laughed at the puppy's antics and the man's willingness to do exactly what the puppy wanted. The little girl said her name was Autumn and she was six years old. She had the bluest of blue eyes and her light brown hair was separated into two pony tails with rubber bands that flopped as she moved about. She held out her small hand and asked him to tell her who he was. He said that his name was Jesus and was very glad to meet her.

As he stood there he realized that he was being carefully watched by the little girl's parents. They were not overly concerned at this point as they were within fifteen feet from where he was standing and all his actions were those of a decent young man who was just accidentally run into by their daughter. Yet as they watched Jesus sensed fear radiating from them with his every move. It seemed like they felt as if he was going to simply disappear with their daughter in front of their very eyes. He realized that parents are very protective of their children but the father appeared ready to spring forward like a deer into the woods with any sign of trouble. His attention was drawn away again by the little girl. She had paused for a minute before saying that he had the same name as God's son who she is learning about at church each Sunday. She told him it was a nice name. Jesus smiled and thanked her for the kind words and said that his father thought it was a nice name as well and he was very pleased that he chose it. Jesus was extremely pleased that his first encounter was with individuals who had faith in god. It was a good sign to him. As he knelt there the puppy jumped to his feet and licked the back of his hand and then stopped and looked up at him again. The puppy then gently rubbed his face against his hand and sat down and gave him his paw. The little girl giggled at the puppy's antics and said that was the first time that he ever did that. Her parents were trying to teach him to sit and give them his paw but without much luck. She said, "Wait until daddy hears about what Boozer did, he will be very jealous".

Autumn's father did not take his eyes off of his daughter and the stranger. His hands were actually starting to shake uncontrollably as his thoughts drifted to what happened to Will. He actually began to slowly inch forward anticipating the worse. History would not repeat it—not on his watch! It was at that moment that he saw Boozer give the stranger his paw and that was enough for him to relax a little while moving forward in the direction of the pair. As he approached them he reached out his hand and introduced himself, "Hi, I am Nathan Bishop. See that you had the opportunity to meet two members of my family, they are two bundles of joy, aren't they?"

Jesus stood up and shook his hand and told him that he couldn't have run into two finer individuals. Then using his first name only, he introduced himself as Jesus and it was nice to meet him also.

For some reason the mention of his name seemed to relax Nathan and caused that tension building up in his body to gradually ease down. Nathan told him that he could not believe that the puppy just sat down and offered his paw to him out of the blue like that. He said that was a sign of a good man when an animal takes a liking to you that quickly. He told Jesus that his wife was just putting some food on the grill and he would be pleased if he would join them if he could. Jesus said that it sounded great and could never turn down some free food. Nathan laughed, lifted Autumn into his arms and turned to walk back to where his wife was preparing lunch. The puppy was hopping up and down against Jesus" right leg and he took that as a sign that Boozer wanted to be picked up. Jesus reached down and lifted the puppy to his chest while cradling him in his right arm. The puppy nestled there, content with his new friend as Jesus followed Nathan to his camp area.

Jesus was introduced to Nathan's wife April. As he reached out his hand to say hello he sensed the same fear exhibited initially by Nathan. She was a lovely woman in her late twenties. She, also, had her blonde hair tied in a pony tail with a rubber band. She was wearing blue jeans, plaid blouse and brown walking sneakers. Autumn looked so much like her that you could have picked her out as her mother from a crowd of five hundred women. She was extremely quiet and simply said it was nice to meet you and immediately dropped any further conversation.

Nathan broke the ice by telling Jesus that they were married for eight years and was taking a few days away to help them with a personal matter. As he spoke it was obvious that the personal issue was serious enough for his voice to start to quaver as he tried to maintain his composure. As he spoke his wife stepped further back as if not wanting to hear anything further on the subject. As much as Nathan tried to put a front that the "time away" would help them with their problem it was apparent that it was causing more anguish for the couple.

The Struggle by R. Cole

Jesus asked if they had any other children and the question was met with silence. He had touched on the very subject that they were having difficulty dealing with and Jesus quickly realized that from Nathan's reaction.

Nathan stared at Jesus for a minute as if contemplating whether to share the information about his son, Will, with him. Yet as he stared at this stranger he realized that talking to someone, beyond his family, may help him to get things off his chest as he felt like a volcano ready to explode. Nathan said that they also have a son, Will, who is Autumn's twin brother but he is in a coma at the local hospital since early January. He and his wife had sat by his bed taking turns, day and night, to assure that someone was with him at all times. Yet for months that has not been a flitter of hope in any sign of improvement in his condition. They, admittedly, were getting run down both emotionally and physically and the doctor advised them to get away for a few days with Autumn. They needed to regain a little sense of normalcy in their lives and to determine what was best for Will in his deteriorating condition.

The doctors' recommendation, based on Will's brain activity steadily declining was to remove the life support system and let fate take its course. In their professional medical opinions there was no possibility that he would come out of the coma and that death is inevitable.

So Nathan and April decided to use the time away from their son to make a decision. Nathan stopped as if in deep thought and tears welled in his eyes. He said initially he had faith that his son would recover—somehow or someway. Yet the endless days and nights with no sign of any improvement has made them realize that they needed to consider other alternatives to release him from his suffering. Nathan said that it was terrible to see the growing bed sores on his body, the feed tubes and needle marks turning his arms black and blue, the obvious soreness in his throat from the constant pressure of the breathing tube forcing air down his throat and into his nostrils. It was becoming an intolerable situation for them to observe.

He said that his son, Will, was a good boy and always full of love and innocence like his sister. One day in early January they had been shopping at a Wal Mart in town for some winter clothes for the kids and something terrible happened. Will and her sister were taking turns hiding between the clothes racks and playing hide and seek. The store was not very busy with other customers so they let them play their silly games as Nathan and his wife picked out some winter jackets for the kids. He listened intently to their playful shout outs as where they were hiding between the clothes racks. Everything seemed normal until Nathan heard Autumn constantly asking her brother where he was hiding. No response. She called his name again and again no response. It was then that Nathan knew something was wrong. He immediately turned his attention to the location where his daughter was standing and quickly ran over to her. He grabbed her hand tightly and yelled out his son's name and told him to come to him immediately. There was nothing but silence. He panicked. He lifted Autumn off the floor and rushed to the front of the store as April quickly followed. He told the store manager that his son was missing and could he make sure that no one leaves the store carrying a little boy. Nathan asked him to call the police because his son would always come immediately when he called for him. He rushed over to the clerks at the checkout counter and asked if they saw anyone leaving with a little boy in blue jeans, white tee shirt with sponge bob on the front and a baseball cap. The first two cashiers said no but the third one a young girl said that a man left a few minutes ago with a boy that fit that description. She said that she thought something was wrong because the little boy was crying and didn't want to go with him. She thought it may have been that he was just tired or didn't get what he wanted in the store so she brushed it aside. She looked at Nathan and said that she was so sorry and that she should have known better.

Nathan ran outside and scanned the parking lot for any sight of Will. He looked for any signs of a vehicle racing from the parking lot or someone rushing to their car. Nothing—it was like his son had just vanished. The police arrived moments later and quickly took as much information as possible from Nathan and his wife to get an Amber Alert out in the surrounding community. Even with all these quick actions, Will had simply disappeared with a stranger without a trace of him anywhere. The surveillance cameras were of little help in getting a good identification of the kidnapper. The man had the ball cap pulled low over his head and wore sun glasses to shield his eyes. His coat collar was also in an upward position against the side of his neck helping to cover the lower portion of his face. The interrogation of the clerk was not much help either. She was overcome with grief and an emotional wreck. She was only able to give a brief description of the man. She had been concentrating more on the crying little boy than she was in the person who was carrying him. The man was described as approximately six feet tall, unshaven, stringy black hair, dark eyes wearing blue jeans, boots, a tan jacket, brown gloves, baseball cap and sun glasses. The description could have fit hundreds of others in this rural community. A sketch of the man and a photo of Will were released to the press within two hours of the incident. Nathan and April were devastated that within a few short minutes that their lives would be changed forever. April was an emotional wreck and she also needed to be sedated because she couldn't stop crying. Her body continued to shake and tremble uncontrollably knowing that someone evil had her son.

The waiting turned from minutes to hours with no news coming forward on the whereabouts of their son. It made the nightly news and photos of the boy were spread throughout the county. Helped by the police the Bishops provided a contact number for any information and also a reward from the limited money they had in a small savings account. Each time the phone rang their spirits were lifted only to be let down with no real leads on Will's whereabouts.

Finally they received the call. It was the call that would change their lives forever. As normal procedure the police had the phone tapped to get any possible clues to the location of the caller that would help them recover Will from the hands of this mad man. As soon as Nathan picked up the phone he realized that something was terribly wrong and his son was in the grasp of a maniac. The man did not seem frightened or intimidated in any way as he spoke slowly and carefully so Nathan could recall every word that he spoke. It was like he was intentionally trying to drill his words into Nathan's head so that he would never forget what he was about to say. He said listen carefully because I am not going to repeat a single word. I truly enjoyed my little party with your son it was a frigging blast! It just didn't last long enough for me to get my full enjoyment out of it but what can you expect with a six year old. Anyway it was fun while it lasted. You can have what is left of the little bastard by going to the intersection of state highway 102 and route 73 just outside of town. Behind the abandoned house there is an old barn that is pretty well hidden from the road. He will be there waiting for you just like I left him. If you are lucky he may still be breathing when you get there but you better hurry. I'm sure that the cops listening in will be of some use in finding the place but not much luck in finding me. I truly enjoyed his company—by the way I wasn't crazy over that stupid tee shirt he wore. Give my regards to your loving wife and little girl. I would have loved to grab her but she was not in striking distance to me so I had to settle for him. I still had a ball for myself, I am sure you will get my drift when you see him. Anyway good luck and with that the lunatic hung up the phone. The call originated at a phone booth outside of town but the suspect was long gone by the time the police arrived. Although they immediately set up road blocks leading in and out of the identified area the man was gone as if he just disappeared. The police conducted a house to house search and gathered names of all those who worked in the general area but could not come up with a prime suspect in the boy's kidnapping. The wacko was thorough and left no fingerprints, notes or other clues that would make the cop's job easy in identifying him.

As the police expanded their search to surrounding states they immediately discovered that Will has another victim in a pattern with the kidnapping of other small children. His tactics, targeting small children, waiting for an opportunity to snatch them within minutes of the parent's attention being drawn elsewhere, and the follow up phone call intimidating and terrorizing the parents all matched similar cases in six other states. He had been carrying out his vicious attacks for nearly three years and it was apparent that he would continue until he was apprehended or killed. The lunatic had already attacked six other children over that span and each attack grew more vicious. His last victim was sodomized repeatedly and beaten severely. The little girl was alive but it took several weeks for her to come out of a coma.

Eventually they finally managed to stop him before he inflicted his perverted fantasies on another child in Nashville, Tennessee. He had waited for an opportunity to grab a six year old boy who had wandered too far from his parents during a party at Dave and Buster's. The child's attention was diverted by the man waving a large bag of M&M candy that he held in his hand. With his other hand he motioned the boy forward by moving his fingers back and forth and smiling broadly at the child. The boy looked up at his parents but their attention was drawn to a couple that was violently arguing in front of one of the electronic game systems. The little boy ran over to him and in one swift move, he handed the child the bag of candy, placed him against his chest with the boy's face resting on his shoulder and exited the building. He quickly mingled with the crowd and disappeared through the exit doors to his car.

The horror of the mother when she reached down for her son's hand and realized that he was not standing there send shivers down her spine. She turned to her husband and asked where Tyler was and he said I thought he was standing next to you. They immediately started calling his name and searching through the crowd to find him. Initially they thought his attention was drawn to one of the many games flashing very colors and making all those fun sounds that kids like. But within minutes they knew that they were wrong and the wife started screaming at the top of her lungs to call the police that her son was kidnapped.

Outside in the parking lot everything happened so quickly that Tyler did not start crying and asking for his mommy and daddy until he was placed into the back seat of the car. The child was concentrating on that bag of multi-colored candy he held in his small hand. But it was that sudden outburst of crying that drew the attention of a witness that saw the boy struggling with a man who was putting him into a 1993 Buick. The witness managed to get his plate number and immediately called 911 in an attempt to get help quickly. An Amber alert was sent out across the county for anyone seeing a blue and white four door Buick Sky Hawk with Colorado plates with a dented right hand fender. He had already done his usual homework spending the week casing abandoned and isolated buildings. He found one, an abandoned warehouse that was used to store tobacco but had been vacant for six years now. He had watched that location for four straight days without noticing one sign of any activity. It was completely deserted without any other signs of casual travelers such as bikers or joggers. It was perfect for him to give the little boy a taste of how cruel life could be at times. He was already getting hard just thinking about it.

The good news was that he was spotted turning off the expressway as he headed down old route 3 into the farming community of Nashville. It was unfortunate for both him and the police that he was spotted by two men bend on vigilante justice. Call them rednecks or citizens fed up with the justice system and the slap on the hand provided to hardened criminals. Call them anything you want but once they smashed into the back of his old car sending it swerving off the road and into a drainage ditch; you can call the kidnapper a dead man.

Before he could react to the loss of control of his car and flee the vehicle they were on top of him. They dragged him through the open window and punched him in the face immediately breaking his nose and sending blood spurting everywhere. As he fell to the ground the second man kicked him in the balls so hard that he actually felt as if he sent them deep inside of the wacko's body as he screamed in pain. As he laid there on the ground one of the men checked on the little boy in the car. The boy was lying on the back floor of the car duct taped hand and foot but otherwise unharmed. As one of the men stood over the kidnapper the other freed the child and told the boy that everything would be all right and just to stay there for a few minutes while they got help and called his mom and dad. Tyler reached out and hugged the man and said please hurry my mom and dad must be very worried about where I am. The man then returned to where his friend was standing and told the predator to stand up. To help him one grabbed his hair and pulled him from the ground while the other grabbed him by the crouch as he let out another low moan of pain. The driver of the pickup returned to his vehicle while his friend told the culprit to run and get away or they were going to blow his brains out of his demented head. Panicked with fear he stumbled to his feet and tried to regain some balance to his shaky legs. As he stumbled down the dirt road that lead to another country road to who knows where he heard the truck's engine reeve with the gravel spitting out from beneath the rubber tires. As he turned to look he had just enough time to see the front of the truck spinning in his direction. As he tried to gather his composure and roll into the ditch running along side of the road it was too late. The massive tires of the truck crushed his body and rolled to a stop about ten feet in front of him. The physical damage was obvious as his skull was crushed from the weight of the truck and he was dead. As the two men high fived each other on ridding the world of a sexual predator they went over their story for the cops about how he tried to run away after they pushed his car off the road and they had no choice but to run him over with the truck. They didn't mean to kill him but he dodged the wrong direction at the last moment causing his death.

With that they called 911 and asked for police assistance and a rescue right away. They said that they were passed by a speeding car fitting the description of the predator on the Amber Alert and a chase pursued. They told the 911 operator that the little boy was safe and the suspect in dire straits lying alongside a road. So ended the terrorism that had been inflicted on so many innocent children and their parents but it did not help poor Will who a few years earlier had crossed paths with the lunatic.

When the police arrived at the old barn where Nathan's son was reported to be, they immediately blocked off every access road and combed the area for anyone walking, riding bikes, or driving and questioned them. The barn doors were old and falling off their hinges and it was obvious that they could not have been used as the entry point. They were heavy and blocked with some huge rocks that someone had placed in front of them to keep them in an upright position. The windows were boarded up with planks of knotty pine and there were large holes in the roof that allowed the birds, wind and rain to come and go as they pleased. At the rear of the barn the police found a pine board leaning against the rotting wall and moved it. There they found a hole large enough for a man to easily crawl through and get inside. When the board was removed one of the state troopers shined his flashlight inside to get a glimpse inside and was immediately startled by a large rat that was settling into the stack of rotting hay that the rat called home. For that split second the officer lost his balance and fell backwards on his ass on the ground. The other officers drew their weapons and peered into the hole. The trooper was totally embarrassed by the mishap as one of his buddies whacked him on the side of his head knocking his smoky the bear hat off. At that point another officer entered the barn and shined a flashlight back and forth but there were no immediate signs of Will. As more officers entered and panned out in search of the boy the barn began to illuminate with the beams of light. It was eely inside as the dark shadows and the abandoned array of old farm utensils cluttered the walls and floor making it difficult to maneuver. The misty smell of rotting hay mingled with the odor of rodent waste filled the air. There was no sign of the little boy on the lower level of the barn and the police officers were concerned that they were sent on a wild goose chase. It was then that they noticed an old wooden ladder leading up to the loft area. It was obvious that it had been recently used as there were foot prints in the mud at the ladder's base and the hay was scattered in every direction as if someone had managed to get up there and shuffle around. With gun drawn one of the officers slowly climbed the ladder and reached the top. As he shined the flashlight into the far corner he noticed something lying on a pile of decaying hay. As the trooper stood up and walked slowly to the object he knew it was the missing boy as the figure took shape. He was overtaken with shock on what he saw as he grew closer. As the beam of the flashlight shined on the boy's body it showed that he was naked and covered with bruises from head to foot. Some of the bruises may have been caused by being deliberately dragged along the ground as there were scrape marks running down the side of his body. He was lying on his back and it appeared that he had cigarette burns on his chest but his face, his face was severely beaten and almost unrecognizable. At first the officer thought he was dead but as he reached out his hand the felt an ever so slight pulse. It was then that he shouted out to get a medic up here right away. Get a damn medic up here, oh god, you poor thing, how could anyone do this to you and live with themselves he said to Will. Get me a god damn medic he repeated as his hand lightly brushed against the boy's face to let him know that someone was there with him.

It was an absolute brutal attack on an innocent child and even veteran officers were emotionally affected with the condition of the child as they lowered the stretcher from the loft. He was just barely breathing but alive as they rushed him to the hospital.

At the hospital the trauma team did all they could to ease Will's suffering and determine if medical science could somehow bring the little boy back to any sort of normalcy in his life. Through the following days the doctors carefully monitored Will's vital signs and ran batteries of tests on his brain to determine the severity of the beatings that the boy absorbed. In the end the doctors knew that the prognosis was not good. The overall results from the MRI's and brain scans conducted on his frail body indicated that he had severe brain damage and any possible normal recovery is impossible. The doctors advised the Bishops of their findings and basically told them that the only thing keeping their son alive at this time was the life support equipment attached to his body. Should it be removed he would surely die. So there Nathan's son lay each day as a decision rested solely on the shoulders of Nathan and April on the fate of their son.

Nathan said that they were a god fearing family and deeply devoted to living life the way that their parents taught them. They were both of the Mormon faith and had deep roots with the church and the foundation that life is about caring and sharing with others. He said that his son's death would seriously challenge his faith and whether there is truly a god who cares about the people. Jesus silently listened intently as Nathan used him as a vehicle to attempt to get what was bothering him off his chest.

When Nathan was done expressing his most personal feelings and thoughts about his family crisis he thanked Jesus for listening to him. He said that it actually helped to relieve some of the tremendous pressure by discussing crisis and difficult decision that they must make. Nathan said that he prays to god every night asking for his son to come back to them but there has been no change or sign of improvement. He said that removing the life support system on his son will seriously affect both he and his wife for years yet it appears to be the right thing to do based on his son's condition and prolonging the situation would be useless.

Jesus knew that this was not a chance meeting with the couple. It was an event that would further test the forces of good and evil and he was ready for it. He carefully studied Nathan and his wife and reached out to them with empathy. He told them never to give up hope. He sat down beside Nathan's wife and placed his hand gently on her shoulder and felt the sadness that engulfed her body. He felt the deep sorrow that was troubling her in having to join in the decision of possibly ending her little boy's life.

Jesus was very hesitant in his actions and words. He did not want to appear to be a religious fanatic nor someone that they would view as a weirdo who happened to cross their path that day. He knew that the world as it existed today was full of a great deal of mistrust and weariness based on the elements of fear and he did not want to add any fuel to that already burning fire.

Jesus told them that he felt their pain and said words cannot express his empathy for them during this difficult period in their lives. He also has shared in difficult family decisions that pressed the very limitations of what a person can endure. Yet he realized that for every trial and tribulation we also become better people because we open our hearts and souls to share our experiences with others in helping them. He stressed the importance of keeping one's faith throughout the most difficult times. It is these times that truly test one's ability to get through the difficult times. With that faith and the will power to carry forth you can become a stronger person and can make things happen that you did not think possible.

They listened intently to him as he spoke. This young man seemed blessed with an ability to listen and also console others. Nathan had wanted to ask him whether he was a minister or preacher but refrained from any questions at this point. It really did not matter as he possessed a natural ability to be a healer in helping us move forward. There was something soothing in his spoken words and the manner that he spoke that gave them a few moments of peacefulness that they had not felt in weeks. When he was done Autumn looked up at Jesus and asked him to help bring her brother back to them. She said that her mommy and daddy are so sad since he was hurt and it made her unhappy to see them like that. She had seen her brother only once after he got hurt and she tried as hard as she could to wake him from his sleep. She talked to him, whispered funny things in his ear and actually told him his favorite story about the little train that could. With tears welling in her eyes she told Jesus that he never woke up and she wondered if he had gone to sleep forever.

Nathan reached down and picked up his little girl hugged her and told her that her brother was not dead. He told her that if her brother did not wake up than he always will be with them in their thoughts and dreams.

Jesus knew that the conversations had lead to everyone losing their appetite and he did not want them to dwell further on the very subject that they tried to get away from for a few days. It was time for him to leave and he told them that he had to get moving along. He reached down and patted Autumn gently on the head and rubbed the ear of the puppy as it licked his hand. Jesus reached inside of his shirt and pulled out an old metal cross that he had hanging around his neck. He handed it to Nathan and told him to place it around his son's neck when he returned to the hospital. Jesus told him that he had worn it for years as a keepsake from his mother and it had provided him with the comfort and security of knowing that everything would be all right. At first Nathan said that he couldn't take something so personal from him but Jesus closed Nathan's hand around the cross and told him to please take it to his son. He told him to always keep the faith and remember the chance meeting that they had that day.

Jesus turned and slowly walked away. As he looked back he saw the couple standing together holding hands while looking in his direction. When they saw him turn his head towards them they each waved and little Autumn blew him a wish. He smiled and waved back. This was his first opportunity to demonstrate to others that he had returned and he so desperately wanted to end the misery that was imposed on the family who he had just met. Evil had visited them and had inflicted its share of pain and suffering that would last them a lifetime. He was going to change that without any doubt in his mind and with that a warning shot that he was going to fight with every ounce in his body to bring harmony back into this world.

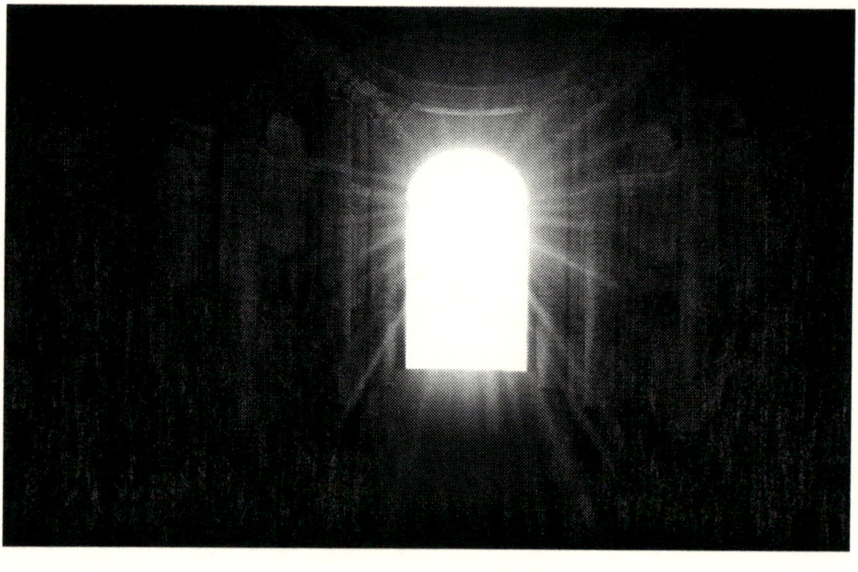

Chapter four

The Decision

The following day, the day that Nathan and April dreaded so much, they returned to the hospital and their son's condition had not changed. The doctor asked if they had made a decision yet and they told him that they needed a few minutes alone with their son. The doctor left the room and quietly closed the door leaving them as they sat by the side of the bed with their little boy. Each of them reached out and grabbed one of his little hands and prayed. They prayed that they would make the right decision for him and them as well. As Nathan looked at his son's face he remembered the first time when he first held him in his arms and kissed him. He thought about the many times that they played together and how Will loved being bounced on his knee until he got the hiccups from laughing so much. He was so innocent and Nathan only wondered how some mad man could have taken pleasure in doing those awful things to him.

Nathan already knew the right decision and studied his wife who was sitting across from him. Her head was down in prayer and she did not see him watching her intently as she gently rubbed her son's hand and patted the side of his face. Just when he was going to say something to her he remembered the cross in his pocket that was given to him by that stranger and he reached into his pocket and pulled it out. He carefully studied it and noticed it appeared to be extremely old and worn. Prior to placing it upon his son's neck he kissed it and made the sign of the cross.

His wife watched him gently lay the cross against Will's chest and she herself reached out and touched it. What she noticed was that the cross was very warm for being a piece of metal just removed from Nathan's coat pocket. Nathan waited for her to sit back down and then kissed her cheek and told her it was time. He asked her whether she had any last minute reservations before talking to the doctor. She said that the conversation that they had with the stranger helped her tremendously as it allowed her to get things off her chest. She realized that they needed to place their faith in god and themselves rather than some breathing apparatus that was being used to keep her son alive. Nathan hugged her and opened the door and asked the nurse to find the doctor and tell him that they had made their decision.

The doctor arrived a few minutes later and they asked him to remove all the life support equipment from their son. They would place his fate in god and let it ride its course. The doctor told them that he believed that they were making the right decision and told them that he knew how difficult it was. He said no matter what happens always remember the good times and you have a wonderful little girl that will surely help you keep Will's spirit alive and well for years to come. With that he turned to the medical team to have everything removed from Will's body. When they were completed Nathan and April managed to see their son lying peacefully on the bed. It was obvious that Will was in a deep coma as there was not a single sign of life in his frail body throughout the process. The heart monitoring equipment was already showing a much smaller and more pronounced erratic beat of his heart. With that the medical team left the room to allow the Bishop's the final minutes alone with their dying boy.

When all the apparatus was removed from Will Nathan realized that it was the first time in month's that he saw his face without some sort of plastic tube hanging from his nose or mouth. Nathan believed that within a few short minutes his son would be released from his torment and assumes his place in heaven along side of his grandparents who would take care of him until they meet again. As they sat there in silence they simply watched their son initially grasp for each breathe that he took. Nathan tried to keep his composure as best he could for his wife's sake but his chest began to take deep breaths as if trying to help his son breathe. He hoped that she

The Struggle by R. Cole

would not look over at him as his face was wet with the tears that were streaming down his cheeks and he could only imagine what his wife was going through at that moment.

As he watched his son he noticed a change—a change that he found difficult to understand. At first he thought that Will had passed way but then he noticed that the labored breathing had turned into a slow up and down rising of his chest. It was beginning to appear that somehow or someone Will was starting to breathe on his own. How was this possible? The whitest tint to his pale face was turning into a pinkest flesh color and Will seemed to be able to tolerate the pressure placed on his frail body without all the equipment attached to him. Were Nathan's eyes playing tricks on him? Nathan rubbed the back of his son's hand and prayed for a miracle. He gently squeezed the hand and continued to rub it as if trying to thrush some of his life into his son's body. Then he saw it. At first he thought it was just a reaction to him rubbing his son's hand but it happened again. He noticed that the fingers moved ever so slightly. There appeared to be a tingle of energy there. Was his mind playing games with him and if so he wanted it to stop or he would surely go insane. He stopped rubbing Will's hand and instead simply glared at his son's fingers and within minutes the fingers moved again. He hesitated about saying anything to his wife as he, himself, could not believe his eyes.

Will had lain in the comatose state for months and outwardly it appeared that he was non-responsive. Will knew something was terribly wrong with him as he dwelled in a world of darkness with the exception of a bright light, a perfectly formed circle that was shining directly in front of him as if it were some sort of a tunnel that he had to reach. The thing that worried Will was that the light grew smaller and smaller and now it was almost completely out. His mind raced as he was frightened that he would be in total darkness and he was so afraid. What frightened him further was that he could hear the faint voices of his mom and dad but could not respond to them. They were always telling him that they loved him and asking him to show any sign that he could hear them and as much as he tried he couldn't. It seemed like he was in a dream and couldn't wake up and he felt so alone. He could also hear the humming of motors and they seemed to be pushing air into his body allowing him to breathe. The noise was constant and never ending and he prayed that it would stop. Will pleaded, "Please, god, let me wake up and let my mom and dad know that I will be all right".

Suddenly Will did not hear the sound of the motors anymore and he was so relieved. But with their stoppage came the halt of the fresh air flowing into his lungs and he was terrified. He saw the light flitter and then it went completely out and his mind screamed out for help but no one was there to listen. He was in complete darkness but he could hear the faint sounds of his dad telling his mom that it was time to put their faith in god. And then there was complete silence. His body was starving for air and Will realized that he was dying. His mind cried for him in the realization that he was being taken away from his parents forever. It was then that he felt it! It was a radiation of energy starting in his chest. There appeared to be something resting there that was totally consuming his entire body. It brought with it a gentle flow of fresh air like nothing that Will had ever smelled in his young life. What was equally amazing to Will was that the light appeared to flitter like a candle and then grow brighter with every passing second. He could feel tingling in his arms and legs as if someone was tickling him. Whatever was happening to him seemed to energize his mind and soul? It was at that moment when he felt it; the gentle squeezing of his dad's hand on his. With all the energy that he could mustard he applied pressure on his dad's fingers to let him know that he knew that he was there. What consoled Will the most was the continued warmest on his chest seemed to be re-energizing every cell in his small body. Whatever it was he never wanted it to go away. Within minutes Will managed to slowly open his eyes and saw his mom and dad sitting there smiling back at him. What was strange was that they both were smiling but they had tears running down their cheeks, how could they do that Will thought to himself—laugh and cry at the same time? Will smiled back and then drifted off to sleep knowing that when he awoke that he would be reunited with his family again.

During the same time Nathan was, also, witnessing a true miracle. He looked directly at his son's chest and again noticed how easily he began to breathe, effect less, and so peaceful. As he peered at his son's face he felt a slight pressure on his thumb that was enclosed within his son's fingers. It was ever so gentle as if you were trying to touch someone they loved without causing them to be startled at their touch. Nathan looked across at his wife and she was staring directly at him. Not saying a word she realized that something was wrong or was it? She looked at her husband and saw a look of absolute amazement as if he had just witnessed something that was beyond words to describe. All Nathan did was look down at his hand and her eyes followed him. At first she just saw the tenderness of the moment where he had placed his thumb between her son's fingers but then noticed more. His little fingers were actually grasping his hand in an attempt to keep it there. Were her eyes playing tricks on her or was Will actually trying to hold on to Nathan's thumb?

As she looked in awe she felt the same tightest begin on her finger as well. She felt it and knew. She knew that their son was sending a sign that he was alive and he knew that they were there with him. She started to cry and she couldn't stop. Overcome with emotion she at first tried to control it but it was impossible—everything she had simply drained out of her body as if someone just pulled the plug. She wanted to reach for her husband but was afraid that if she did the feeling would be gone forever and she would have lost her baby boy again. So she just looked at him and told him that she loved him so much.

They both took in the moment and it felt exactly when he first entered this world six years ago and breathed his first breathe. It seemed as if he was being reborn before their very eyes and they wouldn't have missed this for the world. As they each took in everything that was happening around them they observed the cross lying on his chest. It was no longer that tarnished, worn metal cross but it appeared to be glowing a very soft bluest tint. It appeared to fade and return again and again and then they both realized that it was changing color to their son's heart beat.

Neither one called out to any of the doctors or nurses to come and check out the miracle that was happening before their very eyes. They were content to let the event take its course without any additional intervention from anyone. They simply sat down and with their other arms reached out for one another and created that family circle with their son. They did not know if this was going to be a short lived event or not and did not want to do anything that could jeopardize the situation. Was it them or did the room become brighter than before and a cheerfulness not seen in months. The white blankets and sheets on the bed seemed ever so white and the radiance of the sun light reflected brightly into the room as never before.

It was then that Will opened his eyes and smiled. It was a smile telling them that he would be all right over the coming weeks. No doubt it was delivered from a very sick boy but it was sent with the right message that the worse was over. His mom gently touched his head and told her she loved him so much and was so happy that he knew that they were there with him. He simply used all the strength that he could mustard and squeezed her fingers to assure her that he understood. He, then, closed his eyes and drifted off to sleep knowing that when he woke he would be returning to his mom and dad again.

Nathan gently removed his thumb from the grasp of his son and asked the nurse standing outside the door to have the doctor return to the room as quickly as possible. The doctor arrived within minutes expecting that he would formally pronounce the little boy dead. Instead he found him grasping his mom's finger and breathing easily without the aid of any life support equipment. Nathan told him that Will had opened his eyes for a few short minutes and smiled at them and then dozed back off. Not a word was spoken by the doctor or the nurses who had assembled at the foot of the bed as they could not believe what they were seeing. Every test conducted, every possible medical evaluation performed on the child indicated that it was a lost cause—the boy was basically gone. The only thing keeping him alive was the mechanical devices attached to his body. This was beyond the realm of possibility and was, indeed, an unexplained miracle. The doctor watched the heart monitoring equipment and the steady pulse of the heart beat signal its way across the screen. The blood pressure had climbed to an acceptable level and the child exhibited no signs of distress.

The doctor reached for the boy's wrist to feel the pulse for himself when he noticed the cross lying on the boy's chest. What caught his eye was the fact that it appeared to be slowly changing color before his very eyes as if in rhythm with Will's heart beat. He asked Nathan where he got the cross and Nathan told him that he had met a stranger during their short stay at Yellow stone Park. The man had given him the cross and told him to give it to his son and to never give up his faith regardless of what happened.

The doctor picked up the cross and held it in his hand and carefully examined it. It was old, perhaps, hundreds if not thousandths of years. It was in remarkable shape for its age and the thing that stood out was that it still pulsed in color with the breathing of the little boy. The doctor laid it back on to Will's chest and asked Nathan what the man's name was and if he knew how to contact him. There was something special about the cross and the remarkable recovery of the boy and the doctor had to dig deeper to uncover some answers.

Nathan thought for a minute and said the man's name was Jesus. The doctor initially thought that he was kidding but Nathan did not even break a smile as he stared directly into the doctor's eyes. He said that his name was Jesus Nathan repeated as if taking in what was happening to him and his family. He had said he had come a long way and they were the first family that he had talked to in quite some time. Nathan told the doctor how the stranger listened so intently to him and his wife about what happened and the pending difficult decisions that they were faced with. He was a god sent as his wife managed to open up to this stranger and express herself and the difficult time she was having in coping with the potential loss of her son.

Nathan thought of what he just said—a god sent! He was a stranger coming down a deserted trail who his daughter and puppy took an immediate liking to. A man that easily consoled his wife and whose piercing brown eyes appeared to own their own share of misery and despair. A man named Jesus who asked him to keep his faith so that others would also know that there is goodness and happiness for those who believe. Nathan and his wife had no doubts about who they happened across that day in the park. He had brought their son back from death and returned Will to them with a second chance on life. The doctor sat down in the chair next to the bed and simply clasped his hands together and said a silent prayer. He had no doubt that this was indeed a miracle beyond any medical explanation on how or why. He would not think of taking any credit for the boy's recovery but, instead, issued a commitment to himself that his faith has been restored and he would be committed to doing whatever he could to help those in need whether they had the personal assets to cover his expenses. Today he witnessed a miracle and would do everything in his power to assure that the news carries forth from this day.

Chapter five

The arrival of Satan

So Satan watched from afar. He was the other—the evil one. The one that was so disappointed that the little boy had lived. He had plans for that boy and his parents and he had failed. He was pissed that the event did not turn out as he had planned but he shrugged it off as a very small—even insignificant—defeat. He had so many wins lately; actually far too many to count. He thought of his recent triumphs such as the military officer who went berserk at the army base and killed twenty five innocent people; the terror bombing on the subway system in Moscow where thirty five men, women and children were blown into various body parts; the sicko who went into a children's hospital in Boston and wiped out an entire floor of kids, doctors, and nurses before the Boston SWAT Team shot him in the head from a sniper point from an adjoining building. Satan knew he had more winners than losers as a small smile spread across his face. He simply tossed the thought of the boy being saved by his foe as a fluke situation and he would use every means possible to end this eternal struggle between good and evil by being the ultimate winner.

Satan struggled with the decision of what false identify he would assume while on earth. He could easily pass himself off as a politician, lawyer, banker, or ever a priest since they all deemed themselves so worthy of committing evil acts upon their fellow man. But his intention was to shock the world as it never has been shocked before. In order to win this battle Lucifer would have to be so creative that even the most religious individuals would realize that it was useless to continue to stand by the rightist and turn to the side of evil once and for all.

Satan had to create a situation where the world would surely realize that he was walking among them and there would be no doubt that the other power could not cope with the massive destruction and sorrow that he could dish out.

His thoughts carried him through history as he realized that this journey will allow him to create a path of evil that could easily show mankind that he could retrace some of the most horrific events that would demonstrate his given abilities over the centuries. He would use many of these same events to destroy the minds of the believers and create an environment of hopelessness and madness to lead to his ultimate victory.

Lucifer decided he would be the messenger; the chosen one who would make his presence known by simply being at the right place at the right time so the world could easily understand he is the one responsible. He would simply blend in initially until the high tech communication and observation systems worldwide realized that he seemed to be always there when a disaster hit. Then they would know; then they would come crawling on their hands and knees to him; begging to become a member of his flock for all eternity. Eventually he would announce his presence to the world but, in the meantime, there was nothing like scaring the shit out of everyone.

So Satan sat there for the first time in thousands of years and took his first breath of air and coughed. It caught him by surprise that his first reaction was to gag on his first breath and he initially laughed to himself about the reflex. His smile turned to a feeling of anxiety and fear for a split second as he realized that the gagging reaction could have been caused by the fact that within that breath of fresh air that was also particles of goodness and kindest and life—all the things that he despised. One of the first things that he learned was that the gagging and coughing would not go away no matter how hard he tried to prevent it. He would cope but the uncomfortable reaction of battling goodness would not subside until he was the ultimate winner. He also came to realize that the condition could get much worse if he started to lose the upcoming conflicts he so much desired to inflict.

Satan decided that he would start his journey in Europe and leave the United States alone at this time. Besides his adversity was there and he did not want to truly meet up with him at this point of the struggle. He needed to gain momentum and support; he needed to gain the respect of his followers and the fear of the others who had yet to be convinced to become one of them. So let Jesus do his little acts of kindness in the United States as he had bigger and better plans in store for those in Europe. He had plans that would demonstrate that Satan has returned and is walking the earth.

So it started. Satan decided to demonstrate his power by being the first carrier of a disease the make its presence over 700 years ago in the years 1348 through 1350 AD when it wiped out 30 to 40% of the entire population in Europe. It killed an estimated 75-200 million people in the 14th century but recent research indicated that the figure is more like 45 to 50% of the European population dying off in a four year period. In fact in Mediterranean Europe and Italy, Spain and the south of France it was probably closer to 75 to 80% of the population. Although it basically has disappeared without an absolute true reason as why; he was bringing it back and he would be seen worldwide on news reports, satellite broadcast, CNN and all major news channels. He would be the carrier of "Black Death" he would be recognized worldwide as the person who brought back the bubonic plague that was so feared hundreds of years ago. He giggled at the thought of the pending panic and death that he would instill in millions worldwide. It was just the beginning.

If you are a history bluff you realize that most historians believe Black Death was carried by a bacterium Yesinia pertis and spread by fleas which primarily made use of highly mobile small animal populations like the black rats. The rats then used their ability to get aboard merchant ships and spread their disease to non expecting sailors by infesting them with the deadly fleas allowing them to be the carriers to other humans. The results were devastating.

The plague is thought to have returned every generation with varying results and effects on mankind until the 1700's. More than 100 plague epidemics swept across Europe during this period. The last reported event occurred with the Russian plague of 1770-1772 and then seemed to disappear from Europe during the 19th century.

So man had little idea that such a devastating plague could simply re-appear in the presence of one man who just mysterious appeared one day at a local hospital in London. The man claimed that he had spend the last few days touring the many historical sites in London to include the tower of London, Buckingham palace, and other interesting locations. He stressed that he was overly concerned that he had contacted something that could be contagious and was frightened that he could have passed it along to others. He said as his condition grew worse he had been sneezing and coughing while mingling in the tourist crowds at the sites. He stressed that he hoped that this was not the case but he couldn't shake the feeling that he had contacted something very serious. As he sat there being examined he could not help but to think that he could have received an Oscar nomination for his acting had this been a movie. He knew that his goal was accomplished just by the look on the doctors' faces as they had him remove his shirt and saw the condition of his body.

Satan carried no identification on him. He would be a total stranger of unknown nationality, age, or any other identifying features. The only thing that they managed to get out of him was a name, a first name, a name that disturbed the attending doctors when he voiced it—he said that his name was Lucifer.

The thing that immediately distressed the doctors was his symptoms. They were classic signs of an illness that they had read about but never had actually seen themselves in any patients that they had treated. Initially they each believed that it was not possible. The disease had not been seen in nearly 300 years and this had to be some other abnormality that this man had. But they took all the necessary precautions and isolated him immediately upon seeing his condition until further testing could be done. Lucifer just watched everything happening around him and silently laughed to himself about the pending madness that would develop very shortly with the news that he was the first carrier in 300 years of the bubonic plague.

This stranger exhibited all the symptoms. As they undressed the man they noticed the severe swelling of the growths in the groin, neck and armpits which oozed pus and bled. The man had an extremely high fever of 103 degrees with a splitting headache, nausea and vomiting and aching joints. There were also a freckle like spots and rash covering most of his body. Complete blood analysis and fluid testing was performed to determine exactly what the cause of his illness was. They tried to make him as comfortable as possible while they decided how to attack the disease. Based on the present stage of his condition he was near death. They placed him in an isolated room and placed a security guard at the entrance to prevent anyone from gaining access. Yet Satan wasn't suffering; he was enjoying the pain; he thrived on it. He just lay there patiently while he waited for all hell to break loose!

The results confirmed the deepest fears possible of the treating physicians. They sat in the main conference room also realizing that they, themselves, were also carriers now. They had come in contact with this man; they had breathed the same air as him; they had touched him; they were infected.

How many others over the past several days had he come in contact with? How many more ill people would be flowing through the very doors that he entered into the hospital? It would be just a matter of time before all their questions were answered and they all knew that.

The overwhelming question that required their attention was communication to the masses and how to avoid an overall panic from quickly developing that would cause mass hysteria. They were faced with a monumental task and were unprepared for such a disease striking out of the blue. There was little hope to identify the potential carriers such the stranger was very elusive in his comments by speaking in generalities. He was not fully cooperating with them and they sense it from the moment he walked into the emergency room.

How could they alert the public without starting a panic? They needed to devise a plan that would get anyone showing the various symptoms of the disease to come to designated locations for potential treatment. The doctors immediately contacted the authorities at Scotland Yard and asked for their help to address a pending crisis. As they unveiled the news the chief inspector sat down and placed his head in his hands and said may god have mercy on all of us. How could someone just show up out of nowhere with one of the most deadliness diseases in history without some sort of explanation? Was he a terrorist spreading the results of a dirty bomb or just a maniac who conducted some deadly experiments on his own in trying to duplicate the deadly disease?

Within hours of the inflicted man showing up at the hospital there were others filtering into hospital emergency rooms in the various cities. The emergency rooms were being bombarded with people who were ill, running high fevers and vomiting. Some already were exhibiting the skin rash and the tumors some the size of a small apple or egg all over the body. There were others coming into the emergency rooms with the advanced stages of black or purple spots on their bodies, sometimes a few large ones, sometimes many little ones. These were spots of certain death and the doctors knew that they had a crisis of epic proportions on their hands. The overall affects of the disease was such that the sick quickly communicated it to the healthy that came near them as quickly as a moth to a flame.

Within the next eight hours there were hundreds of people flowing in for treatment and many were wondering about why they were not informed that a new wave of flu was hitting the country.

The doctors did the best they could by informing the medical staff of their findings about a very serious disease in their midst. They had them all gown completely up with personal protective equipment to include respirators, goggles, hair nets, bonnets, shoe coverings, smocks, gloves—you name it and they worn it. But even with those precautions those nurses originally exposed were already feeling ill and were immediately separated from the rest.

After a careful review of their limited options the Prime Minister held a press conference to inform his countrymen of the serious health alert facing his nation. He asked that anyone who had visited any national historical sight in the past six days should report to a local hospital or military site to be thoroughly checked out for the illness. Anyone feeling ill with any signs of flu like conditions should also take the necessary precautions to be seen and treated. The Prime Minister also announced that the borders to the country were closed and all transportation in and out of the country had ceased. These precautions were necessary to help to avoid a further spread into neighboring countries and containment of the rapidly spreading disease.

Lucifer lay in his hospital bed and thrived on every minute of the national broadcast. He was so turned on with the chain of events and the terror that was rapidly spreading that he felt his penis grow so firm that he could have broke down a door with it. It will just be a matter of time before they realize who I am and what I am capable of doing; they will walk in fear each day thought Lucifer.

The first deaths were reported two days later. At first it was two people, a husband and wife, who had toured the Tower of London on Sunday. And then it started multiplying so quickly that the authorities had a difficult time in keeping an accurate body count. Ten, twenty, fifty, hundred, and a thousand—it was astonishing that the death toll grew so out of control within the first thirty six hours. Soon the hospitals were overcrowded and the government used sports stadiums and military bases in their attempts to confine and treat those inflicted. The death spread rapidly and consumed entire families as a whale devouring all fish in its path. It was relentless and unforgiving. Within the first two weeks it was reported that ten thousand people had perished and that number was reported only to keep the masses from further panic. The actual total was close to one hundred thousand people.

The story hit news world wide—"The Black Death has returned". With the ban on travel the major breakouts occurred in the United Kingdom with only a few reports in other countries. These were quickly isolated and kept under the tightest security possible to limit the potential of further contaminating the masses in other countries. As the world prayed for the ill and a cure by the medical community they wondered who was this man that started the spread of the disease and why?

His photo was plastered on every news link in the world. He was famous. The picture showed his face and the effects of the illness that he was also responsible for spreading to thousands. If you looked close you could see a small smile or smirk on his face but it had to be a mistake. How can someone who has spread death and destruction be smiling while in so much pain himself? The puzzling event that amazed the doctors was that he was still alive. Others who were affected days after him had passed away in agony yet he lay on that bed in basically the same condition that he arrived. Although he appeared to be in tough shape he lingered on and the doctors could not believe it.

At the end of the first week of the crisis Lucifer had enough of lying there in that damn hospital bed pretending he was gravely ill. He wanted to get outside where all the action is and see the devastation that he caused. The entire hospital was in disarray with the staff significantly reduced due to many of them catching the deadly disease. Security was lapse and the hospital appeared more like a battle field than a medical institution. He glowed with pride in what he had personally accomplished. One of the nurses had just entered his room fully gowned in protective gear to check on his condition. As she walked to the side of his bed Lucifer could see how nervous she was about being near him. She had not been inflicted, one of the lucky ones, since she followed the specific guidelines set forth by the doctors to avoid contamination. She had been a practicing nurse for six years now and thought that she had seen it all but this disease was beyond anything that she ever witnessed. It was quick, deadly and still incurable although the doctors were gathering the best medical professionals from around the world to come up with a cure. As she reached the side of his bed and prepared to take his vital signs Lucifer grabbed her arm and pulled her towards him. She panicked and tried to break free of his grasp but found that impossible. She tried to reason with him by telling him that she had two small children at home and was trying to help him and to please let her go. She thought she had made an impact on him for a few short seconds as his eyes made contact with hers. However she realized how wrong she was when he grabbed the hood section of her protective suit and ripped it free. She was now standing there breathing the same air as this mad man and she started to scream. He quickly took his clammy, sweaty hand and covered her mouth. He then told her how lonely he was in that room by himself and would appreciate a kiss. She struggled to break free of his grip but he pulled her face to his and stuck his tongue in her mouth and ran it in a circular motion to spread his salvia down her throat. Before letting her break free he grabbed the top of her protective suit and ripped it down the front exposing her bra which he ripped from her body. He then squeezed her breasts and bite on one of her nipples before releasing her. She fell to the floor and tried to spit out everything in her mouth but knew it was too late. She knew that she now was a carrier and her days numbered. She tried to cover her breasts with the torn remains of her suit as she got to her feet. As she ran to the door she screamed at him that he was a lunatic and she prayed that he would go to hell when he died. He started to laugh hysterically at her and screamed out that is my home you fool. Soon each and every one of you pathetic imbeciles will be joining me there. I hope you enjoyed our little affair as much as I did. Come back here and I will give you one of the biggest treats that you ever received from a man. At that the nurse flung open the door and ran from the room screaming at the top of her lungs.

He got out of bed and found his clothes hanging in the small closet and got dressed. He, himself, felt the effects of the disease although in no way was it death threatening to him. He actually felt invigorated from the effects. He swung open the door to his hospital room and walked out into the corridor without anyone paying much attention to him. The security guard was no longer positioned outside his room as the hospital was filled with patients just like him now. He took nourishment from what he saw as he walked by each room and relished in the sorrow and death that surrounded him. As he reached the elevator the doors opened and one of his physicians was standing there. The doctor was in a daze as if he was having a hard time waking up from a horrible nightmare. Initially Lucifer thought the man would simply walk directly by without noticing him but the doctor took a passing glance at the man and his eyes grew to twice their size. The doctor tried to speak but couldn't get any words out as he stared at the man who started everything standing in front of him. The carrier, the man who started the spread of the Black Death, appeared nearly normal. The rash, sores and blemishes were nearly gone from his face and he was smiling at him.

Lucifer stared directly into the doctor's eyes and grabbed him by his neck and lifted him off the floor. He told him to remember his face as he will be seeing him again real soon. He told the doctor to remember this moment and tell the world that the man responsible in starting the crisis simply walked out of the hospital and vanished. With that he started to squeeze the doctor's neck as if he was going to stranger him. The doctor became so frightened that he pissed his pants. Satan noticed the wet spot developing on the front of his pants and started to laugh at him. He then lowered the doctor to the floor and patted him on his cheek. The doctor's legs gave out on him and he fell to the floor as Lucifer entered the elevator and left the building.

Almost two hundred and fifty thousand people would die before the medical professionals from around the world came up with a means to fight the centuries old killer. The new technology and abilities to isolate the germ cells to determine the best method to attack them allowed them to first slow down the spread of the disease and then stop it. Mankind had worked together by joining the best medical professionals and scientists in the world to overcome a plague that killed millions centuries ago. Although a significant disaster everyone knew it could have been far worse and thanked god for the opportunity to avoid a worldwide epidemic.

The authorities searched everywhere for the carrier but he vanished. The doctor blabbered out his story repeatedly to the police investigators and it was very difficult for them to believe it was true. The man's sores and blemishes were almost gone and he lifted the doctor off the floor and was strangling him. How is that possible—the man was close to death? It wasn't until they got a copy of the incident from the hospital surveillance cameras that they believed the doctor. This man was super human and had to be stopped before he struck again. But who was he?

There was a concern that he would spread the killing disease into other countries but it never happened. It was like he just disappeared in a heartbeat. His face became more familiar to the world than Brad Pitt but no leads. He was the most wanted man in the world and yet no one really wanted to run into him. There was just a presence about him that sent shivers up your spine. It was best to just move forward and hope that he never showed up again. The only ones interested he running into him were the authorities who knew that he had to be stopped. This was not an individual who was not going to stop unless he was apprehended and quickly.

Lucifer was angry; things did not turn out the way he expected. He wanted to make a smash on his return—a huge one! This was big but not big enough. Centuries ago this disease killing millions and he managed to inflict only thousandths. Centuries ago it spread to other countries quickly yet today they managed to quickly contain it in the UK to prevent such a disaster. He sat there in the back of a coffee shop and pounded his fists on the table as if he was a mad man. The man behind the counter stared at him for a few seconds but turned away not wanting this loner to flip out. It was late and he had seen enough weirdoes start to cause a disturbance for no reason at all—it was best to let him get pissed at himself rather than be dragged into his personal problems.

Lucifer tried to remain calm but shouted out "Fuck me, I know that asshole had something to do with this!" His face was red with anger and he swept his hand through his hair in a wild motion leaving it standing in so many different directions that he looked ridiculous. He had to calm down and realize that this was not going to be easy. He would be battled all the way. For every event he started he knew that the other would be working to fight back. Jesus would not only attack it but he would do things that will make his job even tougher. He picked up the newspaper sitting on the table in front of him and read the headlines again. It said "Miracle of Miracles—we overcome through World Support". He read on and noticed that the entire article was about how mankind joined together to find a cure and stop the spread of the killer disease. Mankind had attacked and found a cure for the black plague in a few short months. They also found a means to quickly address it should it strike again in another part of the world. The article showed people hugging one another and the doctors with their arms raised in the air in victory. Although the death statistics were there they only took up a small portion of the article; the majority of it was filled with the accomplishments and giving of all those people who gave all they had to others during the crisis. Act upon act of kindness under death threatening conditions were highlighted and everyone in the world was just eating it up. What about all the deaths and despair he thought to himself; why aren't the people talking about the havoc he caused? He shouted out again, "Oh, fuck, fuck me, he actually won". With that he threw his coffee cup against the wall, kicked his chair over and strolled out of the coffee shop just daring the counter guy to say one word to him. Go ahead he thought to himself as he walked by the man—go ahead and I will rip your head off your shoulders and piss into the fucking open hole. The man just stood there, said nothing to the crack pot, and was glad when the door closed and he was gone.

Jesus was handling the situation as best as he could. When he first heard the news about the spreading sickness in the UK he knew who was responsible. He knew that his opponent was going for the homerun right away. Forget about the base hit and the gradual scoring of a run over a period of time he wanted it all and right away. Jesus knew that he could not immediately stop it since each event must also include the help and support of humans to strive through the crisis and exhibit their true colors. But Jesus could be very instrumental in helping to create that aura of love and caring that we all need during a time of hardship and despair. Jesus gave it all and he was thrilled with the outcome.

People everywhere cared and it showed. People from all nations watched the nightly news updates and cried. They cried for their fellow man that was going through a situation where they were surrounded by death. They not only cried but they came in masses to a country torn apart by death carrying germs and assisted those in need. Volunteers thousandths of them streamed into the country to help in any way they could. Many were needed—the professional doctors, nurses, scientists, red cross workers, and soldiers from around the world to assist in finding a cure, helping the sick and providing support to maintain order in a panicked country. Some actually died from the disease and they all knew that was a strong possibility but still they stepped forward and showed that they cared. They loved their fellow man enough to give up their own life and for that Jesus cried.

Jesus knew he had won his second battle with Satan although he knew it was a very costly one. Thousands had died but he ended it without the total effects that Satan had hoped for. Jesus not only ended it but he was proud of mankind for coming up with a cure for it so if it should pop up again somewhere else in the world it would be quickly maintained. Man had helped man to battle through a difficult period and they came out winners. There were celebrations in every country in the world and October third was declared as "World Care" day to recognize the coming together of all countries in tackling a crisis together. What inspired Jesus the most is that at noon time on October third nearly everyone worldwide got down on their knees and prayed to god thanking him for his help in saving the human race. As Jesus sat there he became overwhelmed with emotion. He looked down at his hands and they trembled uncontrollably and his body shivered as if he was extremely cold yet he was sitting with the sun beaming down on him. He wiped the tears from his eyes but another one appeared as he recalled his anxiety of coming forth on this mission. He truly felt that he could easily come out the loser in this battle yet his faith in mankind was being restored with each passing day. He was growing stronger in spirit and his commitment to go the distance for the ultimate championship. He had to; man had suffered enough over the centuries and it was time now to bring everlasting peace on earth.

Chapter six

The drive

Jesus did not push events as his arch rival did; his goal was to demonstrate his presence through his personal contacts with others and restoring their spiritual faith in each other and themselves. He knew word would spread gradually and he would carefully evaluate the results as they basically flowed in. He had no plans to get involved in miracles as making it rain bread, turning water into wine, or helping a blind man see. As he did for Nathan and his family his desire was to restore the faith in each other and god himself. A very simple plan that he hoped would be effective.

Jesus really had no idea what Satan was planning next but he was sure it was going to be another headline splash as that is the way he wanted to proceed with the war. He wanted to strike fear and pain and suffering to as many as possible to indicate that he had returned and he was as real as that last drink that you took. A method to his madness whether it would be as successful as he hoped was another different ball game that still was in progress.

So Jesus prepared to settle back in the car seat and prepared to drive towards Denver where he hoped to further solidify his position as the savior, the one that will lead his followers to a life that they could only dream about. Yes, Jesus was going to drive a four wheel drive jeep. He had practiced for hours in a fairly vacant parking lot inside the national park when the majority of people went home or settled back into their hotels, campsites or RV's.

As he turned on the ignition and heard the engine roar he was startled with the whine of the engine and the various knobs, buttons and switches on the dashboard in front of him. He carefully evaluated what each one did as he turned them on and off. He knew if someone was watching him they would have called the police as he tried each one two to three times to be sure of what it controlled. He would surely have drawn attention from any passerby based on the things he was doing inside the vehicle.

He learned his first lesson pretty quickly as he leaned back in his seat and hit the gas. It was at that moment he realized that he did not have to push it firmly to the floor to have the car accelerate. When he floored the pedal the jeep jerked forward gaining speed much more quickly than he ever imagined. It was entirely different from riding a mule or camel and the forward force threw him for a loop. Luckily he had both hands on the steering wheel and managed to hold on for dear life until he regained his composure and released the gas pedal while applying the brake. He then learned his second lesson as quickly as the first. Never slam your foot firmly down on the brake pedal. As he did, the jeep screeched to a sudden stop and his body rose out of the car seat and his head hit the roof of the jeep. Within seconds he learned his third lesson to always remember to buckle his seat belt as he rubbed the small knot on the top of his head.

With a few more stop and go exercises he learned quickly and had everything under control within a couple of hours of practice. He carefully read the owner's manual about all the safe driving tips, turn signals, head lights, watching your speed to the traffic signs, and other key driving tips. He was pleased with himself on how well he dealt with this new way to travel across the country. It was entirely different than riding on the back of a donkey and he was amazed at the amount of distance he traveled in such a short time period. As he drove he enjoyed the feeling of the warm summer air blowing in his face as he leaned his arm out of the window and started down the highway. He turned on the radio and there was "Elvis on an oldies station singing his heart out. The words caught Jesus" attention—if he could dream of a better land where people walked hand in hand. Jesus just smiled, turned up the radio and hummed along with the song.

Within a few short hours Jesus would cross paths with Henry. Henry Fiddleman. To the few friends he had he was nicknamed "fiddles"; to those who tormented and abused him he was just Henry the jackass. He was their whipping boy for anything wrong in their lives and they used every opportunity to take their frustrations out on him.

Chapter seven

The couple

Henry had been married to Sheila for four years and they both truly tried hard to make a go of it. Both very shy and withdrawn when they had met one day while attending the same discount movie showing of the Michael Cameron's latest 3 D record smashing hit, "Avatar—the Revenge continues". They both fell in love with the dream world of beauty displayed in the Avatar series and as they each left the theater they couldn't help but turn to one another and say that they loved the movie and couldn't wait to see it again. They both laughed at how they each started to say it at the same time and used the opportunity to introduce themselves to one another. Henry was the first one to speak up and ask Sheila if she wanted to stop at the corner Friendly's and have an ice cream and talk about the movie a little more. He felt strange that he was so forthcoming in his conversation with her because he normally would start stuttering due to nervousness around someone he didn't know. She glanced at Henry and saw a person a lot like her in so many ways. Henry was a shy person who basically seemed so alone in such a big world. She could tell by his mannerisms that he would not be any threat to her. As he talked to her his hands were dug deep into the side pockets of his pants and he kept swaying his body from side to side as if he was expecting to be turned down or laughed at. His head was down as if he was afraid to make eye contact and he seemed so insecure almost like a young boy who was constantly in trouble for things that he did not even do.

As Sheila looked at him she realized that she was similar to Henry in so many ways. She was a loner that feared crowds or having a conversation with someone that she did not know. She had gone to her junior prom with one of the most popular boys in her school because he had approached her about liking her and wanted to show it by asking her to be his date for the prom. She was so proud that a boy like that would pick her out of all the girls in the class that she beamed with excitement. It was going to be her first time out with a boy and being at such a social event as the school prom her mom said yes. Sheila was a loner at school by just keeping to herself, minding her business and doing well in her classes. She was viewed by the popular girls as a nerd and fell out of disfavor with most of her classmates due to her constantly grading higher than them on the various tests and quizzes given by the teachers. It wasn't that she did not want to be sociable it was that she did not want to ridicule and talk about the other students behind their backs as so many of her classmates did. She liked to sew and do yarn work which many viewed as old fashion and ridiculous when you could go to the mall and get any brand of type of clothing you could ever want. So she just kept to herself and was satisfied with her simple yet uncomplicated life.

So Alan picked her up in his car, introduced himself to her mom and told her that he would have Sheila home shortly after the prom was over that night. He asked her mom if she would be so kind as to take their picture together so he would have the photo to remember the good time. She took the camera and the kids posed in front of the rose bush that stood beside the house. As she looked into the camera and saw her daughter with this fine young man smiling back at her she was pleased that her daughter was getting away from the isolated style of life that she was getting herself used to. She told Alan that she was glad to meet him and hugged Sheila and told her to have a good time and to come home safe to her. As she walked back into the house she could only imagine what her husband would have thought about tonight. He had passed away three years ago of throat cancer and she was a single mom now trying to the best she could for her daughter to prepare her for the perils of life and her future. As she settled on the couch to watch American Idol she thought about how Sheila was transforming into a fine young woman and she smiled.

Alan did not spend much time with Sheila at the prom. When they got there he introduced her to a few of his friends who basically giggled and made some rude comments about her without him saying much to defend her. He poured her a glass from the large punch bowl and gave it to her and told her that he would be back shortly. He did not return to her until an hour and a half later as she sat in a wooden folding chair that was lined against one of the walls in the dance hall. It wasn't bad enough that he neglected her but she saw him dancing and kissing some other girls who hung on to his arm like he was some sort of a movie star that they were dying to get his autograph. He strolled back to her and sat down and asked her if she was enjoying the music and if she wanted something to eat. He held out his hand to her and she placed her hand in his and got up. They went over to the buffet table and picked out a couple of sandwiches, potato salad, garden salad, and cokes and returned to where she had been sitting. He finished eating his food and got up and told her he would be right back. Right back turned out to be nearly two hours later when it was time to take her home. The hall was emptying and they were one of the last couples to walk to his car. He told her he was sorry that he didn't spend as much time as he wanted with her as he didn't realize how fast the time flew as he talked to his friends who called him away. She almost told him he was full of shit (which certainty was something that she would never thought about doing before his pack of lies but she controlled herself) but held back. He opened the car door for her and she sat down while maneuvering her gown so that she did not rip or tear it in the door.

He got in the car, turned on the engine and pulled out of the lot and on to the main highway. Sheila was counting the minutes to get home and away from this bimbo. As she listened to the music of J Lo on the radio she tried to remain calm and composed about the terrible evening that she had with him. She continued to fiddle with her hands and purse and had not been paying attention to the direction where Alan was driving. When she looked up she realized that he had pulled off the highway and down a deserted side road where he gradually slowed down the car and pulled it off between two trees. He looked at her and said he was sorry and wanted to make it up to her. He draped his arm over her shoulder and tried to pull her closer to him but she pushed his arm away. She asked him to take her home and he refused. He again tried to pull her closer but she pushed him away again and attempted to get out of the car. He grabbed her hair and

The Struggle by R. Cole

told her that she was not going anywhere. He told her that he wanted to kiss her and that he invited her to the prom to give her a good time if she got the drift of his meaning. He told her that she was the talk of the class in that she appeared to be so lonely. The boys joked that she was probably an easy mark and who could be had on the drop of a dime. The girls joked that she was probably as hot as a spark plug under that quiet disposition. Alan looked at her and asked her if she was? He reached for her again but this time his hand grabbed at her breast as she pulled away. Her action caused his hand to slip to the top of her gown and ripped it.

Sheila panicked and she knew that her poor decision to put trust into someone who had constantly brushed her aside at school as if she was a fly on a sandwich led to her predicament. In a few short seconds Alan would be losing it and the only thing that would be driving his mind and body was the overwhelmingly urge to satisfy himself at the expense of Sheila. He would regret his actions later and beg her to forgive him and not to tell anyone and if she did he would say that she was the one who started it. She had to think quickly as his hands felt as if they were everywhere on her body. She turned to him and grabbed each side of his face in her hands and asked him one simple question that stopped him dead in his tracks. She asked him how he would feel if his fourteen years old sister, Rachael, was being attacked in a car after she had trusted the young man who their parents believed would keep her safe that night.

All the energy and emotion just seemed to drain from his body as his brain absorbed her words. He fell silent and he stopped his physical attack on her and stared out the window at the quiet countryside where he had taken her for one purpose. He was overwhelmed with grief on what he had almost done to this trusting girl. It was true that he was looking for an easy mark for that night as his interest in sex was growing with his development into manhood. Sex was one of the main topics of his friends anytime they got together. But her words hit home and he realized that he was no better than those deviants who prey on young girls as they walk home alone from school.

He put both hands on the steering wheel and was embarrassed to look at Sheila. He reached in his pocket for some chewing gum to help settle his nerves and could not think of anything else to say at that point but to ask

Sheila if she wanted one. She was amazed in the change that had come over him and knew the worse was over as she tried to assess the damage to her dress. One of the straps was torn but otherwise it was in good shape. She reached into the small compartment in her purse that she always kept small odds and ends of various items that she viewed could be used in an emergency situation for a small pin. It was nestled next to some thread, buttons, scotch tape, paper clips and small pocket knife. She grabbed the strap and used the small pin to re-attach it to her gown. There good as new she thought.

She turned her attention to Alan and said everything was going to be ok. She asked him to take her home now in a firm yet stern voice. It was not demanding yet the message was clear—the evening was over and they both were much better off with them parting ways as soon as possible. Alan looked at her and said in a trembling voice that he was so sorry. He said that he learned a valuable lesson tonight—something that he would carry with him for years to come. He tried desperately to retain his composure but Sheila could see that he was now as scared as she was a few minutes ago. His reputation would have been shot, his parents destroyed by his actions and he could have been facing criminal charges if Sheila had decided to press the assault against her. Beyond the consequences that he would have imposed on her he would have also exposed himself to some serious consequences for his actions for years to come. Why hadn't he thought about that before the evening ever started—what a jerk he thought to himself?

Sheila saw his emotional condition and told him it was all right. She would say nothing to anyone about what happened and she would expect that he did not take the opportunity the following day to lie to his friends that she was an easy mark and further destroy her reputation with her classmates. She was already thought of as a nerd, standoffish, and strange; she did not want to be viewed as a whore on top of all the other misconceptions. Alan told her that she did not have to worry as he would not spread any further gossip about her to others. She believed him and again asked him to take her home. He turned the ignition on and drove off into the night. The incident further strengthened Sheila's distrust in men and she knew that the road of recovery would be a long one. At that point she did not want to be alone with another man and her anxiety grew to the point where she withdrew into her solidarity world of loneliness. So she decided to live with the whispers behind her back, the little cat calls about being a weirdo, and the silly laughs and smirks from others as she walked by. They were far better than the potential of being brutalized in a god forsaken isolated area where no one could help you.

Sheila had kept her promise to herself and lived a simple life far removed from others. She became more and more withdrawn and shy and she seemed ok with it. Yet that day at the movie theater changed it forever. Seeing that movie led her to get into a conversation with another person who had the same troubling issues as she did. The more she talked with Henry the more she realized that he needed her as much as she needed him. The movie and drinks at the coffee shop lead to others and soon they were an inseparable couple. They loved the simple things in life such as walks in the city park, reading books, taking rides on the local bike trails where they could enjoy nature and get away from the busy city life. They appeared to be chiseled from the same mold and Sheila was so happy the day when Henry asked her to marry him. She melted as a chocolate bar left in the sun when he gave her a small diamond engagement ring and placed it on her finger. He had saved for months for that ring and kept an eye in the Sunday newspaper for any sales that he could afford. It was small and Sheila knew inexpensive but she loved it with all her heart. She kissed Henry gently on his lips and told him that she would be so proud to be his wife. At that moment when they hugged their future could not have been any brighter as they both finally found someone in this world that they could believe in and trust. It was like they each hit the lottery yet they both knew that they had many uphill battles that they must take to survive in this world but they had each other and that is what counted most.

Chapter eight

Henry Fiddleman

Henry was always considered a strange boy. He was the only son of Luke and Stella and was an unexpected and unplanned surprise arrival to the couple. You see Luke was a two time loser working on his third. Luke stood about five feet eight inches, thinning brown hair with long side burns. His arms were covered with tattoos and his face showed the scars from the various fist fights that he always managed to lose in his drunken state of mind. His arms, chest and body was covered with thick brown hair and he was always embarrassed wearing shorts or being on a beach as he thought he looked like a gorilla. Besides that one physical characteristic that made him stand out from others he believed he was a cool character and always had the knack to talk a woman into bed with him. He spoke with a southern accent and tried to imitate Elvis to impress the girls. But in reality he was a user and abuser. He was a real weasel and never managed to hold a real job very long due to his temper and drinking. Between the both of them he always managed to get himself fired or arrested and his track record proved it. One thing led to another and he took the easy way out through petty thief and taking advantage of others for his personal gain. Prior to leaving home for the last time he beat up his father over a pack of cigarettes. He left with his father unconscious on the floor after hitting him over the head with a jar of peanut butter. The glass jar shattered as it opened a large laceration that would take fifteen stitches to close. As he walked out the front door he told his father to go fuck himself and he would see him in hell. He never looked back nor returned home ever after he heard that his father died of a massive heart attack six months later.

Luke had spent the last seven years of his life in state prison for attempted robbery of an old man of his social security check. Luke needed some quick cash and was never up to working a full week to earn it. He used his skills as a petty thief to attain what he wanted. Throughout the years he had gotten into his share of fights and lost the majority of them. He learned from all those lost fights that it was better to give than receive. He liked to inflict punishment and relished in dishing it out to others should the opportunity arise. His last crime had centered on that old man who had just left the Old Stone Bank on West Main Street. Luke followed him waiting for an opportunity to separate the man from his money. The old man was an easy mark and Luke knew it. He ambled slowly down the street supported with a walking cane that helped to balance him on a set of very arthritic knees. His shoulders were slumped forward and he seen to be staring at the ground intent in not stumbling over any crack or crevice in the sidewalk. He finally managed to reach the small, deserted, parking lot where his 1988 Toyota Corolla was parked. As he unlocked the door Luke ceased the opportunity by whacking him on the back of the head with a metal flashlight that he had hidden beneath his jacket. The old man fell to the ground next to his car and Luke fumbled through his pockets looking for the cash that the poor man had withdrawn from the bank. It truly was not Luke's day as three men passing by saw what Luke was doing and rushed to the old man's aid. They were on Luke quicker than bees on honey. One of them bashed Luke on the side of his head knocking him to his knees while the others jumped on top of him and beat the daylights out of him. One of them left the assault long enough to call 911. Within minutes the police and medics were on the scene. Luke was arrested and got seven years in the state pen. There he counted the days when he could get out and get a piece of ass and some cold beer to wash away his sorrows.

The day of his release is when he met Stella. She worked at a local diner that was about a mile from the prison. The place was basically well known by the prison guards as a great place to stop for a cheap breakfast and coffee. Luke had overheard the numerous conversations about the place and was determined that he would do exactly that on the day he got released—walk down that road and have himself a breakfast that didn't taste like that prison garbage that they served every day. So as he stepped outside of the prison gate, took a deep breath of fresh air, and he pointed himself, northward, down that country road to the small diner. There were a few taxis sitting at the front gate of the prison. The cab drivers would always check with the administration department to determine if anyone was being released that day knowing that the majority of the felons would be looking for a ride into their future. But Luke just walked right by the taxis with his mind set on that decent meal, cold beer, and a piece of ass in that order.

There he met Stella. Stella was a small woman standing no more than five feet four inches and weighing about one hundred twenty pounds. She was an average looking woman and those that met her said that she looked a little like Princess Di. She wore her hair short and had sparkling blue eyes that definitely caught your attention upon initially meeting her. But if you examined her more closely you would see that her body gave away signs of a darker side. Her arms were pitted with needle marks and her drug addiction was causing her to age beyond her years. She used any extra money she could mustard to get high. She couldn't maintain a steady relationship and the men in her life were basically one night stands.

When Luke walked into that diner and eyed Stella he knew right away he was going to get more than a meal that day. Maybe his luck would indeed change this time around? On that same night he screwed her brains out in her dingy apartment on the outskirts of town. Nine months later little Henry came along. It was not a pleasant personal relationship between Luke and Stella but they both put up with one another because it was better than having no one. Luke got abusive when he drank and that was quite often. Stella learned quickly it was best not to say anything to him when he was plastered as he would take anything the wrong way and start a violent argument. Afraid to call the police because she was also a known addict she put up with the black eyes and sore ribs that she received when he went into one of his crazy spells. Luke was content to settle in with Stella because it was far better than prison life and he had a roof over his head and a warm body in the bedroom and food in his stomach. Until something better came along he would put up with her and then toss her aside like a rag doll.

Stella knew that she was pregnant—the morning sickness, the swelling of her body and the general change in her body chemistry. She went to the local clinic and was given a pregnancy test to confirm her belief. She was three months along and that night dropped the news on Luke as he had just punched her in the ribs about her remarks about his favorite baseball team losing six in a row. He was going to kick her as she fell to the floor but stopped when she yelled out the news. He looked down at her and said you are what! Instead of picking her up from the floor he simply looked down at her and called her a sorry bitch and walked away and turned on the television as he popped open another beer. This was the loving environment that Henry was born into six months later.

Henry was a small baby weighing less than five pounds. With a splattering of light brown hair, blue eyes, and a dimple in his chin he looked a lot like his mom and for that Stella was thankful. When Henry arrived in this world he was held in the arms of a nurse who wiped his body down, whispered sweet words to him and welcomed him to this world. Besides the gradual love that developed for Henry by his mom it would represent the small amount of tenderness that Henry would experience in his formative years.

His father, Luke, did not even go to the hospital to see him or Stella for the few days that she was there. Being on very limited income with basically no benefits from her job at the diner the hospital kept her only as long as possible to make sure that Henry was breathing and doing well enough to leave the hospital in her arms. One of the doctors asked her about her black eye and the various bruise that covered her body and she lied as she always did about how she got them. The doctor knew physical abuse when he saw it and tried to get her some help before she was discharged. He met a dead end with the local authorities. The cops told him she had a history of drug abuse and was well known by them. They figured she had got into a hassle with one of her pushers as she sometimes did and it was better to just leave the situation alone. Although Stella decided to weed herself off her drug dependency while she gave birth to Henry it was little consolation to the cops. Being drug free allowed Stella to leave the hospital with Henry because her system was clean and they didn't have anything preventing her from walking out of the hospital with her son. It was a sorry day for Henry.

Stella actually tried hard to be a good mother to Henry. She worked extra hours at the diner and was as pleasant as possible to the customers hoping for a few more cents in tips to help pay for Henry's formulas and diapers. But Luke would find where she hid the petty cash and buy a six pack of Bud or some cheap wine. Stella had to leave Henry with Luke when she worked at the diner and he did a great job of totally neglecting him by tuning out Henry as he cried in his crib. Stella would come home with Henry lying in the crib in diapers soaked in urine and covered in feces. He had not been fed and was just left there to wait for his mom to come home to take care of him. The time that she blew up at Luke about his behavior was a mistake as he pushed her so hard that she fell backwards and flipped over the bed on to the tiled floor. Instead of helping her up Luke placed a pillow over her head and tried to smother her. It was the last time she questioned his behavior.

Immediately upon seeing his mother's face standing over his crib, Henry would stop crying and smile. He would smile as he knew she would do something to make him feel better. Even with the severe diaper rash and just maintaining enough weigh to support his fragile body Henry would reach his two small arms upwards towards his mother. Stella initially hated the thought of returning home each night to a baby smelling like a cesspool and dying for her love. Initially she prayed for the baby to be dead when she got home or woke up in the morning; she thought it would be better for both of them. But Henry stuck though it and persevered.

Stella's attitude changed with each passing day and she looked forward to her son waiting for her arrival home from the diner. She loved his ability to take what the world had to offer even at his tender age and get through it. She continuously feared that Luke would do something to the baby while she was away but he basically ignored the kid as if he didn't exist. Each night Henry would stop crying when he saw her and this reaction would bring tears to her eyes. As she reached down for him and carefully lifted him from the crib he folded his two small arms around her neck and hugged her. He became her world and one of the few bright spots that made life bearable for her.

It happened on Henry's first birthday. It was the event that changed Henry's world forever. Stella was at work but was planning to get out early to be with Henry. She was going to surprise him with a small birthday cake that he could reach into with his two little hands and just have a ball for himself. She had brought an inexpensive disposable camera and had planned to take some photos of him. She also had gone to a local dollar store and picked up a small stuffed animal, an inflatable ball and a balloon for him. She had the items in a small shopping bag with some tissue paper with a small birthday card that she could read and tell him how much she loved him.

As she was leaving work for the walk home something terrible was happening to Henry. It was something that would affect Stella for years to come if she did not hurry to prevent it.

Luke was drunk as usual although this time he was insanely jealous about the small celebration planned for his pathetic son. Luke hadn't had a birthday party in years and here is this little brat getting one on his first birthday. Luke decided he would give him a little party before Stella got home, a party that Henry would remember for a long time. He stumbled into Henry's room with a can of Bud in his hand and went over to the crib where Henry was playing with a small plastic rattle with a cute bunny head. He looked up at Luke and became afraid. Each time he heard Luke's voice or seen him with his mother he was doing bad things. He was hitting her causing her to cry or saying things to her in a loud and threatening voice that told him something was terribly wrong. He looked up at Luke and for the first time saw a smile on his face. Henry sensed that the smile had an edge of evil behind it and he wished for his mommy to hurry home.

Luke grabbed Henry by the front of his soiled tee shirt and lifted him from the crib. He moved Henry so close to his face that Henry could smell the rotten breath of soured beer and whiskey that he had been pouring down his throat since the time he woke that morning. Luke stared at the boy with so much pent up hatred that he just wanted to bash the little boy's head against the wall until it took the shape of a smashed pumpkin that a bunch of kids would have thrown on the side walk of a home that did not open their front door for trick or treat on Halloween. Henry looked into those blood shot eyes and realized that this man was not holding him out of love but hatred. Not once did Henry remember this man comforting him since he was brought home from the hospital and now he could feel the evil being generated from his every pore. Luke fought to hold back his emotions, smiled at his son and said let me be the first one to wish you a happy birthday you little bastard. With that he moved the can of bud to the boy's lips, grabbed his cheeks in his other hand and forced Henry's small mouth open. As he started to slowly pour the beer down his throat. Henry gagged on the foul taste and had a tough time swallowing the liquid as it spilled from the mouth of the can.

Henry was getting sick and he felt dizzy as he wondered what this stuff was that was being shoved down his throat. As if it was a reflex action Henry vomited and it sprayed all over Luke's tee shirt, some hitting him in the face. Luke went crazy and threw Henry across the room in a fiery display of anger. Luckily Henry landed on an old sofa in the corner of the room but bounced off the cushion and on to the floor where he started to cry.

Luke looked at him in disgust and said I am going to kill you—you little bastard you have lived a year too long. With that he tossed the beer can at Henry but missed his target as it landed on the sofa spilling the little remaining liquid into the cushion. He staggered over to where Henry was lying and was going to kick him in the head when Stella opened the front door and walked in. Immediately she sensed something was wrong when Luke was not in the front room either passed out or watching a porno movie from one of his DVD collection. She saw the light on in her son's room and immediately dropped the paper bag on the floor while placing the small cake on the counter. On the counter was a set of various kitchen knives and she grabbed the largest one there in a defense mechanism reflective of a mother polar bear protecting her cub from hunters. She ran to the bedroom and she saw Luke standing drunkenly over her son telling him that he lived a year to long and he was going to put him out of his misery once and for all. Stella screamed "no" as loud as she could and raced towards Luke with the knife raised high over her head. Luke was caught by the surprise of Stella's scream turned to face her and realized too late that she held a knife. In one swift and powerful motion she plunged the knife deep into Luke's chest and shouted get away from my son you filthy bastard. Luke's eyes grew to an enormous size as his hands reached for the handle of the knife sticking in his chest. He had but a few seconds to realize that Stella had hit his heart with the blade and he was within a few short seconds of meeting his maker. Without any remorse she pushed him aside and picked up Henry from the floor and cuddled him closely to her chest. He stunk of beer and she saw that he was covered in vomit with a small bruise on his forehead. Otherwise he appeared to be ok. As she held him she whispered in his ear that she loved him very much and that she was there for him.

Stella stepped over the body lying on the floor with Henry in her arms and in one final defiant gesture kicked Luke in the head. She knew he was dead but the fact that she had put up with his constant abuse and intimidation for over a year had built up inside of her to a boiling point and she finally had a chance to release every ounce of anger. She had put up with the abuse but he was not going to take the one thing she loved in her life away from her. Not her son. She ended that problem quickly with the only solution she could think of at that fearful moment in time.

Stella waited to dial 911 for she knew that her days with Henry would be ending for quite a while. She gave him a bathe and whispered soft and kind words to him. She was still trembling and her hands shook uncontrollably as she put clean clothes on him and sat next to him on the soiled carpet on the living room floor. He smiled at her and put his hand on her knee and patted it as if telling her everything was all right mommy. She opened the shopping bag and took out the inflatable ball and other things that she had purchased for Henry at the dollar store. She blew up the ball and placed it in front of Henry and he laughed. He tapped it with both of his hands and it bounced forward. Stella grabbed it and rolled it to Henry and again he tapped it lightly only to see it bounce away from him. She let him play for a while and watched him enjoy himself as she put the small cake on the table and light the candle. She then reached down for him and walked over to one of the kitchen chairs and sat down with him on her lap. She held him tightly as she sung happy birthday to her son with tears rolling down her cheeks.

She blew out the candle for him and removed it from the cake. She then moved the cake close to Henry as he looked up at her as if to say is this for me? She smiled down at him showing him the love only a mother could provide through a simple expression and placed one of his fingers into the cake frosting and moved it gently to his mouth. Henry tasted the sweetness and patted his hands up and down in front of him as if he was indicating he wanted more. She released her hold of his small arms and Henry knew that he could dig into the delicious cake in front of him. She simply sat back and enjoyed the antics of her little boy go to town on his first birthday cake as Luke lay dead in the next room.

There was no sense in running from the law she had no place to go. She had no close relatives and unless she robbed a bank she didn't have enough money to get to the next town never mind another part of the country. As she sat there and dialed 911 she realized that her days with Henry were ending and that he may be better off with someone else anyway. She would surely do time for the murder regardless if they ruled it manslaughter or not. Her track record was not something that she was proud of and it would definitely be held against her regardless of what she said or did.

As she waited for the police to arrive she wished that she had taken her son far away before it got to this. As they say hind sight is a whole different ball game and should of's and could of's now a thing of the past. She felt no pity for Luke lying in the other room with a knife sticking in his chest; she actually felt some satisfaction in the fact that she ended his miserable life. Her focus was entirely on little Henry, the boy who had known just short bouts of comfort when she was around and not getting abused by Luke. He was innocent and would hopefully see more good times than bad over the coming years. She sobbed at the thought of life without him in it and realized at that moment she did not want that.

As she heard the whine of the police sirens approaching her apartment she knew what she had to do to assure that Henry would have a totally clean slate in life to start over with a new family who hopefully would love and take care of him. She had no fear of death as she had been living in hell for years now with demons ripping at her brain and driving her to do bad things to herself to put up with the rigors of life. She placed Henry on the floor with his new ball and balloon and slowly strolled into the bathroom and closed the door. She looked at the small wallet photo of Henry hanging in the corner of the bathroom mirror and leaned over and kissed it. She then took a razor blade from the cabinet and placed it next to her throat and asked god to forgive her for what she was about to do. As she took one last glance of Henry's photo she cut deeply into the tender skin on the side of her neck. The police arrived seconds later to find Henry playing on the floor in the living room and Luke dead in the child's bedroom. When they opened the bathroom door they found Stella lying against the toilet with blood splatter covering the walls. She had left no suicide note and the police detectives had to piece together what they thought were the events that lead up to the double killings that day. They found Henry's clothes covered with vomit and the strong odor of alcohol. They noticed the bruise on his head and the total disarray of the apartment with beer cans and garbage everywhere except the child's room that was the neatest room in the place. They looked at the numerous injuries on Stella's body—some old and healing; others recent inflictions from an abusive hand good at handing out punishment to a weak person.

Their conclusion was that Stella had arrived home from work and found Luke in the process of abusing Henry as he did so often to her and she lost it. She grabbed the knife from the kitchen and without hesitation stabbed him in the chest with the intent to kill him. She knew if she didn't that he would kill her. It then looked like she proceeded to have a short birthday celebration with her son before calling the police. One of the younger detectives involved in the investigation picked up the little boy and held him in his arms and saw the look of despair in his face. The boy was only one years old and yet had experienced a lifetime of agony.

Henry was placed into an orphanage under state control and spent the next four years of his life there. There were not many interested, potential, couples wanting to adopt a son of a suicidal mother and a felon father. A little boy who had witnessed the death of his father by his mother had to be a traumatic event even for a one year old. So Henry just stayed under the care of the state and was deemed a potential mental case by those who knew his background.

So Henry bounced around during his formative years and was the focus of abuse from the bigger kids in the orphanages. He went through every kind of abuse that is imaginable including normal kid stuff of name calling, taking his lunch or treats, being bullied to just cruel comments about his mother and father. It also went to the extremes of being locked outside in the cold, being make to fight kids twice his age and an attempted rape by a couple of homosexual older boys in the gym when everyone else had left. Henry continued to experience much more of the negative side of life than any child should in his early years but he was used to it and actually felt that it was part of his everyday life.

As he got older he was labeled as an easy mark and the abuse continued. Although people are supposed to mature with age there are still many nitwits who take pleasure in tormenting those that they view as weak. And Henry was one of them.

Henry eventually ran away from the orphanage and they did not even bother to contact the local police when he disappeared. He always seemed to be in the center of some trouble although most of it was not his doing. So when one of the staff members reported him missing that was basically the end of the Henry saga at the orphanage. He was now fifteen years old and within another year could go off on his own anyway if he wished to do so. They were relieved of the burden of always watching out for Henry and felt that they had better things to do with their time instead of protecting the son of a convicted felon and a drug using mother who killed herself.

So Henry settled in a small town outside of Denver where he managed to get a part time job doing chores at a small pig farm run by Darren Copley and his wife Thelma. They didn't question Henry much about where he came from or family; they were just happy that they were fortunate enough to have this kid stumble on to their farm one rainy night and ask to sleep in the barn. He began working for below minimum wage and never complained about anything. He just settled in and did anything asked of him quickly and without question. There Henry stayed for the next four years as he just saved every dime he ever received from the Copley's in preparation of moving on when the time suited him.

The only piece of paper that he managed to hold on to all that time was a worn out copy of his birth certification that he stole one day when a couple was evaluating him for adoption. They had left the file on the table top as they went into another room to discuss their decision with the administrator. When they left the room Henry took a copy of his birth certificate and quickly folded it up and stuffed it into his pants pocket. He held on to it all that time and periodically would look at his mom's name and remember the sweetness of her voice and the tenderness of her touch. It was this piece of paper that allowed him to get an identification card with his name and other key information to give him a small place in society. Henry Fiddleman would eventually become world famous and he had no idea that he would play an important role in the pending battle between good and evil.

So Henry had turned nineteen and had saved nearly five thousand dollars over his four years with the Copley's. On his nineteenth birthday he decided to move on and see what else laid in store for him. He packed his few personal belongings wrote a short note in very poor spelling to the Copley's thanking them for their support and left the farm. He left no forwarding information or indication on where he was headed; he was going to be just a figment of their imagination over the coming years as all traces of that young man who showed up on that rainy room were gone. Henry wanted it that way as he did not have any family or friendly ties through the majority of his life and at this point did not care to start.

He ended up in Denver where he got a small room in a local YMCA for sixty dollars a week. They gave him a discounted rate until he could find a job with the understanding that he would be paying seventy five dollars a week when he got one. Henry finally found a position in a video store filling the shelves of returned movies, learning how to work the cash register and how to profile the movies by category and type. It was one of his first opportunities to deal with people and at first it was extremely difficult for him to adjust. He would become nervous and start to stutter and the customers would just stare at him like he was an idiot. Henry learned that if he slowly counted to five before he started to talk than he could get through brief conversations without much difficulty. He really liked his job and the manager let him have an old television and DVD player that was used to display short trailers of the available new movies. They had gotten a newer display unit and were going to throw it away when Henry asked the manager if he could have it. The manager said sure and they became the first electronic devices that he ever owned. He set them up in his room at the Y and each night rented a different movie to watch. It was then that he developed heroes to worship that stood up for the rights of the underprivileged and abused. He loved Clint Eastwood and John Wayne. He also loved all the Disney films as they were able to take his mind to other places that were colorful and safe to live in. That is one of the things that drew him to the Avatar series of movies. He loved the beautiful world and race of people who were so carefree and supportive until the humans almost destroyed it.

That is how he met Sheila. It was simply that casual passing of comments about the movie that would link them together as two of a kind. That night led to more dates and then the eventual commitment between the both of them that they loved one another. They created an undying love that was supported through their difficult childhoods and their upbringing by their mothers who were their sole link to a caring relationship.

Sheila's mom had passed away and Sheila inherited the small house outside of Denver as her own. It was pretty run down but it was hers and she tried to maintain it as best she could with her job at dry cleaners just up the road from her house. She worked forty hours a week and brought home just under two hundred dollars. She got by and that was all that mattered to her besides Henry. Her hobbies of sewing and knitting also helped her to bring in a little extra cash at the local flea market on Saturdays and Sundays with a small booth that she rented each weekend. Henry moved in with her and she was so happy. It was Henry's quiet personality and sense of righteousness make Sheila feel safe for the first time in her life. He never stuttered when having a conversation around her which was quite a remarkable task when you consider his behavior around others. They both started to attend religious services every Sunday at a Baptist Church about a mile's walk from their small home. They quickly fit in with the congregation as good folks who were always willing to help support the church fund raisers through making things or cooking up some cookies or cakes for sale.

Chapter nine

Witnessing a death

So it came to pass that on that very road that Henry walked each day to work at the video store that he chanced upon a stranger in trouble that would change his life forever. It was here on Galilee Road when he met Jesus for the first time.

Jesus had a flat tire on his Jeep caused by some roofing nails that had spilled from the back of a construction truck whose driver had carelessly threw the remaining nails into an old wooden box seated on the end of the flatbed. The nails bounced around freely until they danced their way on to the road where they laid for some non suspecting passerby to drive over. It was getting dark and Jesus felt the initial problem with his tires when the steering became difficult and then the loud gearing sound of the metal rim against the asphalt pavement of the road. He pulled off to the shoulder of the road and got out of the Jeep to realize that his back rear tire was completely flat. He looked around and noticed very little traffic and those passing by had no interest in helping a stranger deal with a flat tire. Let him call for auto service or a friend on a cell phone they thought.

As Jesus gathered his thoughts he remembered the driver's manual in the glove compartment and went to the passenger side door and opened it. As he reached into the compartment he heard the sound of another vehicle coming to a stop behind him. As he turned he noticed three young men approaching him asking if he was in trouble and needed help. Jesus turned to them and thanked them for stopping and told them about the tire but otherwise everything was fine. Something felt strange to him as he looked at the actions of the three men. While one of them tried to divert Jesus' attention to him one of the others was looking inside the vehicle as if seeking anything of value on the seats or the floor. The other seemed to be walking around the vehicle to come up behind where Jesus was standing. The one talking to Jesus was also casing what was happening around him yet still tried to maintain all of Jesus' attention to him. He told Jesus that they will help to change the flat tire as it was the least that they could do to help since they had been in a similar situation a few weeks ago. The man introduced himself as Turtle, a nickname that he got for being slow at everything he did. He said his friends were nick named rabbit, for the obvious reason he said as he laughed, and Jackal for the other.

Turtle then asked Jesus if he had any drugs in the Jeep that they could have a little party with as they helped him change the tire. Jesus told him that he had nothing in the Jeep except a bottle of water and his jacket. At that point Turtle seemed to become much more irritated and turned to Jesus and asked what he had in his pockets. He told Jesus that it would be wise to empty his pockets on the hood of the Jeep for him to take a look at. He told him that it would be a smart thing to do to avoid any misunderstanding of their positions. Jesus was certainty not going to resort to violence. Outnumbered three to one he realized that it was useless to resist and he could easily replace anything of value that he carried on him in a heartbeat. So he laid all the items including his wallet on the hood of the car. Turtle looked at him and told him that was a very smart thing to do as it would stop any misconceptions that may lead them to go in a different direction in getting what they wanted. Jesus just studied Turtle carefully and thought to himself that he was not the first victim of these three. It was just how many others were fooled into thinking that they were going to help them in the past.

Jackal grabbed each of the items and took anything of value to include his American Express Card, the money and loose change he had in his pockets. Rabbit went through the inside of the vehicle and took his jacket as well. Everything was going along as Jesus would expect in dealing with some petty thugs until one of them made the comment about let's get this over with now. Turtle turned to Jesus and told him that they needed to take a short walk into the cluster of trees that were clustered together down the embankment. He watched their hand gestures and realized that they had done this many times to other unsuspecting victims and he knew that the outcome was not pretty.

Turtle told Jesus that there wouldn't be any trouble but they needed him off the main road to give them enough time to get on their way before he could get help. They were going to tie him to a tree loose enough for him to break free after an hour or so and everything would be all right.

Jackal had enough of the small talk and pushed Jesus in the back causing him to stumble and fall to his knees. The image took Jesus back thousandths of years to the point when a Roman soldier had done the same thing to him as he carried that wooden cross that was strapped to his back. Jesus knew it was useless to say anything so he got to his feet and started to walk in the direction of the trees. He did not let on that he saw the knives that each of the goons tried to conceal from his view in their hands.

As he started down the embankment he noticed a young man approached from the east. The man was watching what was happening in front of him and was trying to figure out why they were headed for the clump of trees off the road when he noticed the knives in a couple of the men's hands. Henry knew that he was walking right into trouble of some innocent person being victimized by others who thrived on intimidation tactics and could not fight back due to the odds against them. Henry would even the odds.

The only one noticed that he was heading in their direction was the one that appeared to be in trouble. Yet he was walking casually to the wooden area without any sign of duress or fear. It appeared that the man was using some sort of a hand signal that tried to tell him that everything was under control but was it?

As Jesus slowly walked to the clump of trees with the three assailants he thought about the daily perils of people everywhere coming in direct contact with such evil monsters that want nothing more than the personal gratification of inflicting pain and suffering on others for their own personal gain. This was his first encounter and he had been on earth for only a few months. He found that astonishing. As he glanced at each of the young men he tried to figure out when each of them decided on the path that they wanted to follow in life and why. Was it related to family problems, getting in with the wrong crowd in school, drugs, laziness, lack of love for their fellow man, or a combination of factors?

He looked at Turtle and saw a young man who was definitely the brains of the outfit. The others were following his every command and were obviously dependent upon him on what to do and when. Although unshaven, in need of a bath, and showing obvious signs of drug dependency Turtle appearing to be fairly well spoken and easily personable in his voice tone and manners. If he had chosen a separate path he could have easily been in marketing or some sort of occupation of personal development where his influence over others could have been better served.

Jesus studied the other two and noticed that they appeared to be barely twenty years old. Both thin as if surviving on fast food with the interference factor of intravenous needles driving illegal drugs into their system creating a conflict that their bodies would not tolerate for very long before just turning it to mush. They were probably high school drop outs that got together to pine over their miseries only to decide that they can feast off the weakness of others to get what they wanted. They had started small with breaking into cars to steal whatever they could find, then houses left unoccupied while the owners worked. But that was not providing enough revenue to satisfy their cravings and they started attacking people who were in need of help—stuck along a deserted highway or parking areas that appeared to be easy prey for the three of them.

Recently Turtle had convinced them to take their trade to a whole new level and their previous three victims had been savagely beaten with one of the three on life support and another still drifting in and out of a coma due to serious injuries inflicted by the trio. But today Turtle planned to take them all to a new high; they were going to kill this man and take everything he had. Turtle was sick of all this petty crap and just making ends meet. One way to take that giant leap forward was to be bold enough to go for the gusto and start going for the bigger money out there. They would terrorize some rich bastard enough to get as much as they could and then eliminate him. In order to have balls enough to do that they had to step over that line of humanity when another's life does not matter and that is where this poor, unfortunate stranger with the flat tire fit into their plans. Each would play a role in his death so there would be no one able to plead out a lesser charge with the DA if they got caught. If one sang then he was going down with the rest—at least—that is the way they figured it.

Henry was in a quandary on what to do. There was no help in sight and this young man was surely in dire need of support. Henry had no weapons and was not a fighter as shown repeatedly in the past. He could yell out to startle them and allow the man a chance to run but that could easily backfire and pull the attention to him as well. He could wait and, perhaps, they are just going to knock him out and steal his car and take off. Then Henry thought that he could go into the trees and save him by calling the rescue.

As Henry milled over his options the four men had reached the clump of trees with Jesus standing in the middle. Turtle told him to get on his knees and pray because he had but a few minutes to live. Henry watched from a distance by kneeling in some tall grass that helped to hide him from the vision of the others. He kept moving forward at a snail's pace to avoid detection while gaining the strength and fortitude to help the young man.

As Jesus began to kneel he spoke to the three men and asked them to leave him there and he would not tell anyone of the incident. He told them that he did not want any trouble and he had given them all of his earthy belongings. Turtle smiled at that one and told Jesus that he was not after his earthly belongings now he wanted his others as well. Jackal and Rabbit chuckled at the comment knowing what Turtle meant by the inside joke.

Without any further hesitation Jesus looked directly at each one of them and told them that they were stepping beyond boundaries that they should not cross. He said all those petty crimes that you did pale in comparison in what you are thinking about doing to me. Think carefully about what you plan to do today and I pray that each one of you are man enough to realize you are making a very serious mistake. You will surely regret your actions while you are alive but—in all certainty—when you are dead.

The calmness in his voice and the effective delivery of his words send shivers down the spine of Rabbit and Jackal. It was apparent he meant every word that he had spoken and the scary part was that he was showing absolutely no fear. He had nothing that could possibly harm them yet he was frightening them more than they were to him. The only one of the three not affected by Jesus" words was Turtle. He was pissed that this stranger was not shitting his pants right about now and was quickly losing his temper. Turtle had enough of this word game and told Jesus if he believed in god then expect to meet him in a few minutes because only three of them were going to walk out of there. With one final statement Jesus turned the odds in his favor as he placed his hands together, looked to the sky, and said forgive them for they know not what they do.

The words caused goose bumps to appear all over Rabbit's body and he immediately dropped the knife and said that he did not want anything to do with this. Something was wrong and he wanted no part of killing this man. Enough is enough he said. We can go to prison for the things that we have done but we haven't taken anyone's life yet and I won't start now. Turtle got pissed at Rabbit backing down and he turned to Jackal and asked him if he was chickening out too. Jackal thought as he tossed the knife from hand to hand. He already knew he was a two time loser and questioned whether he really wanted to become a three. He looked over at Rabbit who was begging him to get the hell out of there with him before it was too late.

Jackal dropped the knife and told Turtle he wanted nothing to do with it. If he wanted to kill this man then he could carry that guilt on his shoulders alone. Turtle was so pissed he couldn't think straight. All he saw was all his plans going up in smoke because these two cowards were going belly up. Instead of waiting for any further reaction from Turtle both Rabbit and Jackal hightailed as fast as they could from that clump of trees towards their car. They had no intention on waiting for Turtle to do something crazy with them standing there. They were pleased for taking a stand before it became too late and there was something about that stranger that scared them. He was not intimidated nor threatened by what was happening around him and then like some religious freak prayed for them instead of himself! They reached the car and Rabbit jumped into the driver's seat, started the engine, and sped off. Jackal turned to take one final glance back and thought that he saw Turtle lurching at the kneeling man. He lowered his head for the first time in years, folded his hands together and said a silent prayer for the stranger.

Henry watched the two of them run from the trees and drive off and realized that the young man had much better odds than before in pulling through this. Henry was also positioned now where he could easily see the punk standing over the man approximately thirty feet away.

What happened next was something that Henry would take to his grave. It seemed to develop in slow motion in Henry's eyes and the initial action caused Henry to stand up and scream no, don't do it! Turtle had decided that he was going to kill this innocent man regardless of what just happened with Rabbit and Jackal. There was no turning back now and he thought of how famous he would become. This stranger would be the first of many and he would eventually stand beside Ted Bundy and Charles Manson as cold hearted killers before the cops caught up with him.

Within seconds he lunged at Jesus and swung the knife in a wide circling motion in an attempt to create enough thrust to bury the knife deeply into his neck. But as Turtle heard Henry's scream he stumbled forward and lose his balance. On top of that he could not stop the arm motion that was in full swing and instead of burying it into Jesus' neck he planted it directly into his own chest. Turtle flopped on the ground like a fish out of water and screamed in pain as the blade sliced into his lung and blood vessels. He laid there begging for help and pleading not to die.

Jesus got up and walked over to where Turtle was lying and told him that a few seconds earlier Turtle could have make a decision that would have dramatically changed his life and fate forever. During those few seconds he willingly chose the one option that Jesus would not help him turn around. Jesus had returned to earth to help in the salvation of mankind and those that decided to join him would enjoy the fruits of their choice. Those who did not will suffer the repercussions of their decision. With that Jesus whispered, "May god my father forgive you but I do not". And in that breathe and the touch of Jesus' hand to Turtle's head he was gone.

Turtle had simply vanished leaving behind a pile of gray ashes and his clothes on the ground. Jesus was standing there alone with the exception of Henry who witnessed the entire event.

Henry had heard it all and had not missed a single word. He was the single witness that just seen a body vanishes before his very eyes. At that moment in time, for that split second in Henry's life, he realized why he managed to get through the turmoil and conflicts over all those years. He had seen the worse of the worse and somehow managed to get through the ordeals time and again. And he often wondered why.

He now knew that he survived because he was special; he was so special that he witnessed something that others only read about or speculated about but never knew if it was true. But Henry Fiddleman knew that he just witnessed the second coming of Jesus Christ and he was standing in front of him!

Jesus knew that Henry was standing there in amazement at what he just heard and witnessed. He had initially wanted him to stay out of the situation but knew that was not to be. Henry had persevered throughout his entire life and carried with him a sense of righteousness that Jesus knew was missing in millions of others. As Jesus turned to face Henry the very first thing that he did was smile; hold out his hand; and told him it was a pleasure to meet him. Henry was completely taken back by the gesture as he had expected some sort of religious occurrence with Jesus spreading his arms and angels singing in harmony in the background. Instead he stood there in front of Henry holding his hand out as if he was an old friend that he hadn't seen for a while.

Henry stood his ground and did not move; it was not that he did not want to but because he still could not believe what he just witnessed. He actually pinched his right hand to see if he was dreaming and this was all a figment of his imagination. It was real. Jesus walked over to Henry and simply put his arms around him and hugged him and then told him something that only Sheila and his mom ever said to him; he told Henry that he loved him and everything would be fine.

Henry felt calmness come over him that he had not felt in his entire life.

It was at this point when he had the energy to place his arms around Jesus and hug him as well. Henry's first words to Jesus Christ was plain and simple and Jesus smiled; he said "Boy, it's great to meet you; I didn't think I would get the chance till I passed away".

Jesus looked at Henry and smiled as he could just imagine what was going through this man's head as he milled over the events of the past several minutes. Yet he stood his ground and was not afraid. There was a sense of tranquility in the air as the two stood motionless for a few minutes trying to determine how to move forward with a relationship between two individuals with a secret not yet shared with anyone else but Nathan and his family. Jesus broke the ice by asking Henry if he could help him change the flat tire so he could get on his way. Henry found the request funny because Jesus could do the star trek tele—transport of himself to other locations just by thinking about it—couldn't he? He was going to ask Jesus just that but thought the better of it because he didn't want to look like a fool in Jesus' eyes so he let his thought pass.

As they walked to the jeep Jesus told Henry that he knew that Henry saw the hand signal not to interfere in the incident with the three men and thanked him for sticking around to make sure that he was going to be all right or to try and get help. Jesus told him that he wanted to determine the odds of someone with evil intents of changing their course of action before it became too late. In this case two of the three men decided on doing something good and not getting involved while the third was devoted to the path of self destruction and evil and he paid the price for it. If these odds held true than Jesus felt more confident that he would surely win out in the conflict with Satan. The issue was that each evil person has the tendency to inflict terrible losses on the righteous.

Jesus talked to Henry as if he had known him for years and placed an element of trust into his conversation that far exceeded any expectation Henry could have had. Jesus told him that he was, indeed, Jesus Christ and returned to put faith and trust back into the human race. Not just some of the people but all of the people. If he failed he would be gone forever and the people will know that fact because they would have been key participants in this ultimate battle between him and Satan. He told Henry he had been on earth but for a few short months but was encouraged by what he has seen and slowly his faith in the human race was being restored. He told him that heaven was filled with millions of souls who left this earth uncertain if there truly was such a place. It was a place of eternal rest and salvation that would allow them to reunite with their loved ones that they missed so dearly. But on the same level there were millions in hell who were residing in a place of eternal damnation that wanted nothing more than to drag everyone into their realm of misery. So the battle has begun and there could be just one winner with no more split pots.

Jesus looked at Henry and thought of the millions of other innocents so much like him that were searching for that one glimmer of light that would brighten their miserable lives and he was saddened. Jesus, himself, did a lot of soul searching about why he didn't decide before now to take it to this level. How many others have searched for that answer over the centuries and could have lived in a relative state of tranquility knowing that they would eventually reside in a place they only dreamed about. Jesus was upset with himself each time he thought about his indecision to wait for the best time. There was no "best" time as he witnessed century after century.

Jesus stopped talking and Henry took the opportunity to say that he knew that he would be the winner; it was a no brainer he said. He told him that it was like the Super Bowl Champions taking on a high school football team and it would be no contest. Henry told him that he looked pretty good for being so old and that he really did a good job of improving the way he dressed and his overall appearance; he said that he never did like long hair on men. Jesus laughed hysterically at Henry's comments and before Henry could take it the wrong way Jesus explained to him that he truly enjoyed his remarks about the changes he decided to make on this visit to earth. He told Henry that if he showed up with long hair and appearing to be very old that someone would have taken him for an escapee from an old folk's home or hospital. Also people would not take him seriously when they dealt with him thinking he was just another elderly crackpot going off the deep end. Henry smiled and shook his head up and down in agreement.

As Henry changed the flat he asked Jesus what his plans were and how could he possibly help him. He wanted to tell the world what he just saw and who he met on that walk from work that day. Jesus just smiled and asked Henry if he could meet his wife before he went on his way and Henry was thrilled.

Chapter ten

Dinner with Sheila

Sheila was surprised when she noticed Henry approaching the house with a stranger. It was not like Henry to come home with someone that she did not know and she became a little anxious about who he was and how Henry had met him. She knew that Henry was a kind hearted soul and had a very difficult time turning his back on anyone in need. As she peered out the window she noticed that Henry actually had his arm around the man as if he had known him for years and Henry was talking up a storm. It was obvious that he was not having any difficulty with stuttering as it appeared as if the words were just flowing from his mouth. The man was young, appeared to me in his mid twenties, from what she could surmise. He was thin and yet quite a handsome young man with wavy brown hair and a small mustache. He seemed to enjoy Henry's company and was pointing at the house as they approached. It was then she realized that he was pointing directly at her as she stood in the window. Sheila looked down at herself and realized that she still wore the kitchen apron and slippers on her feet. Her hair was tied up in the back of her head with a small rubber band and her hands covered in pie dough that was drying on her hands from the pie that she just placed in the oven. As fast as a rabbit scooting down his hole she ran to the bathroom and threw the apron into the clothes hamper, pulled the rubber band from her hair and brushed her flowing locks with the brush laying on the vanity. She washed her hands and quickly applied some deodorant to cover the perspiration from the kitchen chores she was doing.

She heard the front door swing open and Henry calling her name as he entered the living room. She called out to him that she would be there in a minute and looked at herself one more time in the mirror checking her appearance. She ran her hands down the sides of her dress as if trying to smooth out any wrinkles and walked into the living room to greet Henry and his guest. It was a meeting that she would never forget.

Henry walked over to her and kissed her on the cheek while giving her a small hug as he always does. He then took her hand and walked over to where the stranger was standing and turned to Sheila and said I would like to introduce you to my friend, Jesus.

Sheila reached out and shook Jesus' hand and said that it was very nice to meet him as Jesus responded likewise. Henry was tingling with excitement and appeared to be so antsy that Sheila asked him what was wrong. Henry smiled and told her that he had invited the man to dinner with them and he had accepted. Jesus said it was a real pleasure meeting her and he heard nothing but good things about her on the short drive to their house. She reached out and gently touched Henry's chin and told him she loved him very much.

About a half of an hour later they were sitting at the dining room table and preparing to eat a meal of roast chicken, mashed potatoes, gravy, sweet corn and corn bread. Henry said the short blessing as he normally did before every meal and Jesus appreciated the moment of given thanks that was shared by the three for the food on the table.

As they prepared to eat Henry could not contain himself any longer and as Sheila placed a spoonful of potatoes into her mouth Henry let out the news that the visitor was none other than Jesus Christ himself. Sheila almost gagged on the potatoes as some went down her throat and the rest flew out of her mouth and into her hand that she placed in front of her mouth when she realized what Henry had just said. Had Henry been tricked by this stranger into actually believing he was Jesus Christ? What were the real intentions of this stranger in their home? She stared across the table at the stranger waiting for him to pull out a knife or gun and tell them that he was going to rob them or worse. Henry should have known better than to put his trust into someone who he had met only minutes before taking him into their home.

Yet Henry was still a bundle of joy and the stranger just sat there with a small smile on his face looking at Henry. Henry turned to Jesus and said I told you that she would not believe me and I was right. Henry just turned to Sheila and looked at her directly into her blue eyes and said he really is Jesus you have to believe me.

Instead of telling Henry that he was being taken as a fool by a total stranger or ridiculing him for his faith to believe in others she looked at Jesus. She saw a quiet young man who was just enjoying the pure happiness of Henry as he unveiled his story to his wife. The calmness and peacefulness of the man amazed her and she began to sense that she was slowly being dragged into a life changing event that descended upon her with the arrival of this stranger.

For the next ten minutes Henry told Sheila the story about what happened up the road and how he had heard every single word spoken and had seen Turtle just disappear as he laid there on the ground. She took in every word and constantly shifted her attention back and forth between Henry and the stranger to monitor the man's reactions to all of Henry's words. When Henry was done he simply looked at his wife and told her that she has to believe him as it was all true.

Sheila sat there for a few minutes and did not say anything nor did the stranger who patiently waited for her response. Sheila got up from where she was sitting and went to the chair next to the man and sat down. She reached out and gently took his right hand and flipped it over and asked him to open it. Jesus did as she requested and she carefully studied it and rubbed the skin as if trying to exam it to see if he gave any hint that he was thousands of years old. She noticed that he had never worn a ring, had no wristwatch and he was so composed that it frightened her a little.

She asked him why he wanted to meet her instead of going on his way and why was she so important to Jesus Christ that he would take time away from much more pressing issues than to meet her. The answer took her completely by surprise and overwhelmed her with emotion when he told her that he was very touched by her prayers the night her mother died in this very house six years ago. How he was touched with her words to her mother that she would miss her every day until they met again in heaven and until that day she would wake up each morning and say hello to her and place a small wooden cross that she made from wooden matches into a small wicker basket in memory of her. Jesus said that she had kept her word every single day for six years and her mom was so happy with her. Sheila had told no one of that pledge to her mother not even Henry and at that moment she understood the joy and pure emotion being exhibited by Henry. She was holding the hand of Jesus for that she was certain.

The mystery on why Jesus had entered their lives would be answered in the future. Until then he was happy that he had touched another couple who were searching for answers to their existence and whether they truly meant anything in this world except to one another. Before leaving Jesus gave them a small worn metal cross and told them to keep it in memory of him and he hoped that they would always remember the day that they allowed a stranger to enter their home. With that he left their home and drove his jeep down the lonely highway.

Chapter eleven

The dam destruction

Lucifer was laughing his ass off. While Jesus was pampering a couple of losers he was in the midst of finalizing another major disaster in the world. He had better things to do than let a few individuals know that he had returned to earth to settle a long standing conflict for mankind. What good is it going to do anyway by letting a select few in on the big secret? Whoever they talked with would think they were loonies who should be put away before they hurt someone. Jesus had no chance in this battle and by whittling away his precious time on these petty relationships would only allow Lucifer to gain more of a strangle hold in his plans.

He had already used a little "germ warfare" to cause thousands of deaths and he was fairly pleased with himself. He had wished to make a much bigger impact but what the hell he made the headline news for months until the white knight came riding to the rescue. What did Jesus do so far—help a little boy come out of a coma and let a couple of losers know that he was real. Big fucking deal he thought to himself.

So he was in the city where the old saying goes—"What happens in Vegas stays in Vegas". Yap the gambling capital of the world where you can buy anything that you desire if you have the cash to do it. He marveled at the rows of casinos stretching as far as the eye could see and was actually excited to be there. It almost felt like home to him as he sensed every imaginable vice possible surrounding him. Gambling, sex, adultery, greed, and envy were evident to him everywhere as he strolled into Caesar's Palace. Go back a few thousand years and they would have been throwing the humans to the lions but today it was Lucifer leading the humans to their slaughter in a few short months.

He walked into Caesar's Palace and over to a dollar slot machine where he slid a twenty dollar bill into the slot, hit max bet and pulled the handle. The wheels spun and when coming to a complete stop landed with three lucky sevens showing across the screen. Bells and whistles went off to alert all those around him that the casino had a winner in their midst. One of the attendants walked over to him and congratulated him on his winning of a jackpot prize of five thousand dollars. Lucifer just smiled and thanked the attendant as he waited for the payout to be delivered to him.

As he waited he looked around and was so pleased with his observations. A couple of old farts were there feeding a slot machine as if it was a hungry dog. There was a wino stumbling through the doorway that was being approached by two security guards assuring that he did not enter the premises and cause a scene. There was a couple arguing over taking more money from the ATM machine while another man at the roulette wheel trying to sneak a last minute bet beyond the eyes of the casino crew. There was a hooker pretending she was playing a slot machine yet her attention was drawn to a man playing a five dollar slot machine a few feet away. Easy prey she thought as she started his direction. There was a man walking by with a blank stare in his eyes and it was obvious that things did not go his way that day and now he had to face the music for blowing the money he had. There were a couple of dudes casing likely victims that they could rob in a parking lot. Everywhere he looked he saw evil and he was on a sky high.

But Lucifer had not come to gamble or people watch; he had come forth to do another near impossible feat. He had big plans, very big plans that would set the world straight. He would demonstrate that the man who showed up in all those photos in the UK as the carrier of the black plague was now in the U.S. This time he was involved in another devastating event that would, hopefully, allow people to realize who he actually was.

Lucifer thought how strange it seemed to have such a booming city surrounded by nothing by desert. There were hundreds of miles of cactus, sand, snakes, spiders, and more cacti. Yet out there on the outskirts of Vegas was also an engineering marvel like no other. It was something that was built to help mankind deal with the hazards of living in such a god forsaken area of the country. He chuckled at his little joke about god forsaken country but continued on with his thoughts. There was a little beaver dam called Hoover that spans the Colorado River between Arizona and Nevada, about 30 miles southeast of Las Vegas. Should something unforeseen happen to that dam it would send further shock waves across the world. The destruction of something that was built to outlast time would make the headlines and he would be in the middle of it again.

His plan was simple but it was the implementation of it that would take his ungodly talents to complete. He was just going to blow such a large frigging hole in the center of it that the entire structure would crumble like those twin towers did on 9/11. He was seriously contemplating duplicating the disaster on the same date but figured it would point all fingers at the terrorist world and decided on a much better date to unleash his fury. He settled on July 4, the country's national Independence Day, as his choice. It will be July 4th he mumbled to himself, so sweet!

Hoover Dam started construction in 1931 and opened in 1936 at a construction cost of $49 million dollars. It was a massive structure of 1,244 feet in length; 726.4 feet in height and 660 feet wide at the base. The entire flow of the Colorado River passes through the turbines and reaches speeds of about 85 miles per hour. The electrical power generated by the dam is about 2080 megawatts enough to generate power as far as Los Angeles, California which is 266 miles away. Lake Mead itself is approximately 157,900 acres, backing up 110 miles behind the dam.

With maximum pressure at the base of the dam of 45,000 pounds per square foot weighing more than 6,600,000 tons with over 4 million cubic yards of concrete it was an unbelievable sight to those seeing it for the first time.

Records vary on how many lost their lives in the construction of the dam. In some reports sources cite the number of deaths at 112. But this number includes figures of personnel involved in the geological surveys that fell into the river and drowned well before the building started. The "official" number of fatalities involved in the building of the dam is 96 from "industrial fatalities". These are men who died from such causes as drowning, blasting, falling rocks or slides, falls from the canyon walls, being struck by heavy equipment, truck accidents, etc. "Industrial facilities" do not include deaths from heat, pneumonia, heart trouble, etc. Regardless to the number that lost their lives in the dam's construction, Satan was going to kill so many more in that one day that any recent disaster would pale in comparison.

Due to 9/11 security has increased around the dam. Some types of vehicles are presently restricted such as trailer trucks, buses carrying luggage, and enclosed box trucks over 40 feet long. Others are subject to inspection prior to crossing the dam. Average traffic across the dam daily is 13,000 to 16,000 vehicles. In a year approximately 8 to 10 million visitors travel each year to see the dam and use the Lake Mead National Recreation Area.

This was the target of Lucifer's next action plan to let the world know of his great return. The problem was that the security was so tight it would tax his abilities in having it crumble and fall like humpty dumpty falling off the wall.

During the construction of the dam they created four diversion tunnels, two from the Nevada side and two on the Arizona side. Following the completion of the dam, the entrances to the two outer diversion tunnels were sealed at the opening and half way through the tunnels with large concrete plugs. The downstream halves of the tunnels following the inner plugs are now the main bodies of the spillway tunnels. What was interesting was that the spillway tunnels have been used only twice in the history of the dam; they were the perfect locations to plant a pleasant surprise to the visitors on July 4th National Holiday.

Although covered with a large gating system the spillways were the perfect entrance to plant tons of explosives that would cause a massive crack in the interior of the structure that would be irreparable. The blast would generate the wallop of a small atomic bomb and a leak of catastrophic proportions would develop within minutes and the Hoover Dam would be forever remembered along with the twin towers of New York—just a memory in time.

Satan had done his research well and also carefully analyzed those humans who eventually would end up as permanent residents of hell when they met their end. From this group he would select the few trusted individuals who will help him pull this caper off. He decided to center on two individuals who worked at the dam and held very responsible positions in the intra structure of the site's daily operations. One of them was Roland Bates the chief security officer and the second a Jonathan Tates, a lead project engineer responsible for the annual inspection of the spillways operational performance. As Jesus had done in his encounters, Lucifer will assure these two men that he was indeed Satan; the one that they were so anxiously supporting in their private lives. Satan met up with them after they had spent the night boozing at "The Hell hole" a local bar off the interstate. Roland and Jonathan were good friends and for good reasons. During their evenings they shared a few hobbies involving society's outcasts, hookers, or unsuspecting travelers who broke down on the highways around the city of Vegas. They would troll the area after a night of boozing and settle on a target. They were extremely careful in their selection process as they did not want to draw undue attention to the authorities that there were serial killers in their midst.

Once they had their target in their control they would do as they pleased with them for a night of fun, take them out to a deserted part of the desert and kill them. They had their own burial site out there in the middle of nowhere and figured that they could continue with their antics for years without being detected if they were careful. Periodically they would spot a local news article about one of their victims being reported missing but it was followed up with some comments about the person's criminal record and run ins with the law. Extra care was taken with the stranded motorist and choosing them as victims was few and far between. There was additional risk in killing them as they would have pesky relatives hounding the authorities to find out what happened to them. Roland and Jonathan were perfect for each other as neither seemed to have a conscious or fear of being caught. They were psychos and the perfect candidates to support Satan's plans.

Satan was standing by their car in the darkened parking lot as they left the club. Initially they eyed him as an easy mark for their night of fun—why go out searching for a victim when there was one standing alone in the parking lot. They sized him up as they approached their car and Roland told him to quit leaning on their fucking car if he knew what was good for him. Roland went to Satan's right as Jonathan positioned himself on his left. Roland had a police blackjack in his rear left hand pocket and was gradually getting it out of his pocket to whack Satan over the head. Then Jonathan would catch him; put him in the back of the car; and they would drive into the desert for some fun.

Satan told both of them to go fuck themselves because he knew the kid's game that they were up to. Roland stopped suddenly in his attempt to free the blackjack and asked him what the hell he is talking about. Satan told them he knew about all the bodies in the desert and their morbid hobbies that they enjoyed so much. He gave them the exact body counts and even told them how much money and jewelry they took off the poor, unsuspecting souls. He said that he should turn their sorry asses into the cops but he had bigger and better plans for the two of them. They both looked fanatically around thinking that there would be twenty to thirty cops jumping all over them but the area remained quiet and deserted with only an occasional passing car flying down the highway. They glanced back and forth at one another as if trying to decide what to do next. How did this man know about their "fun time" and what the hell did they just get themselves into without even realizing it?

Satan wasted no more of his time with explanations of his knowledge of their escapades. He just looked at them and said that you sorry bastards better believe me when I tell you that I am the person that you have been dying to eventually meet. You will definitely be coming my way when you croaked but I need you now. You are part of me as you are also pure evil and you both know it. Goody good shoes during your daylight cover jobs but a holy terror inside your soul that drives your insanity at night. Let me introduce myself I am Satan, your savior, you two bastards.

His knowledge of their every crime, his confidence level showing absolutely no fear, and his glowing red eyes left no doubt who he was. The question now was what the hell did he want with them and is this how you eventually meet your final fate before you enter the hereafter?

Satan told them that he wanted to take a little ride with them and got into the front passenger seat of Roland's car. He rolled down the window and told them to get their sorry asses moving because he did not have all night to screw around with them. He had bigger fish to fry and soon they would understand what he was talking about. It was a ride that they would never forget. As they spun out of the parking lot Satan grabbed one of the beer cans lying in the six pack on the floor. Although warm as piss he popped the tab and quickly downed the can, crushing the aluminum can in his hand when done. He could sense the fear being generated from Roland and Jonathan but tried to make them feel at ease by telling them not to worry—they were on his side and he would take good care of them.

That night Satan laid out his plan and why they were chosen to help him carry it out. Killing an unsuspecting person every once in a while for their personal jollies was one thing—this was involvement in a historical event of catastrophic results. Yet deep down inside they were getting a thrill in being handpicked by Satan himself and could not believe their good fortune. They knew that their final destination was hell and really wasn't worried about that until the day that they died. Now they had an inside track with the man himself and would do everything possible to get on his good side before judgment day.

As Lucifer carefully laid out his plan it took on a certainty that it would work without any doubts in their minds. As long as they were careful they had the means and knowledge to carry it out. One of them had easy access to the spillways and the other was the chief of security who could pull the right strings at the right times to create the voids needed in security. They listened intently to Satan as he laid out in detail their every action and his own participation in the plan. Every minute, every action was carefully planned and any fool could see that it had a very high probability of complete success. The authorized excursions into the spillways will allow Jonathan to carry the explosions easily concealed in his back packs that should have carried his laptop, chemical sample bottles, forms and documents. He would stash the explosives into the various watertight sealed chambers that were spread throughout the spillway and follow up with the wiring schematics that would start the chain reaction of devastation to take down the massive structure. Roland in the meantime would be monitoring the spillway activities personally himself to help avoid detection.

Over the next four weeks the chambers were loaded with enough explosions to equal the wallop of an atomic blast and the plan was moving forward at a pace that sent shivers down Satan's spine. It was three days before the fourth of July and there were an increased activity of tourists in the Lake Mead and Hoover Dam area; just what Satan had planned. This was going to be a thing of beauty he thought as he went over the final preparation with the two clowns that he had working for him.

He had decided to make his presence known over the next three days by being a member of the tourists being caught on the surveillance cameras. On the last day he made sure that he would be picked out by the FBI team that will be so carefully scrubbing them by sending the universal sign of fuck you with his middle finger graphically displayed in front of him as he smiled for the cameras. He repeated the act four times throughout the tour by gradually turning to the camera and slowly chucking it the bird so it was not obvious to those around him or anyone watching the cameras at that time. They would surely pick it up, however, under close review as they methodically scrubbed the videos. There he would be—the same wacko who started the black plague in the UK. It wouldn't be long before some of the experts began to realize who he was or at least consider the possibilities. Actually if they really scrubbed the videos he intentionally wore a v neck pull over to expose the small numbers on the skin of his neck. They read 666.

July 4th started off as any other sleepy holiday across the country. Parades were set on main streets and firework displays would be sparkling in the night skies later that evening. Families were gathering in back yards for barbecues with an endless supply of ribs, hot dogs, potato salad, and burgers. Here in Vegas the steady stream of cars and Recreational vehicles stretched miles leading into the Hoover Dam and Lake Mead area to enjoy the day with outdoor activities. High on a ridge overlooking the scene was Satan with his two goons watching all the unsuspecting wind endlessly down the highway to their eventual doom as the minutes ticked away. He would let them enjoy the last moments on earth by becoming exhausted from the day's activities of boating, swimming, hiking, and biking. He had the explosive set to detonate at 6:06 PM with a secondary one going off 6 minutes later. He was sure that the investigating agents would again tie all the loose ends neatly together.

As Satan waited he wondered what Jesus was up to? Was he helping an old lady across the street; trying to sell Girl Scout cookies, buying a homeless man a hot meal, or kissing up to some poor soul who lost their way? He laughed to himself at each passing thought and was actually proud of himself in the mass hysteria that he was about to unleash on the American public. All fingers would point to the terrorists and the country would be crying out for revenge and blood for those that they believe are responsible. The President would grasp the opportunity to get all the attention away from his political woes and try to recoup some of his long gone popularity. There was nothing better to stir up the American public in your favor than to start another war to stir up patriotism. What a joke he thought.

He was getting antsy as the clock slowly ticked its way to six o'clock. He stood up and folded his arms in front of him and studied all the activity below him. Cars lined up for miles, people touring on top of the dam while others were inside of it as well as people in boats on the lake with people everywhere. As the clock hit 6:06 he heard a huge rumbling sound coming from within the dam followed by a massive explosion. The ground shook under his feet and the power of the bomb sent shock waves across the water that made it look like an ocean in a very bad storm. Security was running in every direction but not knowing exactly what to do or where to go. People were screaming and parents were running with children in their arms trying to get as far away from the dam as possible.

But it was not to be. The second explosion six minutes later did the damage that would send shock waves across the world. The concrete in the center of the dam displayed a huge crack that started at the base and quickly worked its way to the top. As it traveled upwards the crack began to spread wider and wider and water became to pour between the two sections. The huge dam was starting to crumble under the massive pressure and people were falling into the water and swept below the surface with the tremendous force of the surging water.

It took less than fifteen minutes to take down the massive structure as it became just a memory like the twin towers. The water that had created Lake Mead began its travels to new locations and re-creating the landscape into a raging killer that was basically uncontrollable. The electrical power generated from the massive structure was cut off as far away as California with blackouts occurring in numerous communities, cities and states dependent upon the dam.

Thousands of men, women and children were drowned or crushed to death in the disaster and sirens could be heard for miles. All kinds of vehicles were floating or sinking in the water with people still trapped inside them pleading for help and praying to god for their safety. Satan laughed and said that there ain't no god that will save you today he is busy taking a nap somewhere to rest his weary bones.

Satan shook the hands of his two goons and actually gave each a hug. He did appreciate their loyalty and would show it when they showed up at the gates of hell for permanent residence. But now it was time for them to high tail out of town before the authorities start piecing everything together. It wouldn't be long before a back ground search revealed that these two had a less than desirable track record especially when they got exposed to the lie detectors. Satan told them he may call on them again and would know where to find them. They thanked him and headed off before the police set up road blocks and started questioning anyone in the immediate area. Satan, he just stood there and marveled at the destruction and lives that he had taken on this national holiday.

Satan looked down for one final time at the devastation that he caused and raised his arms to the skies and screamed at the top of his lungs for Jesus to bring it on, give him his best shot because he was ready for anything coming his way. You cannot defeat me you pitiful excuse as my equal. You are a no body and should be ashamed of yourself for even taking up this challenge. Bring it on he repeated. Satan had no idea what he had just asked for.

The destruction of the Hoover Dam made instant headlines across the world. As expected the government authorities wasted little time in placing the initial blame on a terrorists group but none claimed responsibility for the act. It was a complex puzzle that fell into the hands of the best investigators possible in determining who, how and why such an event has occurred.

The devastation caused by the destruction of the dam was unbelievable. Six thousand men, women and children lost their lives that day with another 562 still missing and unaccounted for. The overflowing river created an entirely new geographical layout of the land surrounding the dam and it would take years for a full recovery plan to help address the after effects of that day. Electrical power had to be re-routed to those communities and states affected and many homes and businesses were severely handicapped for months with the outage.

The authorities searched for answers for days without any concrete clues coming forward. The two goons who worked for the dam authority and who supported Satan were classified as missing with the other 560 so they did not come under the probing eyes of the investigators. The video security cameras were being carefully screened in slow motion, magnification, backwards and forward to try and locate potential suspects involved in the incident.

It was on a Tuesday afternoon when Satan was first spotted on the video, standing there chucking the bird at the camera. At first the technician thought it was a wise ass playing a joke but as he zoomed in he noticed the smirk on the man's face and that face, that face, it looked familiar for some reason. He immediately reported his finding to the lead investigators and they decided to review the other camera locations for the same man. They discovered that he was also there on the previous days and was doing exactly the same thing as if sending them a sign of trouble to come. A defiant loony who was sending a message, it was too bad that they received it too late. They took all the videos and enlarged photos and stills of him from every possible angle and then gathered in a large viewing room to discuss their options in locating this madman.

The agents profiled thousands of photos into their database in their attempts to determine who he was. The initial search proved fruitless but they soon discovered that this wacko was indeed a wanted man worldwide. His picture had been plastered in web sites, newspapers and television as the one man responsible for starting the black plague in the UK. One day he just got of his hospital bed, threatened a doctor at the elevator and walked out of the hospital and disappeared. He should have been dead months ago yet he was alive and well in the U.S. He was now the lead suspect in the destruction of the Hoover Dam and every law enforcement agency internationally was alerted to the importance of finding this man. Yet who was he—all they had was a face.

Yet that face led to leads as it was plastered all over the news. The counter man at that late night coffee shop immediately realized him. He reported the incident to the cops. He told them that the man sat by himself in the rear of the shop and talked to himself, constantly swearing and threw his cup against the wall and kicked the chair over. The counter man said that he appeared to be in some drug induced state or absolutely insane. He had a terrible feeling that if he said anything to him that the man would go berserk on him.

As they continued to dive into the videos they came across him in one of them talking to two other men. As they continued to investigate they soon discovered that each of the men worked at the dam and both of them became prime suspects as accomplices in the disaster. An all points bulletin was put out for the two men and it wasn't long before they located Roland in the Treasure Island Casino at the end of the Vegas strip with some blonde bimbo hanging on his arm. He was immediately taken to the FBI headquarters where investigators were anxious to interrogate him about his involvement.

Chapter twelve

Smiley Rider

FBI Agent Smiley Rider was the lead investigator and he knew the importance of getting answers on what happened and why. He was in his mid forties but looked much younger. He was about six feet tall and a solid two hundred and ten pounds he as an imposing figure. He was a New Englander, born and raised, but moved to the Mid West with his wife fifteen years earlier. He had settled in quite well and actually enjoyed the hot, dry climate over those cold and snowy New England winters. He still tried to get home at least once a year to see his folks and other family members. He was the only one who actually decided to re-locate while the others remained in the safe confines of Rhode Island and Massachusetts. He was still a diehard Red Sox and Celtics fan and watched as many games as possible thru the cable networks.

He, also, tried to keep his personal emotions in tact as he entered the room with Roland. One of his sisters was visiting on that faithful July 4th weekend and had taken her daughter to see Hoover Dam that afternoon. Smiley did not go as he had seen the Dam so many times before and had to finish up some paper work on a case that he just completed. The report was important for the DA on the following Monday so he stayed behind and told his sister that he would be done by the time she returned for the cook out later that night. She perished with her three year old daughter, drowning with so many others who had little chance to escape the rush of water. They found her two days later washed up on the banks of the newly created water way with her daughter lying a few feet away. Smiley was devastated and blamed himself for the loss of his sister. He thought that had he been there he could have saved her; yet knew deep down inside that it would have been an impossible task.

As he walked into the room he slowly counted to ten in his head to retain his composure and not lose it by taking this wacko by the neck and choking the life out of his worthless body. He stepped over to the other side of the table, sat down and introduced himself while giving a brief description of who he was and why Roland was there with him. Roland just studied Smiley's face and actually wondered how Smiley would take the news about who was truly responsible for the incident. He would probably think he was some sort of a loony tune and bull shitting him but he could give a rat's ass if he did or not. He would play it cool for a while and decide whether to spill the beans or not.

Smiley cut right to the chase and told him that they knew that he was involved in the plot. He told him it would be best to come clean and provide them the support they need to catch the others and they would take that into consideration when the time came for sentencing. Roland thought to himself—yea—instead of frying me they will lock me into a six by eight foot cell for the rest of my life like a caged animal—big frigging deal. Smiley showed him a few of the photos with the other two and told him how they checked his relationship with Jonathan and discovered that they hung together a lot during their off personal time. He told him how they checked the databases at the dam and found that Jonathan had been spending more time than usual in the auditing of the spillways under his direct approval to do so. He had actually recorded log entries that he formally approved a more thorough inspection of the shafts due to analysis provided by Jonathan. It was all tying neatly together in one package and all fingers were pointing directly at him as a main accomplice. Instead of asking for an attorney Roland just sat there and listened intently to the excellent investigative analysis by the FBI in gaining so much information so quickly.

Roland asked for a cup of coffee to settle his nerves; at least that is what he told Smiley. He really just wanted to relish in the fact that he would go down in the annals of history as one of the big three involved in the destruction of the Hoover Dam. Smiley left the room and just shook his head to the numerous agents standing outside the one way mirror closely monitoring the interrogation of Roland. Smiley had a sick feeling in his stomach that when Roland decided to let loose on his involvement it was going to be something difficult to believe. One of Smiley's key traits was to be patient and not demonstrate any emotion even under the most difficult of situations. This specific one was very difficult as each time he looked at Roland he saw his sister and her daughter drowning in that raging water and just wanted to put a gun to Roland's head and blow his brains out.

Smiley returned with the coffee and set it down in front of Roland. Roland thanked him for his hospitality and took a slow sip as he looked around the room. As he looked at the large mirror on the wall he smiled and slowly raised his hand with the middle finger extended to the group gathered on the other side. Smiley caught his gesture and knocked the coffee off the table and told him that he was through screwing around with him. They had enough on him to keep him in the electric chair for an hour as they fried every inch of his pitiful body and people everyone would stand and cheer. He told him he was a sorry animal that should be put out of its misery and asked him how he could possibly look at himself in a mirror. He could no longer control himself no matter how hard he tried and he lifted Smiley out of his chair and held him off the floor by the front of his shirt. He told him that they would make every second of what was left of his miserable life a horror show and he meant it. There wasn't a single person who would shed a tear for him and who would come riding to his rescue when he complained about the treatment he would receive. They would make sure that he was roomed with the biggest and meanest homosexual that they could find as his cellmate. They would piss in his food, keep him up all night, and play blaring music until his ear drums exploded. He would become a walking zombie when they got through with him and if he didn't die from aids they could easily come up with some other miserable way to slowly pine away to nothing.

Smiley then threw him across the room and he landed hard on the concrete floor. Smiley walked over to him and said forget about a lawyer I'm your fucking lawyer and you are guilty as hell and I sentence you to die you sorry fuck. With that he pulled out his revolver and placed the barrel into his mouth and cocked the trigger. It was at the moment Roland broke down and started balling like some little kid. He pleaded with Smiley to let him live and he would tell him everything as long as they could deal and make the rest of his life somewhat more appealing than what he just laid out.

Smiley removed the gun from his mouth and helped him off the floor. He swung him into the chair and told him to start spilling his guts before it was too late.

Roland wiped his mouth and tried to compose himself as he stared at Smiley and noticed the resolve in his attitude and behavior. Roland sat there for a few seconds as he decided how to deliver the news that the world waited for. Who was responsible for this historical disaster and how do they catch him to bring him to justice? Without another moment's delay Roland told Smiley to pull up a chair because he would have a difficult time dealing with the information that he was about to receive. Roland then spoke loud enough to be heard within the entire office area and said that the one responsible for the attack was Satan himself. As he said it he could not help but begin to laugh hysterically as the words sunk into all those closely watching him from the other room.

Smiley asked him what the hell he was talking about and Roland proceeded to spill out the plan, how they met and how the plot unfolded. He told Smiley that every detail was planned carefully by Lucifer himself. He gave out every small detail that was carried out over days of careful planning by Satan with two individuals that he knew that he could trust. Smiley let him talk and did not stop him once. With the recorders taking in every word and Smiley taking notes Roland rambled on nonstop. Nearly two hours later Roland stopped, looked at Smiley and actually realized the sadness and sorrow that he was a willing participant. He started to tremble uncontrollably and Smiley had a difficult time figuring out whether it was because he would be identified as one of the three who took down the dam or whether finally realized the consequences of what he had done.

Smiley asked him how he knew it was Satan and not some loony trying to brain wash a couple of idiots in believing it so he could carry forth his plan to perfection. Roland had nothing to lose now and told him about what else he and Jonathan were involved and told him that Satan knew every morbid detail. He told Smiley to take a look at the photos from the UK disaster and he will see it was the same person. He told him about the three sixes on his neck and his ability to absorb pain and suffering and grow stronger from it. He told him how he promised them a special place in hell whether it is on earth or hell itself. He knew everything as if he had some sort of supernatural ability. On top of that he had seen him change his visible appearance with his eyes glowing as red as hot coals. As he spoke his voice quavered. He said that Satan mentioned that he was back on earth to settle centuries' old struggle between good and evil. He said that the other was here as well and this time there would be just one winner and mankind would surely choose Lucifer when the final tally was counted. How could they not when they experience the wrath of his power compared to the other.

Smiley was taking in everything that this wacko said yet he thought that Roland was one of so many others in history to be influenced by some freak in believing he was more than just another human being. As Smiley was about to challenge him on some aspects of his confession he noticed that something was gradually happening to Roland as he sat in that chair across from him. He was sweating profusely and his hands were shaking uncontrollably. He had a blank stare in his eyes and was beginning to foam at the mouth. As if out of some sort of grade B horror movie Roland's voice changed into a raspy threatening echoing tone that seemed like it was coming from a poorly filmed Japanese movie where the words coming out of his mouth were not in sync with the movement of his lips.

The voice that came forth did not sound anything like that of Roland who had spoken relentlessly over the past two hours. The voice said that he had no further use of Roland and he was taking him to a place where he will be able to better serve the master one. He said that he had served his master exactly how he wanted and the message was delivered almost to perfection. The voice said that the final exclamation point is the termination of Roland in one of the securest places in the country; the local headquarters of the FBI interrogation room under the watchful eyes of trained agents. The voice simply said that everyone should not make a mistake that the chosen one has returned and is walking among you. With that Roland's body collapsed on the floor and with the sudden puff of smoke was nothing more than a pile of ashes lying on the floor under smoldering clothes. It was at that instant that Smiley knew that there was an evil among them. There was no doubting the fact. As the door to the room swung open and the agents gathered around Smiley he simply turned to his chief aide and told him to get the president on the line as quickly as possible we have a crisis.

While Lucifer was getting his jollies off on the reaction of the agents and the realization that the world will soon know of his presence; Jesus was busy seeking forth his plan to combat the rising tide of evil let loose by Satan. He, also, was planning to send a clear message that the battle will intensify and he would not bend or break under the pressure being applied by Satan. He had to demonstrate to the world that they were not alone against the evil one!

Chapter thirteen

An encounter in Rhode Island

Jesus had driven east. He crossed into the smallest state in the union, Rhode Island. He was simply amazed at the massive changes that have occurred in the world today. He could not help to notice the massive highway systems, buildings, and cities—all that were basically nonexistent when he walked the world so many years ago. The technological advancements that have demonstrated man's superiority were overwhelming in the fields of science, medicine, agriculture, space, energy and educational development. Yet through all of these efforts there was always the uncertainty of peril and destruction coming from unknown sources. Whether these sources came from a terrorist group, aggressive military tyrants, common criminals, or frauds and fakes leeching off of unsuspecting victims—they were among us today. That was the thing that bothered Jesus the most—how could mankind condone these maggots of society when they could easily use all their available resources to combat them?

As Jesus reached the state line separating the state of Connecticut and Rhode Island he noticed a sign welcoming visitors to the Ocean State. Rhode Island was but a speck on the world map and even on a map of the United States it was smaller that some cities in the state of Texas.

Yet Jesus' travel had brought him here. Here to the state that was founded by Roger Williams on the principles to fight for religious beliefs and the foundation of a state where all men could live together in harmony. One could drive from one end of the state to the other in approximately an hour and it was a known fact that most Rhode Islanders were truly spoiled in getting from one place to another. Since everything they needed was in easy driving distance they all complained when they had to go "out of there ay" to get somewhere. If there as an event, party, or place beyond those boundaries it was like pulling teeth getting them there. It is a known fact that Rhode Islanders have also experienced their share of crooked politicians, job loss, and natural weather disasters. But in the typical New England spirit they also have overcome adversity and will basically fight for what is right. Instilled by the spiritual fire of their forefathers hundreds of years ago during the revolutionary war the spirit of freedom and justice still resides in all of the New England states. Hundreds of thousandths of visitors worldwide visit these states to see the historic place that generated the start of a new nation founded on life, liberty and the pursue of happiness. Jesus thought—what better place in the world than to demonstrate the importance to instill the same philosophy in all nations?

Jesus had pulled off Interstate 95 and hoped to satisfy his hunger with a lunch at one of the roadside diners that peppered the country roads in New England. As he drove down the two lane asphalt covered road with more pot holes than you could count he noticed a small diner set back from the road. The building stood between two large oak trees and resembled one of those that you would expect to see in a movie that was filmed in the 1950's. It was one of those old metal ones that somewhat resembled to be a cross railroad car and a school bus. There was one set of stairs leading to the front door. There was a neon sign running along the roof with the name, "Scotty's Place" in green letters. There was an old picnic table sitting to the right of the front door with six wooden chairs. On the table were some scattered coffee cans with cigarette butts indicating it must have been the designated smoking area for the customers. Hanging in the front window was a sign that was hand written in pen felt marker. It read, "Keep your pants on, I will be back shortly, visiting a love one". Jesus smiled and said to himself that this is one man I would love to meet.

The owner was a seventy two year old "Yankee" who perfectly fit the mold of the New England spirit. His name was Scotty McNabb and true to his name he still spoke with a slight Scottish tone in his voice with that New England accent that you can recognize anywhere. Rhode Islanders has the reputation of speaking fast, much faster than your typical American. They run their words together in sentences so you have to listen carefully on what the hell they are really saying. Put Scotty's accent into the mix and you have a real problem on your hands. His wife had died three years ago and he kept the diner open to help him pass his time as he would surely go stir crazy without the interaction of passer byes or the locals who stopped in to see how he was doing. His sons had long ago moved to other areas of the country and would periodically contact him to assure that he was all right but, otherwise, he was on his own. He truly didn't mind as he still had his health and was able to do the little things that meant so much to him. After he closed the diner in the afternoon he would grab his fishing pole and head down the road to that small salt water pond where he could catch a few flat fish to grill for dinner. He could also do some periodic clamming at low tide and sink his feet into the muddy ooze of the salt marsh with his claw rake seeking out the clams hidden slightly below the surface. He would drop them into a canvas bag that he had wrapped around his waist with a nylon rope. When he had dug enough to satisfy his craving he would take them home and clean them thoroughly. Then he would sit down at his table and decide what to make with them—clam cakes, chowder or just steam them to eat with some melted butter.

He loved meeting new people as he as always fascinated with their stories about their travels or home states. For the few who wandered off the main road and stopped by his diner he managed to openly share stories with them that brought some enjoyment into his, otherwise, dreary days. Although some certainty enjoyed the interaction with Scotty, many just wanted a quick meal and wanted to get on their way. Scotty still missed his wife, Sally, and he would stop by the small town graveyard at least twice per week to sit in one of those old folding beach chairs that he kept next to the old oak tree that shaded the place where Sally rested. There he would softly talk to her about the various interesting things that happened during the course of the week in an attempt to keep her alive and present in his heart. They had been together for over fifty two years and been through the highs and lows that life had to offer. Through it all they make the best of it and grew more closely together because of them. It is almost as if they each would know what the other was thinking without even saying anything. The last day he saw her alive was his worse day on earth. The cancer had overrun her body and she was just a shell of the person that she once was. She weighed mire eighty pounds, she was always a fairly slender woman, but it was so obvious the toll that the disease was taking on her. Yet as the sun rose each day she smiled through her pain on seeing his face and reached out to touch his hand. He would always kiss her lightly on the cheek and tell her that he loved her as much as he did the first day he met her. She would always kid him and tell him that she knew all about those pretty young girls in town who were always after him and made it quite clear that she wasn't going to give him up without a fight.

He always smiled at her and told her that she had nothing to worry about since she was all he could ever handle and he wasn't the man that he once was.

He loved her so. Without her saying much he knew that day was the last one that they would be together until they met again on the other side. He read it in her eyes and the tightest of her fingers wrapped around his right hand. Scottie knew that she fought the battle as long as she could and could not hold on any longer under the conditions that she now suffered through every day. She drifted in and out of consciousness and when awake she always felt as if she was on some sort of high due to the medication and was not at all comfortable with this state of mind. When awake with the pain medicine wearing off the pain was unbearable as the cancer was destroying her internal body organs at a more rapid pace with each passing day. As much as she tried to be the good soldier and tolerate the pain and suffering she knew that she could not hold out any longer. She did it for Scotty not herself since the day she was diagnosed. The doctors had told her it would be a fruitless path to seek treatments or recovery as the disease had spread to her vital organs to include her kidneys, liver, lungs and brain. Yet she persevered for Scotty each day. She tried to conceal how terrible she felt and her longing to just rest in peace. She knew where she was headed and had no fears that soon she would be in the hands of god.

She had pleaded with Scottie to die at home in a place where they shared so many memories. Scottie had gone outside to gather the mail and returned a few minutes later finding her lying on the bedroom floor curled up in a ball. She had passed out and as Scottie lifted her up and laid her gently on the bed he knew that she would be leaving him soon. He had difficulty coming to the reality that he had to cope with the significant changes in his life without her.

She awoke as he pulled the woolen blanket up to her shoulders and she looked into his eyes and told him how much she loved him. She also told him not to worry about her and she would be fine. She told him to always keep her in his thoughts and periodically she would send him a small sign that she was still around watching over him. With that she reached out her hand, touched his face, closed her eyes and was gone.

Scotty never felt as all alone as he did at that moment. The one person whom he entrusted with his life was gone and he thought seriously on joining her at that moment. If he only knew that he would be by her side he would have done it in a heartbeat but he wasn't sure. He wasn't as religious as his wife and had a difficult time believing in a god that would allow such a good woman to suffer as she did. Why didn't he just let her die in her sleep rather than put her through months of hell? So with those thoughts he had decided to wait for his natural time to die. During this period he could pay his respects to her in his own way and on his own terms.

Jesus had decided to explore the area a little bit and then circle back to see if Scotty had returned. As he drove slowly down the road he noticed an old man in a grave yard leaning against a tree. He decided to stop for two reasons. The first was to see if this was Scotty who had indicated he was visiting a loved one or someone who needed to get a few things off his chest. Either way it would help pass the time until Scotty returned to the diner.

As Scotty sat there under that oak tree talking to his wife he noticed a jeep drove up and parked along the small fence at the front of the cemetery. The man got out of his car and walked a few steps towards him and waved his hand as he said hello. The man asked him if he knew anything about the small diner just up the road and whether the food was good enough to stick around until the owner returned. Scotty got to his feet and walked slowly towards the stranger. He said it just so happens that this is your lucky day as I am that proud owner of that diner and will be more than happy to fill that empty stomach of yours. Scotty noticed that the car had

Colorado license plates. Scotty thought to himself that the least he could do for a man who had driven half way across the country was to be able to offer a decent meal. He certainty looked like a friendly enough individual. Scotty told him that if he gave him a ride to the diner he would fix him up. The stranger smiled and in a reassuring manner said no problem there. As Scotty climbed into the jeep he introduced himself and asked the man for his name. The stranger reached out his hand and said hi Scotty I'm Jesus it's great to meet you. Scottie said Jesus huh, well, if you are the real thing then you need to forgive me. Don't you get pissed at me but I haven't been to church since my wife passed away but I'm sure that you aren't going to hold that against me when you taste one of my special sandwiches. Jesus just smiled back at him and said to himself, "No Scotty I certainty won't hold that against you".

Within minutes they arrived at the diner and Scotty got out of the jeep and unlocked the front door of the diner. As he entered he turned over the door sign to show that he was open for business as if some crowd would be pushing each other out of the way to get through the doors. He told Jesus to make himself comfortable as he started the small gas grill behind the counter. He told him that there was a paper menu laying there that he could pick out his choices. He told him that the corned beef was out of this world and he actually puts some personal touches to it such as a little cabbage, onions, and carrots while spicing it up with some hot mustard on a hard roll. It comes with a side of Cole slaw and baked beans at no extra charge. Scotty smiled and said that it was somewhat of a strange combination overall but sure works wonders with the digestive system later at night. He said he could kill mosquitoes with one blast from his rear end if he knew what he meant. He said that Sally would get so mad at him that she could barely talk when he would let out the silent bombs as they sat there and watched television. He would get the biggest kick out of it and promise not to do it again while waiting for another unsuspecting moment to surprise her again. Scotty's eyes beamed as he recalled her expressions and scolding him to knock it off.

So what do you think do you want to try your luck on one? Jesus smiled and said sure why not and with that Scotty was scooping all the ingredients into the hard roll and placing it in front of him to take a good bite. Jesus asked for some lemonade to go with it and Scotty grabbed a Minute Maid one from the cooler and placed it on the counter. As he did he had another chance to look the young man up and down trying to learn something about him without being overly nosy. Dressed casually as any traveler he was someone that could easily blend in with the crowd, but there was something about him that didn't seem right. Was it the distance look that he had a lot on his mind? Also he wasn't very talkative or inquisitive for someone who was new in this neck of the woods? How come he wasn't asking about the various points of interest in the area or directions or places to stay?

Jesus was extremely hungry and as he took a bite of that sandwich he told Scotty that he was indeed right about it being delicious. He washed some of it down with the lemonade and sat back on the stool and thanked Scotty for taking the time to open the diner. Scotty smiled and said no problem you are my first and probably last paying customer today so I hope you spread the word about me. A little publicity never hurt anyone. He told Jesus that he kept the doors open to keep him busy or he would go stir crazy if he didn't. It helps pass the time he said as he bend his head low and gently tapped his fingers slowly on the counter top.

Jesus knew what and who he was thinking about as he stared at the old man. He knew that Scotty wished that he could be with someone else and in a different place. As much as Scotty tried to move on with his life he found it difficult to keep Sally out of his thoughts. She was getting into them more than ever before and he knew it. He had thought about taking a short vacation or going to see his sons for a few days but wherever he thought of it would bring back memories of her. Even visiting his sons did not really entice him much since they looked so much like her that it would upset him more than help. He was a man losing the desire to live and it was becoming very obvious where he really wanted to be. We all know of loved ones that have just given up after the one they most love is taken from them and they also pass away a short time later. It is a given fact that their loss is too emotional and stressful to them that they really don't care about living any more. There is nothing sadder in this world than to be a lost soul who wants a way out and will do what is necessary to achieve it. Jesus knew that Scotty had reached that crossroad and was gradually starting down Path of self destruction and needed to understand that all is not lost.

Jesus looked at Scotty and said you truly miss her don't you? It was over three years ago and you still truly grieve Sally like it was yesterday. The moment she left you and told you not to worry about her that she would be all right was the moment that I met her he said. I did not see a frail cancer ridden woman but a spirit alive with love and dignity that knew where she was headed and that someday she would be seeing you again. She told me to tell you that she always enjoyed your attempts to sing her that song, "Only you" to her on special occasions and the way she would laugh at how out of tune you were but that you didn't really care as she was the only one hearing you. She said to tell you that she held on as long as she could for you and she believed that you knew that. On that day she felt the calling from the other side and that it was time for her to gain the peace that she needed so desperately. That is why she told you not to worry because she knew and she felt it. Her final message to you is to enjoy life for as long as you can as she will be waiting for you and you could bet your favorite pair of red wool socks on that one. She said to visit our sons, have the grand kids get to know you better before you are gone forever and do the things that you would have done together as if she was still there by your side. Jesus reached his hand out and gently opened Scotty's right hand and placed a small bracelet ornament of a gold plated angel that Scotty had placed into Sally's hand while she lay in the casket. Jesus told Scotty that she wanted him to keep it in his pocket to know that she is still with him every day and to carry out her wishes until they meet again.

Scotty almost collapsed on the floor when he saw the angel in the palm of his hand and he grabbed the edge of the counter to regain his balance and composure. He stared at Jesus and thought of every single word that he had just said. He knew every small detail of some very intimate moments between just him and his wife. He knew exactly what she said when she passed away, his favorite socks, song, and the angel. He knew it all.

Scotty looked at him and said that he did not know what to do or say to him in recognition of realizing who he was talking to. He said that he was too old to bow and too proud to admit that he was not taking care of his body so he could join his wife. He told him that he was not a true believer in heaven or hell and had actually loss faith in god because of the way of his wife died. How could there be a god when he treats decent human beings like this he shouted in anger even though he knew who was sitting directly in front of him. Yet with each passing moment his anger subsided with the realization that there truly is a god and his wife was actually resting in peace and he will be seeing her again.

As Scotty came around the counter and sat down at one of the empty tables, Jesus joined him. As he sat down he told Scotty that he was pleased to meet such an honest and sincere man as he. He said that he could not think of many who would stare him directly in the eye and voice his displeasure and blame over his wife's death. Scotty went to apologize but Jesus stopped him knowing what he was about to do. He said that an apology was not necessary and he understood exactly how he felt and also how his own father felt when he was hung from the cross.

Jesus told him that he had no control over how humans died. The very day we are born we also know that there will be a day we die and we all realize that. Death is an unknown and depending upon so many variables—too many to count—we will surely pass away. Our bodies could be brought down from a deadly disease; die in an accident, violent encounter, in our sleep or just from old age. No one is assured of an exact method of death and so good people die in some very bad ways. What happens after that second of death is a whole different story and the way you lived your life plays a vital role in your next destination. That is where evil and good play the determining factor and you are in destiny's hands from that point. As Jesus died on the cross with nails embedded in his hand and feet with life draining from his body as hundreds watched he had no control over his method of death. So it is with every other person who is faced with that dramatic event in their personal lives.

Scotty knew that he did not have to go through the details with him yet he deeply appreciated the fact that he felt his agony and despair and was trying to help sooth it.

Scotty asked him what next and what is expected of him now. Scotty said that I know you are real and I can tell the world about meeting you and try to get people to understand that there is a life after death. Perhaps people around the world can change and be kinder to one another with such a message?

Jesus listened intently to Scotty words and was very careful with his response. He told Scotty that what happens next is really up to him. He has the message from his wife and she expressed her wishes that he make good use of his remaining years in a positive and construction manner while leaving a legacy to their children's children. As far as telling the world about his chance encounter with him he said that he could do as he pleased with it. He said that he honestly felt that most people would have a very difficult time believing an old man who lived by himself. Jesus told him that others knew that he had started down the road of losing the desire to live and would seriously question his reversal. The future was entirely in his hands and he should do what he thinks is best and that he had no magic formulas for Scottie to use. He said I am but a messenger and I have done the job that I set out to do. With that he got up from the chair and started to walk to the door.

Scotty shouted wait I have one more question, please do not go yet. Jesus stopped and Scotty walked over to him and asked him if he heard of all the terrible things happening around the world lately and whether he could do anything to stop them. Thousands were being killed by some crazy mad man and they have not found him yet. He asked Jesus if this was one of the reasons why he returned.

Jesus told him that he knew of the tragedies and could not personally stop them. There was a struggle going on right now that should become evident to everyone what needs to be done and by whom. Society has reached the point where it cannot tolerate both evil and goodness in the world because the impact is basically destroying the world as we know it. There can be only one solution to the turmoil and that decision rested with the human race. Beyond that he will demonstrate that he is truly a real spirit while the other also demonstrates in his own way his presence as well. They both have different tactics and the one who has chosen the best one will be the ultimate winner with the human race as the prize.

With that Jesus reached out and placed both his arms on to Scotty's shoulders. He then reached into his pocket and gave him an old metal cross—the same type that he had given Nathan to place on his son and told Scotty to wear it in memory of him. With that he walked out of the diner, got into his jeep and drove away.

Scottie placed the cross around his neck and looked down again at the small angel resting in his hand. He slowly raised his head and whispered I love you so much Sally and I am so sorry for not being as strong as you. Knowing that you are all right has brought new meaning into my life and I will not waste another moment of it. With that he picked up the phone and dialed his son, Jason, and asked if he was up for a visitor for a week or so. As his son's voice expressed the surprise and happiness of the message Scottie wiped tears from his eyes in the realization that he was just re-born this day. He would forever be thankful and would have an opportunity to repay the debt in the coming months.

Chapter fourteen

The news spreads

Sometimes it takes a small news story to suddenly blossom into a major event and that is what happened as Nathan's son recovered from the maniac's hands. As Will recovered the news caught the attention of a reporter who was at the hospital covering another story about a politician who had drunkenly stumbled down a flight of stairs after getting into an ugly shouting match with his mistress. He had broken both of his legs and nearly bit his tongue off. He was bleeding like a stuffed pig when the rescue arrived and would be the butt joke of all the talk shows due to his tongue problem. "Guess he is really licked" now Leno would say while Letterman chimed in about another politician speaking with a forked tongue. As the reporter was getting ready to leave the floor he noticed a large gathering of nurses and doctors in this one little boy's room clapping and cheering him as he stood on the bed.

The little boy was surrounded with stuffed animals, a baseball glove, ball, bat, candy and other things that would be the envy of every kid in America. The reporter stopped at the door and asked what was going on to one of the nurses standing there and she told him that the boy should be dead yet he miraculously survived and was getting ready to leave the hospital. She looked at him and said you must remember it is the young boy who was kidnapped from the Wal Mart months ago by some wacko and left to die in an old barn off the old highway. He was basically brain dead and they took him off the life support apparatus expecting him to die within a few hours but he came back and everyone is so happy. The reporter thought now is a story! He asked if the treating doctor was in the room and she pointed him out.

Doctor Pappas was standing in a corner just watching the joy and happiness of the others in the room. He did not to be standing in the forefront as if he was trying to take credit for the kid's miracle recovery. The reporter walked over to him and introduced himself and asked if he could have a few minutes and the doctor said sure. The doctor grabbed him by the arm and said let's get out of here for a few minutes and we can talk; my office is just down the corridor. As they walked the reporter could not help to feel the jubilation of the doctor. When they entered the doctor's office he sat down and Doctor Pappas offered him a coffee but he declined. The one thing on his mind was to get to the bottom of what happened on that day the boy had awakened from his coma and near death experience.

The reporter introduced himself as Stanley Fry and he worked for the local paper called the Denver Chronicle. He asked the doctor if he could take some notes and also record some of their conversation about the recovered boy and the doctor said that was fine. Cutting to the chase Stanley asked the doctor how he pulled off the miracle in saving the boy's life; was it some sort of new drug, therapy, or treatment that could be effective on others. The doctor smiled at that one and said it would work wonders on others if they all took advantage of it; actually he was positive it would.

The doctor explained what happened to the small boy and how close to death he was when he arrived at the hospital. The boy had tremendous trauma to his head with his brain severely swollen due to beating the boy incurred while under control of the predator. The predator was extremely careful to assure that the boy was found barely alive and incapable of ever identifying him in any police lineup. He apparently relished in what he did to the boy because attached to the pile of the boy's clothes was a note thanking his parents for bringing him into this world and that he had actually brushed, accidentally, against them a number of times in stores because he could. He wanted to let them know that; that they were so close to him and yet never knew it. He wanted them to always try to place that stranger's face yet knowing it was improbable that they really could.

He told the reporter that the medical staff knew how badly off the boy was and had he been found an hour later he would have been surely dead. After their initial evaluation it was actually recommended to the parents that they refrain from putting him on the life support system as it was basically just a frantic attempt to save a life that was already gone. They could not convince the parents which was certainty expected since no one wants to give up the hope that a loved one will be gone forever. So the child remained on the equipment for months until they received approval from the parents to remove him in a heart breaking decision. Over that period of time the boy's condition had not improved at all and he had lost weight and had developed all the negative conditions of a body exposed to endless bed rest.

The approval came after the doctors convinced the Bishops that they should get away for a few days to discuss their son's faith. They took his twin sister to Yellowstone Park where they decided to place his fate in god's hands. When the doctors were summoned to remove the equipment they figured it would only be a short time before they would be called back to the boy's room. However, this time it would be to officially pronounce him dead. The call came thirty five minutes later.

But when he walked into the room with the nurses and a resident physician they saw Nathan and his wife smiling and Nathan pointing to Will laying on the bed and breathing normally. He told the reporter that he could not believe his eyes and walked to the side of the bed. There he checked the boy's pulse and vital signs. All appeared to be near normal and the boy, besides being extremely weak from his ordeal was definitely holding his own. The doctor looked at the reporter as if recalling the moment when he realized that Will would survive and he whispered quietly that it was a miracle.

Before the reporter could ask him what he meant about the miracle the doctor said, "The cross, I saw the cross". After checking the boy's vital signs he noticed a small metal cross hanging around his neck that glowed a very soft color. It was pulsating as if in rhythm with Will's heart. As Doctor Pappas held the cross in his hand it still remained glowing in beat with the boy's heart as if it didn't care that he held it in his hand. He asked Nathan where he got it from and who gave it to him. The father said that he got it from a stranger that wandered out of the woods at Yellowstone National Park who told him that he hadn't talk to others for a very long time. Nathan said what amazed him about the young man was the fact that his daughter and her puppy took an immediate liking to him even though she was told to be very cautious around strangers. And his wife, his wife, seemed so at ease as she laid out in detail what the family was going through at that time. Always a private individual he found it strange that she opened up to this man within moments of meeting him about the tragedy centering on Will. The stranger told them to always keep their faith and to always remember their chance meeting with them that day. With that the stranger walked away but told Nathan to put the cross around his son's neck when he visited him at the hospital. Nathan did just that and within minutes his son was breathing on his own and into a full recovery mode that all the doctors found astonishing. When he was done he looked up at the reporter who noticed tears welling up in his eyes. He looked directly at the reporter and said that Nathan told him that the man identified himself by the name of Jesus.

The reporter could not utter a single word as the doctor continued to look at him and repeated the stranger's name, Jesus, it was actually Jesus. The reporter had recorded every word and was still trying to take in everything that was discussed. He asked him what the father thought about it and he told him that Nathan, his wife and daughter all believed it was Jesus who visited them that day and who saved Will. As Will recovered the cross returned to its normal metal color and ceased glowing. It was checked thoroughly in the hospital test labs and found to hold no supernatural powers but was simply a very old religious cross and held no super powers that could be used on others in the same coma like conditions. Will still kept it around his neck and would for the rest of his life. Although he never met the stranger that happened into his life he felt a closeness to him that would only grow stronger over the years.

The reporter did interview Nathan and April and got exactly the same story from them as the doctor. He asked them if he could write a story about their experiences and they agreed. They knew for some strange reason that Jesus would not mind as he had told them before departing to always remember the chance meeting with them. They believed it to be some sort of a message to also let others know about his meeting them. He took photos of the happy couple and the doctor and also one of the cross still hanging around Will's neck. Initially the story just made the local newspaper but it was sent to others within hours by people who happened across it and used the web to spread it to family and friends. It was soon picked up by the Today Morning Show and Nathan, April, Autumn, Will and the doctor appeared on the show a few days later.

Their heartwarming and sincere story should caught international attention and people were talking about them worldwide. Some said that they were in cahoots with the doctor in some sort of elaborate plot as some religious fanatics who wanted to bring spiritual religion back into many lives? Was the boy on his path to recovery anyway and by removing the life support equipment provided the needed boost to accomplish it? Were they simply coots who decided to become temporary media stars through a story with partial truths mixed with lies? They were the main subject on talk shows to include 20/20; Nancy Grace, Dateline, etc. Through it all they retained their composure and never once got caught in changing their story. Each time they told it they gained more and more credibility to those watching them and many started to believe that Jesus was walking among them!

Next to come forth were Henry and Sheila in their own simple way. They contacted Nathan and April with the news that they also received a visit from Jesus. Their description of him perfectly matched that of Nathan and his wife and the topper was that Henry had a cross; the same type of cross that was placed around Will's neck. At that point both Henry and Nathan knew that they had encountered someone very special and for a very special reason. To be the present day disciples that would help Jesus convince others that he was indeed the savior and he was real—very real!

Again the national news reporters went crazy with the stories that a second couple hundred miles away had experienced a similar encounter with the stranger. This time it was no life saving events as it was with Will but different much different. Only Henry had witnessed the life threatening incident with the three goons who were trying to mug Jesus on that lonely road and Henry was very convincing. When he was contacted by the police to go through the exact events leading up to Turtle losing his life through self-inflicted wounds it all tied together.

There was Turtle's blood in the clump of trees just as Henry said it would be along with some of the ashes from his body that had not blown away. His clothes were still piled there on the ground as if he was just lifted from them for some strange reason. His DNA confirmed that it was Turtle a petty thief with a history of crimes escalating into more and more violent acts. With the information provided by Henry they managed to track down his two accomplices that day and during a thorough interrogation they spilled their guts to the detectives. They confirmed Turtle's intentions to murder that guy with the flat tire that day but told the cops that they got cold feet and wanted nothing to do with it. They had almost participated in the grand finale of killing this stranger but basically backed out when the stranger looked up at the sky and said forgive them for they know not what they do. It was those words that hit home with them and they couldn't carry forth with the murder. They both claimed that they dropped their knives and ran as fast from the clearing as quickly as possible. Even as Turtle pleaded with them to stay they couldn't; the words haunt them to this very day. Rabbit said that he wasn't a religious person, actually far from it, but he remembered those words that Christ spoke so many years ago and they hit home that day. It was the way that this man said them and the emotions that they stirred into him to not get involved were overwhelming. They ran from the clump of trees and high tailed to the car and sped off down the highway. They said that they had waited at the local bar that night for Turtle to show up and tell them of what happened but he never showed and never tried to contact them. They figured he was just pissed at them and decided that it might be better that way anyway. They were actually happy that he did not show up because they really wanted nothing further to do with him and were prepared to tell him so. They took this as another sign to square their lives away and start down the straight and narrow path so to speak.

Their stories tied up exactly to that of Henry so we now had two "bad" guys actually confirming the statement of Henry. The police did not hold Henry nor further question him on the story. It was obvious this man was telling the truth and he did not stray from the facts once in the many times that he was questioned. Turtle was gone forever and everyone knew that. The police also verified that the cross that Henry and Sheila had was an exact clone of the one given to Nathan in every detail. The stranger did not do any bodily harm to Turtle according to Henry's story with the exception of touching his dying body and telling him that he would not forgive him but asked his father if he could. The two separate stories centering on the same stranger hundreds of miles apart added more fuel to an already growing belief that Jesus was truly back on earth and had plans for mankind that only he really knew at this time. Both Henry and Sheila came forward and participated in the various televised events watched by millions and telling them that someone special was walking among them. They now understood the value and importance added into their otherwise simple lives by getting the message out to all that would listen.

Next up to bat was Scotty an elderly man who lived in New England. Scotty read the stories in the morning newspaper and then turned on the world news and listened intently to the others who crossed paths with Jesus.

Scotty reached into his pocket and once again held the cross that Jesus had given him and compared it to the photos of Nathan and April and Henry and Sheila holding it. It was the same make no mistake about that. Yet as Scotty sat alone in his small restaurant drinking his cup of coffee he knew what he had to do. The next morning Scotty got up, showered, walked down to the grave of his wife where he confined in her on what he was about to do. He felt a calmness coming over him that he had not felt in years and knew that he was making the right decision. As he sat there and looked at the tombstone of his wife a beautiful blue and yellow butterfly fluttered slowly down and landed on top of the stone. It appeared to hover there but for a few seconds before going on its way yet Scotty knew that it was a sign from his loving Sally that he was doing the right thing regardless what others may think about him. With that he got up, threw her a kiss, waved bye to the butterfly and walked to his diner to call a local news reporter.

Scotty became the third reported incident of someone actually meeting Jesus across the country and with each passing day the momentum was gathering speed about the real possibility that he walked among us. Scotty came under more scrutiny than the others with the nay sayers calling him an old crackpot dying for some attention in his pitiful lonely life. Many were much crueler to Scotty than the others because they felt that he was one of the many who would be coming forward with meeting Jesus and it would become more and more difficult to investigate every loony who called for the national attention. Some pranksters actually went so far as to paint a huge cross across the front of his diner in yellow paint while others had paint balled his car as it sat in his drive way. Scotty was shaken by the non believers and people looked at him differently than before—people who he had known for years as if he was some sort of a leper.

What caught everyone by surprise is when Scotty actually displayed the small cross that Jesus had given him like the others. He gave it to a FBI analysis lab to confirm that it was indeed exactly the same as the other two. The analysis came back a week later confirmed the originality of the cross in every detail to the others. The report was published in every major news outlet the day the report came back verifying it's authentically. It was then that millions became believers and looked to the three separate families that were touched by Jesus for guidance to help them mend their ways.

The struggle had changed course over the simple beliefs of three separate families that came forth and told the world that they believed in Jesus. Without causing a worldwide disaster Jesus managed to touch the hearts of millions who waited for years for any sign to confirm that he existed. Through love and caring Jesus took a significant lead in the struggle to change man's destiny forever. It was a remarkable achievement.

Chapter fifteen

Washington, DC

Satan could not believe what was happening all around him. While he created chaos and fear in millions worried about his next move here was the other gaining the support of millions through simply personally meeting a few American families in need of faith being restored in their lives.

The line was drawn and Satan realized that he had taken his opponent far too lightly in his assessment. He promised himself that he would not make the same mistakes as the stakes were much too high to screw around with. Satan stood on the steps of the Grand Cathedral in Washington, DC, the very church that most United States Presidents attended each Sunday morning along with hundreds of other who showed their religious devotion to Jesus. It was nearly two o'clock in the morning and with the exception of a few cars or street people trying to find a place to settle down for the night; the area was basically pretty deserted.

It was here that Satan decided to send his message to Jesus that he had no respect for him or the "kind acts" of friendship that he bestowed on the few people he had met. As he stood on the top step he turned and faced the huge wooden doors that were securely locked at nighttime. He unzipped his pants and proceeded to send a steady stream of his piss spattering against the front door and dripping down to the concrete steps. Immediately upon the urine striking the surface it started to smoke as if it was some sort of an acid that was going to burn its way through the doors and concrete. At first Satan laughed at the results of his act and was taking personal pride in the smoking effect of the urine when he began to realize that it was a counter reaction to what he was doing. It seemed like there was nothing left on the door or steps of any sign of his urine—no stains, no odor, and no nothing! It was like a strong cleanser was used immediately to purge the surface and this infuriated Satan. A homeless man seeing him at the top of the stairs yelled to him hey, what the hell you doing up there? Get your ass down from there or I am going to come up there and knock you off those stairs. I may have lost some of my dignity and self respect but what you are doing isn't right and I will kick your ass if you don't come down right now.

Satan lost it completely at that moment. In one gigantic leap he jumped off the top stair and landed in front of the homeless man and grabbed him by the front of the raggedly coat that he wore. Satan kicked aside his wire shopping cart that held all of the man's earthly belongings and told him that he wouldn't need them where he was going. As the cart rolled down the sidewalk he told the man that he just screwed with the wrong person at the wrong time. With his eyes raging bright red he squeezed the poor man's neck and asked him if he wanted to be one of Jesus disciples too. Yes, you do, I know you do said Satan as the poor man now knew that he got into something way over his head and there was no good way out.

Satan told the man that he truly appreciated his balls of standing up to him for pissing on the steps of the church but he should be a little more careful with who he decides to mess with. The man trembled and tried to apologize but knew it was too late. Satan with drool running down his cheeks used the poor man to vent some of his rage. He lifted him high over his head and flung him in the air. The poor man with arms waving as if he was some sort of a bird trying to regain its balance in high winds saw his destination. He was in complete free fall and was impaled on top of one of the sharp wrath iron fence posts that lined the front of the church as if he was a human sacrifice. As Satan walked by the impaled man he grinned and told him that he wouldn't be hanging around too long and he would greet him in hell. As he walked away he was laughing hysterically to himself on his gutter humor.

The poor man was found shortly after by a passing patrol car. The officers tried to sooth his suffering until the rescue arrived. The man tried to babble out the story of what had happened but it was far too incoherent to try and provide a fully accurate detailed account. He seemed delirious and scared out of his wits. With a blood curding scream he cried out it was Satan, may god have mercy on my soul because I don't want to meet him again. Oh, god, have mercy on me he shouted out again and closed his eyes and was gone. Satan stood in the small crowd that had gathered across the street who were drawn by the flashing lights. Acting as one of the innocent bystanders, he gloated at the scene unfolding in front of him. The medics were placing the body into the back of the rescue and the cops were scratching their heads as if they couldn't believe what they had stumbled across. One of the woman in the crowd said that she knew the man and he never did anything to hurt anyone. Yes, he lived on the streets but he never stole or harmed anyone. He had lost his wife and children six years ago in a house fire, lost everything he had and just couldn't put things back together again. She began to say a prayer for him when Satan told her to shut up. He said that the man was nothing but a worthless piece of shit and the world would be a better place without him. Now he is at rest in a much better place that will keep him very warm for eternity, I can guarantee that! So don't pity the poor bastard he must have said or did something that really pissed someone off. With that he buttoned up his coat as he felt a chill in the air—must be someone meeting the cold reality of death he thought—as he walked off into the night.

Even the killing of the bum could not stop Satan from beginning to feel the pressure and was not at all happy about it. Everything seemed to be, initially, going his way yet Jesus was turning the tide and he knew it. Through a few simple acts of kindness word was spreading throughout the country that the savior may have returned and is walking among us. The story had begun to spread into other parts of the world and the general perception is that something inspiring was happening in the general attitude and behavior of the people. Satan knew that he also had to do something that would inspire others—others who believed and supported the dark side while also sending the warning shot to the goody good shoes that he was a force to be reckoned with.

As strange as it may seem the threat of losing the struggle created a fear factor that he had not known or experienced in centuries. He was used to calling the shots and basically determining the faith of those coming his way at the point of their untimely deaths. He was always in full control and he didn't appreciate how things were gradually changing. He would surely change that situation and he would make a great deal of people pay for his troubled state.

He had in a very short period of time created havoc in the world and he was the most wanted man walking the face of this earth. He realized that it was time for him to take full credit for his acts of terrorism and show the world that he was an equal to the other and there would soon be choices for every one of them. Being in Washington he couldn't help but to visit some historical sites that were of extreme interest to him. His first stop was Arlington National Cemetery where he seemed at home as he viewed the thousands of tombstones stretching as far as the eye can see. It was the resting place for soldiers who fought for their country and died for the right to keep it free. Although many went to heaven he attained his share of souls that exhibited enough evil and contempt for their fellow man that they won a spot in his realm of eternal damnation.

He actually spotted some of their names on the stones as he passed by and grinned in the realization that they now belonged to him. He chuckled to himself that so many of them thought that they did not believe that they would have to suffer the consequences of their evil acts until they stood frozen with fear before him. They really didn't believe in the afterlife and truly felt that their bodies would eventually turn to ashes and they would fade to just a memory to those who knew them. The surprise on their faces when they appeared before him was priceless. These men who faced death on a deadly basic in the various wars that they fought in now trembled in fear as Satan stood in the entrance to the fiery gates of hell. As that old saying goes, "Seeing is believing" and they were sure seeing. The pity of the situation was that he knew that each would of them would have lived their lives differently if they only knew and believed that there was a heaven and hell. As they were dragged through the gates by other demons they knew that salvation was unattainable and they were at a place where no man wanted to enter.

He relished in their pitiful, apologetic attempts to convince him that they were in the wrong place and something had gone wrong. Perhaps they were confused with someone with the same name or did something that they did not even realize was evil enough to be standing before him. With a quick flash of his hand he managed to bring forth before their eyes the evil deeds that brought them to him. Many were so shocked with the realization that they were cornered like a rat in a basement that they started to whimper like a child being scolded. The vivid images were so graphic that many of them just wanted to vomit as they knew what their eternal faith was going to be.

Satan did not say a word as he signaled his demons to escort the poor souls into the dens of hell. Their screams were music to his ears and he longed to have so many more join him on a daily basis.

So he toured the sights and gained more and more confidence in his ability to be a powerful foe to the other as he liked to think of him. He toured the holocaust museum where he was thrilled with the many exhibits of the dead and dying from the Nazi concentration camps during World War Two. He spend hours there studying the photos and documents that were preserved as a permanent record of man's inhumanity to man. He had so many Nazi soldiers in his den that he actually loss count. It was surprising to him how many "righteous" soldiers would support the forces of evil in the guise of just performing their duties. How could they possibly believe that murdering, men, women and children day after day be all right? The majority of them grew accustomed to what they were doing and actually enjoying doing it. They would blame the Jewish people for every wrong thing that was ever done to them and use that as a means to convince themselves that they are doing nothing wrong. Using the same principles as instilled in the Nazi soldiers Satan hoped to incite others to raise up and be counted. He could just imagine the satisfaction of those who choose to follow him by blaming anyone with a job, a bank account, a happy family, an education, white skin, healthy, intelligent, good looking for their troubles and despair. The world was in turmoil now for the same reasons that incited the Germans during World War Two and he would take advantage of the general discontent and forge forward in victory.

Countries were going bankrupt, people losing their jobs, homeless rates growing, people losing their homes, bank accounts being squashed as the stock markets continued a down ward trend. Prices rising uncontrollably and everywhere you looked there were growing seeds of discontent and a beckoning for someone to step forward to make things right again. It was time to level the playing field and bring some satisfaction to the discontented that those smug individuals who are so happy with their lives feel the same pain and suffering as those who have been living a life in hell. Satan was sure that he was the one individual who can surely satisfy their hunger for revenge that they were so thirsty for.

Washington D.C is a beautiful place when you visit the tourist sites and stay within the acceptable boundaries of the city. Security is tight, police presence is everywhere and the landscape and buildings are so well maintained that you are not afraid to walk the streets at midnight. Yet just on the outskirts of the tourist areas there are slums and scenes of violence that would make your skin crawl. Here is where the addicts and pushers dwell. Here also are the petty criminals and the people barely scraping by on that small income that are so disgusted with their lives that they just want to puke their guts out. Anyone wandering into their midst are subject to their wrath for something better whether it be the car that you are driving, that wallet in your back pocket or that shirt on your back.

It was here that Satan set his sights for support and a plan; a plan to set the record straight that life is not just a bowl of cherries but that of the most foul, disgusting things that you could possibly imagine. Leading the discontented into a new frontier or Promised Land has been a mechanism used by so many fanatics throughout history so successfully. Attila the Hun, Adolph Hitler, and Charles Manson are but a few of these role models. They have successfully enrolled others into a world of evil and devastation through simply convincing others that they can make things better for the inflicted, poor souls, who society has forgotten about and want nothing to do with.

Satan's plan would ignite a flame that he hoped would carry forth throughout the country and eventually the world for the commitment of others to choose him as the ultimate leader for all eternity.

What better place to start then a known neighborhood that was a hot bed of discontent with crime running rampage. As he walked slowly down the trash littered streets he couldn't help to notice the obvious signs of despair for those who called this place home. The broken windows, the bars on the doors, the graffiti covering the walls of buildings and homes, the stripped autos sitting alongside the curbs, and the darkened street corners caused by broken lights in the lamps making strangers easy prey for those who waited for them in the darkened alley ways. Through the open windows he could hear the sounds that were music to his ears. He heard drunken men cursing their wives for some petty thing that they did wrong, babies crying for their mothers or a bottle of milk that just wasn't there, women screaming for help as they were being beaten or abused by a pimp or a john, and even gun shots with no one really caring or doing much to help those in trouble.

His destination was a dimly lit building at the end of the next block where some thugs were standing outside. It was one of the few buildings with any sign of real activity and he surmised that it was a focal point of drug, and sex. As he neared the building he noticed a few of the "spotters" pointing him out to some others standing in the doorway of the dilapidated building. Two of the ones that were sitting rose slowly to their feet and were preparing to let this stranger know he is not welcome in their neighborhood.

As he reached his destination he was greeted by one of the thugs with "What the fuck do you want here you piece of shit?" "Don't you know better than to just walk down this street like you own it you cock sucker". "If you know what is good for that scrawny white ass you better get the hell out of here before we stick this baseball bat lying up there until it comes out your mouth."

Satan just smirked at the goon and told him that he wanted to talk with the man in charge. He told him that he had little time to exchange pleasantries with losers standing in his way. He said that he had a proposition, a very good preposition, for the man and it was a once in a lifetime opportunity that he better not past up.

Now he had the attention of all the thugs standing there. He counted at least six of them and there were probably a few more hiding in the darkness. The one who appeared to be in charge of those on the stairs had listened intently to what Satan had just said and just started laughing. He chuckled for at least a minute before he stopped and said man, you got balls for someone who is going to spend the next six months in a hospital ward probably on some sort of a respirator while you piss and shit your pants every day from the beating that we are about to give you. The boss just doesn't talk to every wacko who comes here to see him and especially for some honkie like you. Now let's set the record straight. We don't want you here; we don't need you here and never what to see that ugly face of yours around here again if you are able to walk when we are done with you.

He walked down the stairs and stood directly in front of Satan and pulled out a switchblade knife and tossed it back and forth between his hands and said he was going to do a little craving on him all by himself. The others gathered around forming a semi-circle with Satan and the man in the center. Should things go astray and this stranger get the better of their friend they would surely pitch in and assure that the stranger would be the loser. Satan told him that it did not have to be this way and again asked him to see the man in charge and that he didn't want any trouble. The goon said it was far too late for that and he took a quick swing at Satan's right arm with the knife. Satan had decided that he had to sacrifice this whacko to get the message to the others about who they were truly dealing with. As the man swung the knife Satan simply placed both of his hands directly in front of him with the palms in an upright position and moved them slowly upwards to the sky. The goon who had started to attack him was lifted off his feet and dangled there approximately three feet off the ground with an astounded look on his face. As he dangled there Satan told him that he screwed up his only opportunity to do the right thing. But all he did was to run his mouth and try and intimidate him. The others standing there were so shocked by the fact that their friend was hanging in mid air and not being touched in any way by this stranger they did not attempt to get involved.

Satan turned to the rest of them and demanded to be taken to their boss. His glaring eyes went from face to face of the startled observers until he settled on the biggest one standing at the top of the stairs. He peered directly at him and said, "You, in the door way, I have chosen you to get my message to your boss, and you better deliver it now before the same thing happens to you as your buddy who is dangling here. With that he simply took his index finger and seemed to aim it at the man's mouth and at that instant the knife in the man's hand swung violently into the opening and buried itself so hard that it protruded out of the man's neck in the rear of his head. What was amazing to all who witnessed it was the fact that the man still hung there off the ground with blood spurting out of his mouth as if he was a water fountain. As his head snagged to one side all knew he was dead and that the stranger standing there in front of them had done it. He had instilled a true sense of fear into each one of them and they were terrified to even move one muscle in retaliation. The stranger just smiled and dropped his hands to his side and the hanging man dropped to the ground with a huge thump.

Satan turned to the man at the top of the stairs and asked him if he was going to help him or not. Without hesitation the man told him to follow him into the building as the others cleared the way for him to walk up the stairs without interruption. Satan just rubbed his hands against his pants, brushed his hair back with both hands, started to whistle the tune when the devil went down to Georgia and followed his new found friend into the building.

They climbed the stairs in silence up to the fourth floor where there were two men standing guard beside a thick wooden door with a brass plate with the words "Ice Man" carved into the metal. At first the two men quickly pulled out a couple of forty fives and pointed them at the stranger but the one leading the way told them that everything was cool and he had already checked the dude out. They stepped aside and the one leading Satan turned the door knob and walked into the room with Satan right on his heels.

Chapter sixteen

The ice man

There sitting at a large wooden desk with stacks of cash, cocaine, heroin and crack in various packages and envelopes was the leader of this motley crew, a character called the ice man.

He was an imposing figure weighing in at least 350 pounds, shaved head, very thick glasses that caused his eyes to appear to be twice their normal size, unshaven with a small goatee resting on his chin. He wore a large gold earring in his left ear and a gold chain with a medallion of a snake dangling from it. His shirt was open down the front with coffee stains and dribble spots everywhere. On each hand were three to four rings encompassing his huge fingers and showing just above the pants top was a semi-automatic pistol positioned within easy reach in the event of trouble. He carefully watched the two men enter his chamber and walk towards him. When they got approximately ten feet from him he told them to stop and asked his man what the hell was he doing bringing in a stranger to his office? He told him that it better be good because there was a strong possibility that the man was not leaving alive based on what he just saw in the room. Ice man then asked where the hell Rattles was anyway. The man told him that Rattles was lying outside on the side walk dead as a door knob and that he killed himself with his own knife. He babbled that he stuck it through his mouth and out the back of his neck as he dangled three feet off the ground. Ice man looked at him and asked him if he was out of his mind or something. Before the man could answer Satan spoke up and told him that it was true because he not only witnessed it but he was the one that was responsible for the poor, misfortunate death of Rattles. Ice man asked him if he was crazy as he had just signed his own death warrant. Satan just smiled and said not today. He told the ice man that he should listen very carefully to what he was about to say as his future depended on it. He told him that he was simply a man possessed in winning a struggle, a very important struggle. A struggle that would make the Ice Man a very wealthy man if he wanted to throw his support his way. Ice Man had already reached for his gun and was pointing it directly at the head of Satan and was contemplating on whether to pull the trigger or not. He told Satan that he was already a very rich man and didn't need his white ass to make him any richer. He told Satan that he was not going to kill him out right because he was going to suffer for killing his friend. He wouldn't die for days and he would beg for his death by the time that he was through with him.

Ice Man noticed something strange and even unsettling in this man. Others who have stood in front of him and heard the same threats started to tremble and beg for their lives. Yet this man just stood there with a little smirk on his face as if challenging him to try and do those things to him. Ice Man studied the stranger carefully much more than he even did with people that he had just met. The face—the face was so familiar. Where had he seen it before? He didn't have much direct contact with white dudes yet this one was definitely one that he had recently seen but where? And then it hit him like a ton of bricks falling from the sky; this guy was the same one that every law enforcement agency in the country, if not the world, was looking for. He blew up the Hoover Dam and started that virus that spread through England and there were news articles about him being tied directly to Satan himself.

Satan could tell that Ice Man recognized him it was as obvious as his mouth actually hung open and the huge man stopped with the threats and lowered the gun pointing at him. Ice Man said you are the one aren't you; you are the most hunted man in the world right now and you are standing here in front of me. What the hell do you want with me?

Satan reached out and grabbed one of the Cuban cigars from the box on Ice Man's desk and pulled a lighter from his pocket and lit it. As he puffed out large rings of smoke as an Indian sending smoke signals he told Ice Man that he wanted his help in gaining support in his personal quest. Ice Man asked him what the quest was and Satan simply said "the world". With that Ice Man told his goon to leave the room and he wanted to be alone with his "friend". In a surprising move Satan reached out and touched the man on his shoulder and told him that it was a very smart thing he did when he decided to bring him to see the Ice Man. With that he actually pinched the man's cheek as an old grandmother would do to one of her darling little grandchildren and smiled at him. The man knew that he was being make a fool but didn't really care—all he wanted was to get the hell out of that room as fast as he could. This man was pure evil and he felt it through every bone in his body. The fact that Rattles was lying dead downstairs was a strong indicator that he was not anyone to mess with. How could this "stranger" take his life so easily and not be afraid of the consequences of doing it? He appeared to be fearless and that in of itself was frightening. The man had some sort of supernatural powers and was not afraid to use them. As he opened the door to leave the room he turned one final time to glance at the stranger and noticed Ice Man and the stranger shaking hands and smiling at one another as if they were long lost buddies. He thought to himself that this is a marriage make in hell and he wasn't too far from the truth.

Satan sat down in the old wooden desk chair in front of Ice Man's desk. He said let's quit beating around the bush and come to a clear understanding on what I want. I need your help to convince the masses that I am here to stay and I walk among them. He said it is I who rule the kingdom of death and who most people are afraid to even mention my name. I need you to spread the word that those who join us will be the chosen ones, the ones who will be my chosen flock of disciplines where everything that they ever longed for will be at their beck and call. Every personal, evil desire that they even dreamed about will be theirs by joining me. We will control who lives and dies and those who do not join us will be our servants to please us in any way that we so desire. Just look at what I have already accomplished in a few short months. I spread a deathly virus that had not been seen on this planet in hundreds of years. I destructed one of the largest and most secure man make structures in the world. I did all of this under the watchful eye of the best security forces in existence and I am far from done yet. Join us or serve us it is that simple.

Satan told Ice Man that he wanted to have him gather a massive protest, so to speak, in the large public field near the famous monuments of Lincoln, Jefferson and Washington on Saturday. Make no formal announcements. Let the news travel by word of mouth to get the message out to the discontented that he would be making his first personal appearance there. He would be able to show the world that he was indeed serious and real!

Ice Man listened intently and knew that he wanted to play a huge role in the upcoming plans. His mind raced with all the opportunities that will be at his disposal by becoming Satan's right hand man. He was so excited with his pending position that he almost came in his pants just thinking about the power that will be his. He got up from his chair and walked around the desk and shook Satan's hand as he promised his undying support. With that he bowed his head in total respect of the one person that represents evil in its purest form. Satan smiled as he looked at the loser standing in front of him. He will use Ice Man as he has used every dead soul that came his way over the centuries—to do anything that he needed them to do and then toss them aside like a tumble weed bouncing aimlessly across the desert.

Over the next few days Ice Man sent the word that there was going to be a very special event on Saturday in the public field area near the monuments at ten A.M. The message stressed the importance of showing up or being on the short end of the stick again. For those who don't show they better not come crying to him after the fact about missing out. Word spread quickly through the ghetto and the surrounding areas about the special event. They came out of the woodwork like cockroaches when the lights go out. The crowd gathering caught the police by total surprise and they were certainty undermanned to handle the growing mass of people. The thing that bothered them the most was that they were not your typical tourists sightseeing on a weekend but a much more dangerous mob that was looking for trouble.

As the police officers watched the growing mob scene they studied the faces of those in the crowd. There were the pushers, hookers, street gang members, petty felons, street people, homeless, and other malcontents who easily fit in with their fellow constituents. There were thousands of them and the numbers were still growing. It quickly got to the point where the area was swelling to abnormal proportions and they started harassing innocent tourists who happened to be in the area. It was obvious to the tourists that the best possible option was to get the hell out of there as quickly as possible. The police presence was limited and crowd control was growing more difficult by the moment. The mob quickly realized that they quickly outnumbered the police and started to take advantage of the situation. Many of them were already ganging up on families or couples trying to exit the area. They would block their way and rob anything of value—jewelry, pocket books, wallets, jackets, lap tops, you name it and they took it. Some of them began to manhandle some of the woman and were getting into fist fights with their partners. As the violence grew in intensity a few of the women tried to run for help but their clothes were stripped from their bodies before they could break away. Men were getting beaten, kid's bikes were stolen and it was fast becoming a free for all to the mass of degenerates that had gathered there.

As police reinforcements gathered together on the outskirts of the crowd they were careful not to initiate any actions that could start a full scaled riot. It was already developing into a volatile situation that just needed one small spark to ignite. Donning riot gear, full face shields, batons, tear gas guns, bullet proof vests, and helmets they were waiting for further instructions from their superiors on how to deal with the unruly crowd. The issue troubling all the cops there was what the hell was going on and who could be responsible for this?

It was nearing ten o'clock and what started as a low mummer in the crowd grown quickly to air deafening proportions as the crowd spotted Ice Man. With him was another man that none of them knew. Ice Man had his arm around the man's shoulders and kept pointing at him as they walked through the crowd. He kept saying here is the man, here is the man, here is the man that will solve all your problems and give you life as you have never known it. He kept repeating himself time and again and as he did it seemed to incite the crowd more and more. Within minutes they were all cheering a stranger—a man that they never met—as if he was a conquering hero returning from a war. The noise was deafening and the stranger had not even spoken a single word.

As they made their way through the crowd people were slapping the stranger on his shoulders and attempting to shake his hand without much success. Ice Man had him pretty much surrounded with his personal thugs and didn't want anyone pissing him off. Satan was taking everything in and was enjoying every minute of it. The Ice Man did a great job in drawing out every low life possible and he couldn't be happier if he was shoving a pitchfork up the ass of the other—which he soon hoped that he would have an opportunity to do so. Satan told Ice Man to clear the way to the top of the stairs at the Lincoln Monument where he could stand and look out at the massive crowd gathered there. As he was led up the stairs he was in his own fantasy world of ecstasy. He was thinking about how the entire world was going to handle the communication occurring on June 6, 2066 (6/6/6) in Washington, DC.

The police placed "spotters" in the crowd and tried to get as many as possible close to the stairs where they could gather as much information as possible on what the hell was going on. Already the major news networks had got wind of the trouble brewing and had placed mobile vehicles for broadcasting directly from the site. Everyone anxiously was waiting to hear from this stranger and who the hell was he?

Chapter seventeen

Satan speaks

As Satan reached the top of the stairs he turned to the crowd and raised his arms high above his head as the mob went wild. Women were screaming as if they had just been touched by a movie idol as grown men were stamping their feet and acting like they were in the Roman coliseum as Christians were being fed to the lions. For the mob they knew that the man standing in front of them was evil and they were eating it up all the more. They had waited so long for a savior, a man who would help them get the revenge against all those who looked down on them as if they were some sort of society outcasts as they passed them on the street.

Satan absorbed the cheers, screams and outpouring of emotions as if he was a sponge soaking up water. In a comical act he actually encouraged the mob to keep it going by inciting the crowd to keep it coming. After a couple more minutes of deafening noise he raised his arms and motioned the crowd to quiet down. With the slow lowering of his arms the crowd grew silent as if one was turning down the volume on his television set. When his arms reached his sides you could hear a pin drop as everyone waited anxiously for this man to speak about their future.

It was Satan who was taking the giant leap forward and letting the world know he was among them. He wasn't going to pussy foot around like the other and has people play guessing games on who he was and what his intentions are. He was always the more direct one and he believed he was always feared because of it. Beating around the bush was for pussies he thought to himself; people respected those that come directly to the point even if it is bad news. Satan knew that he had the power and the fortitude in his own kingdom. There each person trembled as he walked by and their pain and suffering gave him the all the strength necessary to realize that he was unstoppable in his quest.

As he started to speak his voice rang out as clear as a church bell on a Sunday morning. There were no speaker systems installed in the area yet his voice carried to people standing in the far reaches of the field. The words echoed through the crowd as he voiced the words, "I have come to end your misery and sorrow and together we will team together for a better tomorrow for those who chose to follow me. I am Satan, I am Lucifer, I am the Devil, and I am the worse nightmare for anyone who chooses sides against me."

As if it was something from a bad horror movie, as he raised his arms to the sky there were lightning bolts flashing in the sky and thundering roars in the background. The sky which was blue with just a few scattered clouds had turned dark gray as the wind seem to grow in intensity. The sudden change in the weather frightened many in the crowd but they stood their ground waiting for him to continue his speech.

As he waved his arms wildly back and forth the skies cleared and he continued. He told them that he had come to restore their dignity and self-respect and bring them the joy and happiness that they so deserved. He sold them on the facts that they needed someone who cared about them and would do everything in his power to turn the tide on those who ridiculed them and forced them into this basic survival mode that they faced each and every day. As he spoke he raised his voice at the right times, and emphasized the right words, and spoke in such a righteous tone that he caught the attention of everyone listening. Even the police and tourists were taken by his speech. He spoke of centuries of abuse and destruction by those who represented themselves as the righteous. These were the ones that gobbled up all the fruits of life while leaving others to wallow in their misery and despair. He spoke of kings, queens, rulers, premiers and presidents and gave vivid descriptions based on facts on how these so called leaders was totally responsible for the separation of classes in the world today. When he said the rich get richer and the poor get poorer the crowd went crazy. A saying that we have heard a thousand times before but when coming from Lucifer himself it further drove the point across that things must change.

He told them that he returned to take them to the Promised Land and it sure wasn't heaven. He said how could anyone choose the one location where all those rich bastards resided? They got there through their generosity to the church and back stabbing their co-workers, neighbors and friends at every opportunity. Yes they were all up there basting in their satisfaction that they successfully conned their place into a rest home for the despicable. Who the hell wants to be exposed to that for eternity after you lived it for so many years on earth? He asked the crowd how many wanted that every passing moment forever! The crowd shouted no, led us to hell, show us the way, and make us strong. Satan' said that if everyone joined him in his quest that he would put those bastards in a place where we can expose them to what you have been through. Hell is where they belong and you can help me put them there he screamed.

The intensively of his speech was overwhelming. The crowd was in a state of hysteria and his performance was like an uncontrollable salvation show. The mob was hearing everything that they ever wanted to hear and they had the one person in this universe that would surely come through for them. He had already demonstrated his supernatural abilities to the world and his following was growing with every passing minute.

As the crowd grew more and more out of control the police knew that they were on the verge of a full scale riot that would spill out into the streets. Satan knew that he won over the majority of the mob and sucked in the air of victory. These lunatics were on side and all he had to do was ignite that flame that would start the newest fire.

The police knew it was useless to wait any longer and received the order to try and disperse the crowd. As they moved forward each knew that the outcome would have terrifying results since they had similar experiences with a feeding frenzy like started today. The crowd had gained an inner strength through the motivational words spoken by Satan and they believed the world at their disposal with nothing standing in their way. In some dark corner of their minds they had prayed for such a fanatic to step forward and bring some satisfaction into their mundane lives. Here they had the champion of evil and the one person that could lead them and not have to worry about the consequences.

The mob was now uncontrollable. It was like a bunch of college students let loose in a whore house or escaped cons facing freedom for the first time in years.

Captain Roger A. Hopper, Chief Washington, DC officer in charge of riot control situations gave the order to work through their systematic methods of trying to minimize any serious after effects of using police force to disperse the crowd. The thing that troubled each cop was the fact that this man was claiming to be Satan himself and had already demonstrated his powers with the destruction of the Hoover Dam and the Black Plague Virus in the United Kingdom. The police goal, as crazy as it may seem, was to arrest this self acclaimed prophet and make him pay for his crimes to humanity.

The police circled the massive crowd and began to move forward. Since the start of the event re enforcements had arrived and they numbered at least three hundred strong now in full riot control gear with enough fire power to destroy a small town. The goal was to get through the crowd without causing a major incident and arrest the "guest" speaker. They had hoped that with him removed from the situation the crowd would break up without much of a problem; the issue was that they totally miscalculated the man in front of them.

To begin with he was not just an ordinary man he was one of the two walking the face of this earth right now with powers far beyond anyone's wildest imagination. As Satan stood there he couldn't help but smile and personally enjoy the sight of the police closing in on the top of the stairs of the monument where he stood. They were making every effort to move slowly through the crowd without any pushing or shoving that would send the crowd into frenzy. He watched and waited until the majority of the cops were so encased with the crowd that it would have been difficult to tell them from anyone else with the exception of the riot gear and blue uniforms standing out from all the rest.

He waited for the exact moment for the police officers to be in the worse possible position to handle the mob. He raised his arms in the air and spoke in a clear and calm voice when he said, "I am your savior and I am your salvation, yet within a few short minutes the police come to take me away from you forever". "I need your undying love and devotion now to show them and the world that you will not let this happen to me nor to you." Stick by me and I promise you your every desire. I promise you eternal life in my kingdom of hell in a world that is made for all of you.

That was all it took for the crowd to go absolutely crazy. Before the police could realize what was happening to them they were battered and beaten from every direction. Since the majority of them were already mingled in the crowd they were at their mercy. There was little opportunity to fight back successfully. They were struck with boards, fists, knives, clubs and anything else at the disposal of the hooligans in the crowd. Within minutes the majority were beaten to the ground, many unconscious and unable to defend themselves. The rioters grabbed their guns, rifles, helmets, and actually stripped many of them of their uniforms to make it more difficult to the cops on the outskirts of the crowd to determine who were the good guy and the bad.

The rioters were now well armed and had prisoners in their hands to further reduce the possibility of the remaining police from opening fire on them. It was a serious tactical error that Hopper now realized was his fault. Rather than keeping the incident as a simple discontented crowd gathering it had mushroomed into an uncontrollable riot with projected causalities much higher than anyone could have expected. Already the fanatics were cutting the throats of the cops lying on the ground or bashing their heads in with anything that they could get their hands on. There was no mercy shown that day to anyone who was not in support of Satan. With arms folded and standing in total defiance he enjoyed the magic of the moment where the world realized that their future truly rested in his hands.

Now armed with semi automatic weapons, bullet proof vests and the other weapons taken from the cops the crowd became more brazen and opened fire on the cops and people who were standing outside of the gathering. It was an absolute slaughter as the remaining police were afraid to fire back due to the large number of their fellow officers encased in the crowd. Some of the goons went to the top of the stairs to surround Satan to make sure that he was not attacked or injured. Others fanned out in every direction to wreak havoc on those innocent people in striking distance.

Innocent man, woman and children were mowed down by the fanatics. Some started to burn cars parked in the streets while others wandered into the tourist area of restaurants and museums attempting to set things on fire and destroying anything in their path. One man trying to protect his wife and three year old daughter was shot in the head as if he was just a wild animal while his two loved ones looked on in total horror. Men pulled the wife into an alley way while another guy grabbed the little girl and tucked her under his arm and ran off. As Satan stood there he turned to a couple of the goons next to him and pointed at the statue of Lincoln sitting just beyond where they were standing. He told them that he, Satan, would be the great proclamation and the one who will be freeing them from their bonds. He commanded them to take care of the statue for him. Each turned and walked to the base of the statue and aimed the semi automated rifles at Lincoln's head and pulled the triggers. Bullets ricocheted everywhere and after a second burst of fire the head broke free, hitting the marble floor and tumbling down the stairs. Satan laughed hysterically at the sight of the headless statute of Lincoln sitting there knowing that this was just the beginning.

Over the next thirty six hours the fires and killing spread through the city at an alarming rate. It took the immediate intervention of the National Guard to restore order through the enforcement of martial law to stop the looting and killing. When all was said and done nearly four thousand innocent people lost their lives and it took the fire departments days to stop the spread of the numerous fires set across the city. It was a national disgrace that such an occurrence developed in the nation's capitol. With orders to shoot to kill martial law kept anyone off the streets after dark. The damage reached millions of dollars and those captured relished in the fact that they were part of it. Standing defiant the rioters promised that it was just a small sign of things to come across the entire country. It would grow until it started to also affect other countries and there would be no stopping the momentum led by Satan. It seemed as if every one of them were possessed by his appearance that day.

That one man, the self proclaimed savior of men, the one that named himself after the biblical character of Satan, Lucifer or the devil—was the one totally responsible for the uprising. During the disturbance he seemed to have just vanished with a few of his body guards and has not shown up anywhere. Even with an all point's bulletin and house to house searches by the authorities they could not find him. It was like looking for a needle in a haystack. The same man that created havoc in the UK and Nevada was successful in Washington, DC—where would he strike next?

It became the top priority of the law enforcement agencies to find and stop him before he struck again. A combined task force consisting of the FBI, CIA, National Security advisers and top cops from across the country gathered in the city of Arlington to utilize their technical expertise in trying to figure out his next move. They needed to capture this maniac before he strikes again. The presidential order was to use every resource possible in nailing him before he incited another incident. As they laid out the facts and observations by those who had come in contact with this individual they all realized that this being had powers and abilities far above the normal man. They filled an entire conference room with photos, drawings, places, locations and witness accounts of this one man's impact to catastrophic events in the past several months. The one terrifying factor that no one could deny was that so far he has succeeded in bringing a new level of terror into their lives. Here was a very powerful, controlling, and evil being that would stop at nothing to attain his goals and objectives. They managed to get some audios of his speech in the park and at each pause in his speech they realized the mob was getting more worked up. It was more styled after Adolph Hitler but magnified at least a dozen times in his intensity of convincing others he was the chosen one, he was Satan himself. It was a frightening thought that this thing, this spirit, this purest of evil specimens was real. Yet if that was the case then there also had to be the other—the one that was a perfect match to combat him to a final conclusion. Jesus had to be also walking among them.

Chapter eighteen

Jesus remembers

As the authorities pieced together all the possible scenarios they took credence in the fact that there were sightings of Jesus in the United States by numerous parties who had encountered him. Initially the stories made good press and good human nature stories. The more they researched the individuals and events surrounding them the more they took on an appearance that they were true based on facts and actual things that happened to these people. All their descriptions matched up with the same person and each witness had been left exactly the same item as proof that they had met the same person. The old metal cross, thousands of years old, was a prized possession of each one of them and they had documented accounts from doctors and nurses on the cross that glowed in rhythm with the beat of that little boy's heart. The accounts appeared to be undisputable evidence that another super human being was also walking this earth and it was Jesus Christ himself. The question was where was he?

Jesus had traveled into New England. He loved the ocean and decided to rent a room in a small inn in Jerusalem, Rhode Island—a small fishing community on the outskirts of Narragansett, Rhode Island. When he heard the town's name it immediately reminded him of his childhood and brought back so many memories.

As he looked out over the Atlantic Ocean and the small fishing boats coming into the dock area he thought back about his mother and father on that cold night so many years ago on Christmas. Both of them knew that the baby that Mary carried was special and they did everything possible to assure his safety from the point of his birth through his formative years of growing up. Not much has been written about him during those years because it was the intent of God to protect him from those who would do evil upon him if his true identity was discovered. So Mary and Joseph raised him up like any other child of peasants trying to scrape by on the little that they had and to show him the way through their strong religious beliefs.

Yet he could not get Bethlehem out of his mind as he sat there on the rocks and watched the incoming tide wash the small sea shells on to the beach. Of course he did not remember anything about that night when he was born but his mother relived it for him numerous times as she reminisced how much she loved him.

Mary smiled as she enjoyed re-living the events for her little boy. Joseph did not view the night entirely in the same light as Mary. He recalled the difficulty in finding a place to stay, the cold weather and his fear of not finding shelter before his loving wife had their child. It wasn't until they stumbled across that Inn keeper where he was told that they could stay in the shelter for his animals. At least it was enclosed and they had some protective shelter from the weather if the baby is born. Joseph would always remember the kind act but he was not totally sure whether the man did it out of kindness or just to get them out of his hair because the hour was growing late and he wanted to get to bed himself. Besides what harm is there to provide shelter to a woman carrying a child on a cold winter night?

Mary, however, took Jesus on her knee and was not afraid to repeat the story time and again to him about his birth that December night. She knew the time was near and had repeatedly told Joseph that they must find a place soon. She felt his stirring inside of her and his desire to enter the world that night. She said that she was concerned that something would happen to him if shelter was not found and it frightened her. Even now as she told him the story her eyes began to tear as she remembered the fear of a mother losing a child at birth. She told Jesus that when Joseph had told her that he finally found a place that she was so happy until she realized it would not be the inn but a shelter behind it. As he tied the mule to the post and helped her get down off its back she asked him with a crackling voice—is this where I am bringing our son into this world? Joseph could only manage a slight nod of his head as he took the small sack of clothes that were tied to the mule and laid them on the pile of hay covering the floor of the manger so Mary could lie down. As she looked around she noticed that the animals seemed to be welcoming her into their domain by being extremely quiet, almost respectful, to her condition. There were a couple of sheep, a small mule and a few chickens tucked into a small coop in the corner. As she checked out her surroundings she turned to Joseph and smiled. She told him that she really appreciated that she had a standing audience for the birth of her child. Joseph touched her hand and gently run his fingers down her face. He told her that everything was going to be all right and no harm would come to them that night.

Mary told Jesus that his father was right as they settled in the manger for the night. The pains and cramps were becoming overbearing and she couldn't help but feel scared that something may go wrong. She always managed to reach out and touch Jesus' face at this moment of the story as if she was remembering the first time she touched him that night. She told him he was beautiful wrapped up in the small blanket as she held him in her arms as Joseph kissed her on the forehead. She couldn't resist telling him that shortly before he was born these three men appeared at the entrance of the manger and knelt down beside her and praised god for the gift being delivered that night. She felt so at peace and secure with them there with her and Joseph. As they gathered around the fire she thanked them for the gifts that they brought to welcome Jesus into the world.

She whispered to Jesus that she was amazed that he settled in quite quickly with his surrounding and it appeared that nothing mattered more to him except to go to sleep in her arms. One of the wise man placed a small metal cross around Jesus' neck as a small token of life and the importance of his birth that night. The cross meant a great deal to Jesus as he grew and it brought fond memories of the day that he was brought into this world. He knew that he had a special mission that was bestowed upon him that would test his limitations for all mankind.

Jesus thought back to his life on earth so many years ago and marveled at the changes that have occurred over the centuries. Transportation, food, energy, housing, medical care, technology, education, and personal growth and opportunity flourished compared to his first time on earth. Man had so many more opportunities to make things right now because they had everything at their disposal. Yet there still remained those obstacles that have plagued man that still existed today. The greed, envy, distrust and abuse of power were still presiding factors that seriously jeopardized the ability of man to make it a better world for all. Dictatorships in poor and developing countries abused their countrymen to gain more power and riches while also threatening their neighbors. Good and evil were constantly battling for the upper hand over the other on a daily basis.

Jesus was doing some soul searching on his personal ability to create the change necessary. He had to stop on this nonsense and convince everyone that they could make permanent changes if they set their minds to do so.

Jesus remembered the events leading up to his first death. The Jewish high priests and elders of the Sanhedrin accused him of blasphemy and sentenced him to death. But first they needed Rome to approve his death sentence so they took him to Pontius Pilate, the Roman governor of Judea. Pilate found him innocent. Yet Pontius Pilate was unable to contrive one reason to convict him but fearing the crowds he let them decide Jesus" fate. Stirred on by the Jewish chief priests, the crowd declared, "Crucify him". Jesus remembered the severe beaten with the leather-thronged whip. Tiny pieces of iron and bone chips were tied to the ends of the leather thong causing deep cuts and painful bruising. He was mocked, struck on the head and spit on. A prickly crown of thorns was placed on his head and he was stripped naked. Too weak to carry his cross, Simon of Cyrene was forced to carry it for him.

He was led to Golgotha where he would be crucified. They nailed him to the cross with stake-like nails driven through his wrists and ankles thus fastening him to the cross where he would hang between two criminals. The inscription over his head read, "The king of the Jews". Jesus remembers hanging from the cross for six agonizing hours as the soldiers cast lots for his clothing and people passing by shouted insults. Prior to dying Jesus

spoke to his mother Mary and the disciple John and also cried out to his father, "My God, my god, why have you forsaken me?"
At that point Jesus remembers the darkness covering the land and as he gave up his spirit an earthquake shook the ground, ripping the Temple Veil in two.

It was then that Jesus knew that he had, indeed, sacrificed his life for man. When the curtain or veil of the Temple separated the Holy of Holies (where the presence of God dwelled) it symbolized the destruction of the barrier between God and man. The way was opened up through Christ's sacrifice on the cross. His death provided the complete sacrifice for sin so that all people, through Christ, can approach the throne of grace.

Even after he died on the cross and they removed his body to the tomb that they sealed with a large rock he had tried to relay the message that a savior did die for the people. The Roman soldiers found the stone removed from the opening and his body missing and although searches were conducted no one had seen or heard a thing about what had happened to the body of the man named Christ who died on the cross. A small tear formed in the corner of his eyes as he thought to himself what else will it take before they believe?

As hard as he tried he could not break through his memories and return to the task at hand. They had seemed to grasp him and hold him paralyzed in their grip of memories from the times gone by. The memories were so alive and so vivid to him that he could not help himself but to recall those that most affected him in his development in being God's child.

His mother, Mary, often told him stories about his youth. Her goal was to demonstrate that although he was special he was also one of us and that the importance of blending the two together was critical for him to fully understand his role in God's kingdom.

Jesus believed that the technological advances of mankind had actually played a major factor in the growing belief that mankind evolved through the simple generic factors. Many believed that these factors were the main contributors to the development of life and the necessary survival tools to sustain it. This philosophy allowed the non believers to sustain a constant attack on the very existence of a "savior" and a "creator". It also allowed them to fuel the forces of evil and despair in every corner of the globe. Ashes to ashes and dust to dust principles were becoming the catch phase. This lead to the conclusion that once man died he is gone forever except in the memories of those who knew him. There was no such afterlife existence such as heaven or hell.

Overcoming this hurdle was a major problem for Jesus. He took a personal commitment to assure that this time there would be no questioning his presence before he left earth forever. Win or lose he would give each and every person the opportunity to understand the very existence of he and Satan. With that information he prayed that man would help to become a key factor in their destiny.

Jesus witnessed Satan's constant bombardment and his self gratification of his growing influence on the people. Satan had managed to strike fear through his devastating events that had caused the deaths of thousands. The recent riots in Washington, the disasters in the UK and in Nevada were all indications of his presence. He made it known that he could inflict pain and suffering while also easily avoiding capture. This was not the normal trademark of any terrorism organization but someone very special. Satan also initiated the assembly a band of followers who were thirsty for blood and revenge for their miserable lives on earth.

It was much too easy for Satan to start a riot of unbelievable consequences in a few short days. He was certainty relishing in the fact that it placed the world on high alert and send the world in a state of turmoil. Jesus knew that Satan was feeding off all the masses across the world that was angry with their lives in poverty and discontent. They would jump at any opportunity of making things better. The violence demonstrated on the day of the riots was difficult to comprehend especially when you consider that the crowd inflicted pain and suffering on anyone they could get their hands on. Man, women, children and even animals were cut down as if they were blades of grass by a power mower. They destroyed anything in their paths and took pleasure in doing it. In all the arrests that followed the riots the police were amazed in so little remorse shown by the participants. They all seemed to be in some sort of a hypnotic state. Regardless of the consequences they voiced that given the opportunity they would do it all over again.

Jesus knew that Satan was probably calculating already how easily he could use the same tactics in other cities to incite riots. The sad truth was that Jesus realized that people generally felt that it was more likely that something bad was going to happen to them than something good. Every participant in the riots exhibited the belief that another person got what was going to them and in many cases deserved it—regardless of how bad it really was. Jesus actually began to believe that it may be easier for Satan to convince the masses to come to him rather than Jesus himself. Although in comic books, movies and stories the good guy always wins, in reality is that what will really happen?

Chapter nineteen

Signs of trouble

Even now there are probably hundreds of serial killers enjoying themselves without the possibility of ever getting caught. On even footing are the child molesters, kidnappers, and murderers that exist to create sadness and havoc wherever they go. Reality is the fact that evil is as present in society as good. The big difference is that evil must conceal their ghastly deeds from others. Jesus knew that deep down inside each person's soul that an element of evil existed. Thus under the right conditions each person could be swayed to negative behavior and could easily be converted from a righteous one to an evil one in the skip of a heartbeat. Jesus realized that Satan was on his way to such a major harvest and he had to use everything in his power to stop it.

There were too many examples that led Jesus to realize that he had to do much more than just show up and convince everyone he was indeed real. He witnessed the reaction of humans and realized the complexity involved in human emotions. In many cases he did not like what he had seen. He started with the simple things that provoke people to consider doing something wrong to another. A simple drive on a Sunday afternoon is a great starting point. How many of us have experienced that reckless driver who is tail gating us, chucking us the universal "bird" sign for not getting out of his way more quickly, or trying to gain a small advantage over others in construction areas by passing in a breakdown lane? Deep down inside we may want to punch that person in the face, or curse them out, or have them get into a fender bender to demonstrate to them that their behavior is uncalled for. That one person was able to spark that negative emotion from us. Yet it sparked an immediate negative reaction but really wasn't that important when you consider the act itself. In a matter of minutes that person would be out of sight and we will carry on with our lives as nothing happened. But for those few short minutes we let our emotions turn to thoughts of evil and revenge. Magnify that one example by others that create a serious impact on our lives and you can understand that given the opportunity evil can easily flourish in today's society.

How would you react if someone hurt your child or killed someone you loved? How about someone who has broken into your house or stole your car? Your deepest and most personal thoughts are that you want something very bad to happen to that person. In some cases you wish that you could inflict the pain and suffering yourself. So regardless of the circumstances Jesus knew that mankind was teetering on the edge on what direction to head and could be easily strayed in one way or the other. It was a very delicate situation and all indications were that he was dealing with the master of deception and he could easily lose this struggle if he was not careful.

Jesus thought back on the recent riots and knew that he had to respond in some manner. The news was basically nonstop with the numerous events involving the "mystery" man who was responsible for all this devastation and there appeared to be a growing discontent that the authorities were fumbling clowns when it came to handling the situation. If this person can puzzle and baffle the best law enforcement agencies in the world how would the third world countries handle him when he showed up at their door step? Many people were thinking that it was time to join his flock as he was shaking things up and could make things better for you if you joined his team.

The stories on the other "mystery" man (Jesus) had taken to the back pages of the daily news. Initially the stories about common people being contacted by Jesus had a very positive impact on everyone and strengthened the believers that there truly is a savior waiting to take them to heaven's gates. But the incidents paled in comparison with what Satan had done. Sure these were good will stories many drew comfort from.

Who could possibly resist the story about a little boy coming out of a coma, or a criminal meeting his just end, or an old man claiming he met Jesus in a small town in Rhode Island who gave him a new perspective on life and its importance. And the only link to all three was a small metal cross that was centuries old that was given to each of them by a stranger, a stranger that wore hiking boots, in his early twenties and claimed he was named Jesus. Their stories were continuously being torn apart by the critics as poppy cock and lies. Immediately the peddlers out for a quick buck used the opportunity to begin selling a small metal cross and a tee shirt with the words "Has Jesus crossed your path yet? If so kiss the cross and tell a friend". It was becoming more of a joke than anyone truly believing that Jesus was walking among us. To further complicate things Jesus had not been reported in another incident that could be authenticated in weeks. That further weakened anyone's belief that he was really walking among us.

Meanwhile there were still pockets of violence on a continuing basis in Washington as Satan planned to keep the pressure cooker on high temperature. His immediate goal was to make it clear that the times are changing. Letting loose his team of cut throats to continue to terrorize anyone in the path continued to strike fear into the population of the capital. Senators and congressmen had returned to their home states for safety precautions and those remaining were escorted by armed security personnel. In some respects Washington, DC, the capital of our great nation, was under siege. Armed National Guard troops patrolled the streets and looters were arrested or shot on sight. Even as things calmed down and it appeared that normalcy was returning to the everyday lives of the residents there would be another attack that killed ten to twelve more innocent people for no apparent reason. The situation had reached the boiling point and the frustrations of the American people were reaching a fever pitch. Satan had everyone soul searching their religious beliefs and many religious, god fearing, people were starting to consider turning their support to the dark side.

Chapter twenty

Jolly

Satan sat back in the dimly lit living room where he was absorbed in watching the continuous updates on CNN on the 42 inch large flat screen television. He had selected a handful of the toughest thugs to be his personal bodyguards. He turned to his top henchman, Jolly, and asked him whether they have struck fear into the people. There were more and more incidents of violence being reported and they were all being attributed to his presence and motivational speech to stand up and be counted on his side. Satan was their man and he would help solve all their problems. Jolly just stood there with that stupid grin on his face as if he just pissed his pants and didn't really care that he did. He was a big man, standing over seven feet tall and weighing almost four hundred pounds. What Satan liked about him was that he always had that stupid smirk on his face even in the most dangerous of situations. He always appeared cool, calm and collected. It was that smirk that made him dangerous as people would hesitate for that split second. That hesitation was all he needed to gain the advantage whether it was throwing the first punch, shooting the first bullet or making the first move—it was always Jolly.

Jolly peered at Satan and told him that he had never seen one man generate so much terror in such a short period of time. Jolly told him that some characters make their marks in one country or state by striking fear into a local populace. Yet he was sitting in a room with the man of all men, the one that is evil and powerful enough to strike fear into the hearts of every man, woman and child walking the face of this planet. He then told him how much he truly admired him. Satan never one to take a back seat when it came to accepting praise just ate it all up. He actually thanked Jolly for his observations. Jolly took the opportunity to ask Satan if there was an equal to him, someone who could pose a threat to their plans. Jolly was an opportunist and was already planning ahead to be on the winning team and he would not hesitate to change sides as quickly as he would if someone puked where he was sitting. He was a dangerous man, a man with little principles or moral, yet intelligent enough to be extremely careful in being on the winning side.

Satan had been in a very good mood up to the point of Jolly's question. He was sitting on top of the world as everything he had planned was playing out to perfection. Yea, he did not inflict the death toll that he had expected with the black plague but what the hell he got his point across to the masses. He destructed a national monument that many believed could never be taken down and he caused riots in the streets in one of the most secure cities in the United States. He was actually gloating in his accomplishments until Jolly asked that stupid question and his mood changed. Jolly felt the mood in the room change completely within a few short seconds. It was as if he had rained on Satan's parade and he was really pissed about it.

Satan walked over to where Jolly was standing and shoved a finger into his chest so hard that Jolly initially thought that he had penetrated his skin. For any other man Jolly would have punched him in the face but this was no ordinary man and Jolly was not as stupid as he looked. Satan still steaming from the question reached out with his other hand and grabbed Jolly's chin and squeezed it like a school teacher would for a misbehaving kid. As he squeezed it he also forced Jolly to look directly into his eyes, those eyes, that witnessed more death and destruction than he could imagine. For just a split second Jolly thought he had seen his own image reflecting back at him and what he saw terrified him. He was hanging from a beam with chains that glowed red hot from the intense heat that was everywhere. His skin was continuously peeling from his body and he appeared to be screaming, an endless scream that could not stop. Yet as the skin peeled and dropped to the floor more appeared in its place and it also ignited and dropped to the floor only to be replaced with more burning flesh.

Jolly was not a man to be frightened of anything or anyone but in those few brief seconds he was terrified that he had just witnessed his destiny in the hands of this mad man. He was so afraid that his big arms started shaking uncontrollably.

Satan had intentionally gave the image to Jolly and he did not want to leave any doubt in this nitwit's head that he was the master and the one that would control the future. Just to make the point quite clear to Jolly Satan asked him if the cat has got his tongue or something. He told him that the mind can play tricks on your imagination, but sometimes, sometimes it is a premeditation of things to come so beware. He released Jolly's chin from his grasp and wiped the drool from his lips with his fingers and stuck the liquid into his mouth. As Satan tasted it he told Jolly that it tasted like fear and had the scent of urine. He tapped Jolly on the shoulder and patted him on the back and said what could possibly happen to you? You are my right hand man and you are protected from any harm as long as you are totally devoted to me. You are—aren't you? Jolly could manage to just shake his head up and down and stutter the words, yes, master I am.

With that Satan then told Jolly he would answer his question. He told him that there is another, one who has been in an eternal struggle since the beginning of time with him for full control of everyone and everything. He told him that just when one of them had thought he had the advantage the other would counter attack and re-gain the edge. It was been a constant battle with neither one gaining enough of an upper hand to acclaim victory. Sometimes they just let things ride their course and not get fully engaged in what was happening. Other times they tried to initiate an event that they hoped would be the one action that could turn the tide in their favor. But it did not.

But this time, this time, it is different. They both agreed that there would be a winner and a loser. So, Jolly, there is the other and he is also here on earth and planning his next move. His problem is that I keep staying ahead of him because I am better than him and I am stronger than him. He knows it and I know it. When he is rational, I am irrational, while he is sane, I am insane, where he is forgiving I do not forget, while he is the creator I am the destroyer and people will flock to join me when he is destroyed. So, Jolly, you big ape, you belong to me and you will help me destroy him because you do not want to end up like him in some god forsaken place begging for mercy that will never come. With that Satan walked over to the television and flipped on the CNN News just in time to see another neighborhood go up in flame in the ghetto area of the city.

Chapter twenty one

What next?

Jesus prepared for his counter attack in a way that was totally unexpected by Satan. Had Satan anticipated the move, which he probably should have in hind sight, he could have probably used his goons to easily stop it. But Satan was basting in all his recent glory being made and the continued support drifting his way. There were rallies being initiated in nearly every city in the country. They were held for Satan as the one who was standing up for the rights of the poor, under privileged, and persecuted. Many viewed the riots and devastation as a means to an end. The end would create a common ground between the wealth and happiness of the privileged few and the needs and desires of the masses deserving of something better.

That morning Jesus had made three separate phone calls. It was time to call on those families that have met him and know of the coming struggle. He asked them to join him in Boston, Massachusetts on Friday morning. He told them that he needed their help and had prayed that they would join him. He told them that he realized the inconveniences of such a short notice but their immediate assistance would help him to control a situation that appeared to be getting out of hand. He asked them to meet him at nine o'clock in the morning at the Paul Revere House located in the historical section of the city.

As Jesus sat there on that Friday morning he thought about how importance it was that each and every person needed faith and spirit. Without faith and a dying spirit man cannot survive. It was an obvious fact demonstrated time and again throughout history. The millions of Jews who gave up hope and walked time and again into the mass chambers of death during World War Two is a prime example of what he was thinking. He needed so badly to restore hope and faith into the people today and if he failed he would just fade away into the night and leave everything at the disposal of the other.

It was a beautiful morning and the sky was a deep blue with scattered puffy white clouds blending in perfectly with the crispness of the day. As he peered out the small window of the inn where he waited for the others he was pleased to see a normalcy in the air that was not present in the city of Washington at this time. People were going about their business and doing the normal things that you would expect to see on such a beautiful day. Some were walking their dogs; others were riding their bikes, jogging, or couples holding hands as they strolled through the historical area. People were smiling or waving to others that they knew as they went about their business without any obvious sign of trouble or discontent.

It was at that moment his first guest arrived. It was Nathan and his wife April with their daughter April and son Will. Nathan immediately spotted Jesus sitting in the corner and pointed him out to his wife who smiled the biggest and brightest smile that her face just radiated in the happiness of seeing him again. As they approached the table Nathan turned to his son and said this is the man that we have told you so much about. This is the man that gave you the cross and helped us believe that everything would be all right if we had the faith and courage to make the right decisions in your recovery. Will walked over to the edge of the table where Jesus sat he extended his small hand forward and said I would really like to shake your hand. It is an honor to meet you sir. My sister can't stop talking about you and how nice you were when she first met you. We left the pup with our grandparents but he wanted us to say hi to you as well. I still have the cross that you gave me and I wear it all the time. Here, look for yourself. As he lifted the tee shirt hanging around his neck was that old metal cross that Jesus had given him. As Will pointed it out to Jesus he looked down and saw the cross shining with the brightest bluest tint that it nearly matched the color of the sky. The family gathered around Jesus and all held hands as if they were in some silent prayer ceremony.

Jesus asked them to sit down and welcomed them to Boston. He told them that he expected a few others over the next half hour so he just initiated some small talk about how things have been and how was Will.

Will spoke up first and said that he was doing fine and was back in school. He said that all his friends have been very supportive and the school had fund raisers to help the family pay for the medical bills. He said that he had a lot of new friends and told him about the thousands of cards he received from people all over the world wishing him a speedy recovery. The boy exhibited no after affects of the terrible beating he had taken from the mad man and it was apparent that the memory of the night mare was erased from his memory. Jesus had made certain that Will never recalled the horror that he experienced and had erased them from his memory forever.

Jesus reached out his hand and brushed it through Will's soft brown hair and said that he was very happy to meet him. He told him that he looked a lot like his daddy. Will smiled and hugged his dad's leg and said that he loved his mom and dad very much. Nathan was still taken back by the gentleness and sincerity of Jesus and thought to himself that there was not one evil bone in this man's body. This man has had a tremendous impact on his family's lives and their faith had been restored in the human race by his one act of kindness. It didn't matter if they would periodically struggle to put enough food on the table or they have periodic struggles that life is bound to throw at you; they knew that Jesus was there and in the end they all would be fine in this life and the next.

April had stood silently beside her husband taking every word in as a flower trying to absorb sunshine. She watched her son interact with Jesus and then the personal exchanges between Nathan and him. The first time she met him she was emotionally drained and was having a difficult time just holding her life together without having a complete mental breakdown. She marveled at the power that this one man had over those whom he came in contact with. Without raising his voice or creating lightning bolts in the sky he exhibited the ability to give people the strength to believe and that itself was a very powerful tool.

Jesus caught her staring at him and looked up at her and smiled. He said April how the heck are you anyway, the last time I saw you was burning burgers on the grill. She couldn't help but laugh at his comments and told him that she would be happy to do a better job next time if he gave her the opportunity. Before he could response she said thank you, thank you so much Jesus for bringing our son back to us. Jesus said that it wasn't really him who brought their son back it was their faith that allowed it to happen. When they disconnected those tubes and placed their faith into doing the right thing for the one that they loved. The end result spoke for itself.

Jesus invited them to sit down and have a cup of coffee or a soft drink while they waited for the others to show. He told them that he needed their help and he would explain the situation when the others arrived.

It wasn't long before Henry and Sheila as well as Scotty NcNabb also arrived at the inn. As their eyes adjusted to the dimly lit inn they saw Jesus waving at them from a corner booth and motioning them his way.

As they approached Jesus stood up to shake their hands and thanked them for traveling to Massachusetts to meet with him. Before he got started with his plans and proposal he asked each of them how they were doing since the last time they met. Henry and Sheila spoke up first telling him that their lives were turned upside down for a while when they came forward with the metal cross and their personal encounter with him. Henry said that, initially, it was a very trying and difficult situation for them as they were interrogated by the police numerous times and then it was the hundreds of reporters getting the scoop, followed by the believers and non believers who taunted their every move. They had mass gatherings outside their home and at times were afraid to leave because they would be immediately swarmed by the crowd. At times they were praised as being the chosen ones who Jesus contacted. At other times they were ridiculed as wackos using the holiest of saints as a means for worldwide attention. Their home was egged, their car spray painted and rocks were even tossed through their windows. Sometimes they had both supporters and non believers standing outside their home and it would turn into a free for all with fist fights and name calling blossoming out of control. The police would have to come and break it up while arresting the main combatants.

It was a very rocky road for them and wherever they went they seemed to be recognized as the Jesus couple—you know—the two who claim that Jesus actually sat in their home and had dinner with him after he finished off a criminal who accosted him along the highway. Some would giggle and point at them while others would come over and praise them and thank them for restoring their faith that Jesus was well and watching over everyone.

They told Jesus that no matter how difficult it got for them they did not stray, for one minute, from their love and support of him as the true savior. They viewed themselves very special individuals whose difficult lives resulted in an opportunity to try and spread the truth about the one man that could change the course of history. Jesus sat and listened, taking in every word and thanked them for their support.

He then turned his attention to Scotty who had silently listened to the stories told by Henry and his wife. As everyone's eyes turned to Scotty he simply stated that he could not believe or understand the fact that man can be so supportive or so cruel to others. He had gone through that same roller coaster ride and he told them it was very difficult to handle on a day to day basis. People whom he had known for years questioned whether he was becoming senile or simply using this "story" as a means for attention in a very drab and dull existence since his wife died. He was nick named Saint Scotty by the neighborhood kids and many of them would mock him by bowing and making crude comments as he passed them on the street. Sometimes drunks loitering in his small restaurant would ask him for power ball numbers or whether they were going to hell when they died. He said it hovered on the fringe of the ridiculous and yet all he did was smile and walk away from them. For the believers it was a different story. Scotty said he could feel their trust and faith that they truly believed and wanted to hear each small detail about his experience with Jesus. He said he would spend countless hours with individuals or small groups repeating himself time and again on the day that he met Jesus Christ.

As he told the story no one said a word as they listened intently to Scotty spill out every detail. As he spoke many in the gathering sometimes held hands while holding rosary beads. As Scotty unleashed the story with his heart and soul into every word, some of them would start crying in the realization that he was providing them the faith that they needed to survive in a very difficult and changing world. What was interesting was that they did not view him as a spiritual leader but that of a common man who was touched by Jesus. The bottom line was that for every non believer there was a believer and that is what helped Scotty and the others get through the roller coaster ride that they remained on every day of the week. And the believers made it all worthwhile.

When Scotty finished Jesus looked slowly around the table and felt a satisfaction and inner warmth that everything would be all right. These innocent people had crossed his path, whether it was intentional or not, and were able to provide him the spark of inner energy and spirit to fight to the death for the believers. It was clear to him that all these people needed was a clear understanding that they soon would be involved in the choice of their lives as destiny awaited them.

Jesus told them that he needed their support to drive forward with his simple plan to demonstrate to the world that he is walking among them. Scotty asked him if Satan was truly responsible for all the riots and other events occurring in the world that seemed to possess a true sense of evil in its purest form. Without hesitation Jesus said yes he is. Without pulling any punches he told them of the present conflict and the potential outcomes dependent upon the winner. He could not exactly say what the total plan for Satan was but he expressed sorrow and empathy on the human race if Satan won. Eternal damnation is a very long time and Satan would utilize every ounce of his power to have each man, woman and child understand that. He would know each person's worse nightmare and would enjoy the fact that he would impose it on each and every one of them. While they screamed he would laugh. While they begged he would ridicule them. When they asked for mercy he would make them beg for more. There would be not winners except him and you could take that to the bank.

As he spoke April hugged Will in her arms and told Jesus that he did not save Will to be exposed to that and told him that she would help to fight Satan to her dying breath. Small Will turned to his mom and said everything will be all right Jesus is here with us and nothing bad can happen to us—you know that. Little Will had broke the ice and everyone at the table chimed in as well saying—yea, Jesus is here, we have nothing to fear as he will protect us. Jesus smiled at each of them and then whispered that he prays to God that it will turn out that way. But he truly is not convinced as he had tried to win this struggle for centuries.

It was not his intent to make a formal announcement that he was indeed back on earth like some politician running for public office. He did not want to become a celebrity or be plastered on the cover of every magazine in the country as some sort of an action hero. Yet he had to fully demonstrate to the world that there was a crisis and each and every person would factor into the final outcome.

Chapter twenty two

Jesus speaks

As the months passed and the situation grew into more occurrences of disturbance in the world, Jesus had laid out his plans. The first action was the meeting with the few that realized he was not a figment of everyone's imagination. It was nearly Easter and Jesus knew that it was one of the holiest of Christian holidays. Thousands traveled to the holy land to experience the somber and spiritual experiences of that sacred place. People who did not normally attend Sunday mass would dress up in their best Sunday clothes and show up much to the amazement of their neighbors and friends. Families prayed together and with the exception of the Christmas holiday demonstrated that millions believed in Jesus and took the time to demonstrate it through their actions.

It was on this holy day that Jesus planned to send the message, a sign that he was there among them. It would leave no doubt that he was real and not the figment of someone's wild imagination. It was the day before in the Boston Commons that a crowd gathered around Nathan, April, Autumn, Will, Scotty, Henry and Sheila. It was announced on the local television and radio networks that the people who claimed that they crossed paths with Jesus Christ would describe their encounters. A massive crowd crammed themselves around the center stage that was set up for the event. Prior to two o'clock the park had filled and there were still people trying to fill a way to maneuver their way into the crowd to get within seeing distance of the speakers. The park was set/up with video screens and a sound system that would enable those people in the rear the ability to catch a glimpse of the group. The event took on an aura of high importance as the crowd hoped that it would provide them hope against the evil being spread throughout the world through Satan.

As they stood there on stage they were overwhelmed with the turn out. Nearly half the people that they have previously encountered ridiculed and abused them as crackpots who were using Jesus as a means to gain national attention. They had taken their lumps and were deeply concerned that some in the crowd intended to give them a few more. Yet, in some strange way, they felt that things would be different today. The crowd was orderly and was settling in with a stirring of emotion in support of the upcoming religious holiday.

As they looked around they saw men, woman and children of every race and nationality imaginable looking back at them. Children were waving hi to them and they caught a woman throwing kisses their way. There were men standing there with children sitting on their shoulders as if they were waiting for a parade to pass by and they did not want to miss a single thing. There were elderly people in wheel chairs being maneuvered to the front of the stage so they could get a better look at the guest speakers. The event took on an aura of something wonderful as if you could feel the warmness in the air.

As the clock neared two o'clock Nathan approached the microphone and the crowd grew silent in anticipation of him beginning the event. As he stood there and took a deep breath he noticed that some people in the crowd were pointing and starting to cheer for no apparent reason at all. It was then he realized that Will got to his feet and ran to stand by his father's side. As he reached him he grabbed a hold of his pants leg and held on for dear life. As he did he also raised his left hand slowly into the air and waved to the crowd. The crowd went hysterical and applauded the little boy. He was the same boy that numerous doctors evaluated and told his parents that he was beyond saving and would be better off if they took him off life support. Everyone knew the story and Will was one of reasons why so many showed up. It was such an inspirational story that even the most hardened individual could not help to applaud the little boy. Will did not realize how much easier he just made his dad's job in talking to such a large crowd. It helped to create the perfect entry into a subject that everyone was waiting to hear.

Nathan told the crowd that he wasn't much of a public speaker as a matter of fact it scared the daylights out of him to speak much even in the presence of a bunch of friends. He was asked to do this today by a very special person and could not deny him. He looked down at his son and ran his hand through his hair and told the crowd that his son would not be standing beside him if he had not ran into a total stranger at Yellowstone National Park one afternoon. He said the man appeared to be just a typical tourist who had casually strolled up a walking path in his family's direction. He was a young man, no more than twenty five years old, clean up, and very personable. His daughter, Autumn, happened to ran directly into him as she chased her puppy and started a conversation with the young man. Nathan said he watched them very closely as a few months earlier a lunatic had taken his son from him in the bat of an eyelash and he swore that would never happen again to his family. Nathan said he could feel the warmth and peacefulness generating from this young man even though he was standing twenty to thirty feet away from him. He smiled and told the crowd that the rowdy puppy who had a mind of his own sat down and gave the stranger his paw as if he had known him for years. He said that he had tried to teach that trick to the dog for weeks without absolutely any success. Nathan said that is when he walked over and introduced himself to the man.

Nathan invited him to have some grilled burgers with his family and the man graciously accepted. The crowd listened intently to every word that Nathan spoke and for some strange reason his voice generated throughout the park as if a Bose Sound System was installed for the event. Nathan motioned to his wife to come forward and stand beside him on the stage. There was light applause as she stepped forward and Nathan introduced her. He continued by telling everyone how difficult it was for both of them to realize that their son was diagnosed as clinically dead and they were in the final stages of approving the medical staff to remove him from life support. He sincerely meant it when he told the crowd that he prayed that they never have to experience such an ordeal in their lives. He told them that he repeatedly prayed to god to take him in place of his son but his prayers seemed to go unanswered as his son's condition worsened each day. The helplessness of seeing the gradual digression of their son's health day by day was an overwhelming ordeal.

Yet that stranger, that stranger in a few short minutes with them gave them hope and the ability to prepare for the unforeseen outcome of their son's future simply by talking with them. He comforted his wife and daughter and give Nathan, himself, the ability to know that regardless of what happened when they returned to that hospital everything would be all right.

Many in the audience were extremely emotional as they listened and watched the couple on stage. Their words rang with honesty and truth that they had been involved in a life shattering event that could easily happen to anyone sitting there.

It was there that Autumn spoke up and allowed her husband to regain his composure. She said that it was every mother's worse nightmare to have one of your children disappear but it is far worse when it happens before your very eyes. She said that she and Nathan blamed themselves for Will's disappearance and they were reaching the point when they couldn't stand to look in the mirror at themselves. They should have protected and watched over him and not take it for granted that the world is full of nothing but good and honest people who love life and children. Yet in one heartbeat he was gone and into the hands of a mad man who used and abused the boy before tossing him aside like a rag doll in an old barn. She told them that she cried and cried when she first saw him at the hospital with his face swollen beyond realization and his body covered with cuts and bruises as if he was literally tortured like some small animal caught in a trap. Although alive deep down inside they knew that his chances for a full recovery were slim. He was nearly dead when he was found and they had to resituate him three times on the way to the hospital. But he didn't die he fought as hard as his little body could to return to his mother and father but the cards were stacked against him. The best doctors in the country had reviewed all the tests and they all came up with the same conclusion; he would not recover from the massive injuries. Autumn told the crowd it was at that point that their belief that people were generally good was questioned and their belief in god was losing its glimmer with each passing day. Should they pull through this ordeal they knew that they would approach life entirely differently and would not be that same god fearing and trusting family that they once were? They were speaking with their hearts and they held nothing back as the crowd was hypnotized by their complete honesty and genuine feelings of emotion.

Yet something happened to them when they met the stranger. He listened intently to their family ordeal and gave them faith to realize that a decision had to be made for the good of their son. He restored their confidence that as bad as things are and appear to be that there will always be hope and faith. He told them that true faith will result in true miracles. It was at that point that they understood what they had to do. Prior to walking away he gave Nathan a small metal cross to place around his son's neck. It looked like any old metal cross, nothing special, and Nathan took it, thanked the stranger, and put it into his pocket. It wasn't until Nathan remembered to put it on Will that something happened. It started to softly glow and then change color with the beat of Will's heart. Initially it was so faint in color that it was not even noticeable until Nathan happened to spot it as he stared at his dying boy.

It became more and more visible and was obvious that it was in rhythm with his son's heartbeat. It was then that he drew Autmn's attention to it. At that moment they both also felt the squeeze of his hand on their fingers and they realized that their son was going to live. It was a miracle, a miracle that the doctors could not explain regardless of all the additional tests that they performed on Will shortly after his remarkable recovery. The obvious damage to his brain was repairing itself with each passing day and with the exception of his lost of memory of what happened on that horrific day he was beginning to resemble any other normal boy of his age.

They told the crowd that the treating physician and attending nurses gathered together in a corner of the room and prayed. The doctor was shaken beyond words and had vowed to dedicate his practice to helping others who have been similarly exposed to the wrath of a lunatic because of the boy's remarkable recovery.
With that Will asked his dad for the microphone to say a few words to the crowd. At that point everyone started to stand up and held hands as if they were in total unity with the little boy.

Will told the crowd that he didn't remember the accident, as he called it, but he does remember one thing that he wanted to share with everyone today. He told the crowd that while he was unconscious he felt an emptiness and loneliness that frightened him. He said that he did not remember much except that it seemed to be getting darker and darker as time passed and he was frightened that the time would come when he would be in total darkness and he just wanted to be in the arms of his mother.

That is when it happened Will said. I felt warmness on my chest as if someone had laid a blanket on it or placed a nice winter jacket on me to keep me warm. The light started to get brighter and I could hear the faint sounds of someone whispering in the distance. I couldn't make out the words but for some reason I felt safe and I was not afraid. The warmest in my chest seemed to spread and I felt a tingling in my fingers and at that point I knew. My fingers were holding the finger of my mom and dad and I was so happy. My eyes wanted to open but I was having difficulty at that moment doing that. Yet my chest, my chest was coming alive and it seemed to be reaching the point where I felt as if I wanted to chase our puppy across a field. I laid there for a few more minutes and was then able to open my eyes and I saw my parents standing there and smiling and crying at the same time. I thought to myself how they can be possibly doing that at the same time but was sure glad to see their faces again. I smiled at them and closed my eyes as they knew that I was all right and I knew that they would be there when I woke up again. Just before I closed my eyes I saw it, I saw the thing that was warming my chest and making me feel so much better. It appeared to be a small metal cross and it was glowing and seemed to be changing color with the beat of my heart. I knew that was the case because I could feel and see it like it was actually a part of me. I felt so good. Will ended his talk by telling everyone there that my dad told me that Jesus Christ gave it to me.

With that the audience burst into a thunderous applause; men were whistling; women were shouting praise Jesus, praise the lord and everyone there could not help to be emotionally moved by the little boy's story.

The family received a standing ovation that must have lasted for three minutes before Nathan raised his arms in the air and asked them to please quiet down as there were a few other speakers that wanted to say a few words.

As the crowd quieted down it was Scotty's turn to take center stage. Scotty went into similar detail about how his life had gone down the tubes since his wife died. He told them about how much he missed her and the fact that he was contemplating joining her because he had nothing to live for now. But the difficulty of the decision purely rested on the fact that he did not really know if there was an afterlife; somewhere he could meet her again and spend eternity together. So he kept up his visits to her grave site where he could talk with her and share with her his continued love and determination in silent conversation as he hoped that she could hear him.

Then a stranger entered his life; a man that he had never seen before yet changed an old man's perception of the value of faith and believing.

You see, said Scotty, I was devastated with the loss of my wife and as much as I selfishly asked her to hang on and fight that incurable disease I realized it was a losing battle. Yet each day I watched her try to stay around for me and inject doses of pain killers into her system until she became just a shadow of the person that I once knew. I knew she tried for me and I will never forgive myself for my selfishness knowing that she was in so much pain. She knew where she was going and she had no fear of the unknown because she was a righteous and spiritual person her entire life. Me I was one of those fence sitters; always wanting to believe but always skeptical that it was all hogwash and when we died that was all there is.

Scotty continued with his story. So that is how I lived. I hung on by spending my days visiting her grave and wanting to be with her yet afraid to end my life for fear of never having the opportunity to at least sit by her grave and talk with her. I know that she heard me: I could just feel it . . . . Yet the uncertainty . . . . was overwhelming. With that he started to cry but composed himself quickly as he didn't want to make a fool of himself in front of so many people.

Then one day this stranger appeared and asked me where he could get something decent to eat. Lucky him he found me as I make some of the best sandwiches around. I took him back to my small restaurant and opened the place up just for him but really to get my mind off her and my loneliness.

As we sat there he talked to me and right away I felt at ease as if I knew him for years. He was a compassionate individual and I could tell by looking in his eyes that he was feeling my pain. As we talked he told me that everything would be all right and then he told me things and showed me things that only my wife and I knew. He actually gave me a message from her and it opened my eyes and jump started my life again—at least what is left of it he said with a smile. But the kicker . . . . the kicker . . . . was what he dropped gently into my hand . . . . that is when I knew who he was and that everything would be all right.

People raised up from the folding chairs that were set up for the event and woman were standing there with their hands grasped together at their bosom in anticipation of what the old man was going to say. You could hear a pin drop or an acorn fall from one of the trees as the old man continued with his story. He looked out at the crowd and extended his right hand. He opened it wide and there sitting in his palm was the small gold ornament of an angel that he had placed in Sally's hand as she lay in the casket. Woman placed their hands over their mouths and men reached for their wives. Everyone there felt and empathized with this old man who was spilling his guts out.

Scotty continued, uninterrupted, as if in some sort of daze as he tried to visualize his encounter and express in detail his story to the people who intently listened to his every word. He said that the stranger told him that his wife wanted him to live the rest of his life to its fullest, visit the grandkids and let them be able to remember him. It was amazing because the man told him about his special socks and special song and how Sally had tried so hard to tough it out for him as long as she could. She would be waiting for him, in a better place, one where love reigns eternal.

With that Scotty told the crowd that he was given something by the stranger who told him to always remember their encounter and the words of his wife. He gave him a small metal cross just like the one that was given to Nathan's son who lay dying in the hospital. He simply said—Jesus gave it to me. With that the crowd rose to its feet and in unison shouting out praise Jesus, praise Jesus—he is walking among us!

Scotty stepped aside and called Henry and his wife Sheila forward to the center of the stage. As he handed the microphone to Henry he said tell them the way it is son, tell them and they will know it is the truth. Henry stood there looking at the crowd and it seemed to be growing with each passing moment. The news of the event now was being carried live on CNN as a human interest story and the word was spreading quickly about the band of people who claim to have personally met Jesus Christ telling their stories in the Boston Common. The police were amazed that the crowd remained so orderly without one reported incident of trouble. This was extremely unusual for a crowd of this size as one small disagreement would spark a conflict of some sort. Yet nothing, no sign of trouble and the story continued to build to become worldwide news with each passing moment.

Henry told the crowd that he was not a gifted speaker and was actually afraid of big crowds but he would give it his best shot as he deemed it important to get the truth out to as many people as possible on this important day.

He told the crowd of his abusive upbringing and had it not been for his mother he would have died on his first birthday. Although he doesn't remember her, he has a couple of photos of her that he has kept in his wallet that he periodically looks at and kisses. He told them about his abuse growing up and the way that he was picked on and singled out by others as an easy mark. He told them how he ran away at an early age and managed to survive through working hard and mining his own business while taking shelter from those who would give it. He met Sheila and fell in love with her because she was so much like him and she made life worth living again.

He then told them how he ran into the stranger on that day by the highway. He said he saw three thugs forcing him into the woods and he realized that they were up to no good. He had decided to try and help the man; he just didn't know how. It was then that he saw the stranger motion to him with his right hand that everything was all right and not to intervene. He hid in the tall grass and behind some trees deciding whether he still should try and help this man whose life was in obvious danger.

As Henry moved closer to them he could listen to every word being spoken and he was amazed at the stranger's calmness under the frightening situation that he was in. They make him get on his knees and the leader had told him that only three of them would walk out of that place and one of them wasn't him. He said any other man would have probably panicked, but this man, this man, just remained as calm as a pond on a hot summer's day. It seemed as if the man looked at the three thugs with pity. In a calm and clear voice he looked to the sky and said forgive them for they know not what they do. Those simple words were enough for two of the thugs to re-evaluate their involvement in the pending crime. One spoke to the other and within a few minutes they had changed their minds and chickened out of any further involvement in hurting this innocent man. They dropped their knives and ran from the woods to their vehicle; jumped in, and sped off down the road. The third man, the leader, was really pissed and you could tell that he was going to kill this stranger. He had made up his mind. The thug swung his knife, appeared to have lost his balance and stabbed himself as he fell to the ground. Some in the crowd shouted out that he deserved it while others shouted amen. Henry said he heard the words of the stranger as he approached the man lying on the ground bleeding profusely from his self inflicted wound. He told the man that he hoped god the father would forgive him because he would not. And with that he touched the man's head and the thug disappeared. His body had turned to ashes on the ground and he was gone.

The crowd was now growing hysterical as if in a frenzy from the stories that they were told. Many had dropped to their knees while others were hugging one another as if realizing that something speculator was happening, something that no one would have ever predicted. People in today's society of technology were actually realizing that the theory of a superior being actually existing was possible. As they all stood there someone in the crowd started to sing Amazing Grace and within a few short minutes the mass of people joined in as if it was a church choir. It was very touching and it seemed as if the world stood still, listened and watched this breath taking event.

There was not a single person watching who was not touched by what they were witnessing. It was the coming together of thousands in a Boston park in an event that was not even broadly announced or planned in any detail. On top of that it was held by common people, like you and I, who had an opportunity to speak from the heart and who managed to touch so many within a few short minutes.

It was then that it happened. It came on so unexpectedly that even Nathan, Will, Autumn, April, Scotty, Henry or Sheila realized what was happening. Initially there appeared to be hundreds of white sparrows flying left to right in the sky above the stage. As they passed a magnificent rainbow appeared to arc over the stage except that it contained every color imaginable. Beneath it was a light, a circular light that hovered approximately one hundred feet in the air. As people watched it; it seemed to slowly descend to the stage. Although it glowed it did not cause anyone to look away but rather cause them to closely follow its path until it settled directly in the center of the stage. And then it ever so slowly changed shape and loss it's glitter. As everyone watched in amazement the shape had changed into a man, a man standing before them with his arms raised above his head as he looked to the heavens above as if embracing the world as he did so many years ago when he hung from the cross.

The crowd was in awe and the beauty of his appearance was that it was happening in real time in front of a worldwide audience. No hidden tricks or magic, it was visible to everyone that something spiritual was occurring before their very eyes.

As Jesus looked out over the massive crowd he was, truly, undecided on whether he had made the right decision. He could have decided to make contact with others through similar personal occurrences that he was among them but felt time was growing short in his battle with Satan. On top of that Satan was gaining momentum and was beginning to win over normally good folks to join his cause. Jesus thought he could possibly decide to choose a final location to battle Satan in a win take all that could have devastating results. Somehow, he knew that the path he chose was the right one and he decided to let it run its course and carefully monitor the situation.

As he scanned the audience he was touched with the reaction of the participants. He saw women trying to reach out to him, couples hugging one another in joy as everyone seemed overwhelmed with the fact that Jesus Christ was standing before them. What was amazing was that no one was rushing the stage and trying to carry him off like some sort of a conquering hero but were content to continue to stare at him in disbelief.

With the gradual lowering of his arms to his side the crowd seemed to grow silent in anticipation of what he was going to do or say. He took a few seconds to gather the words that he wanted to say. These words would probably be the most important that he would ever speak to a gathering; even more important than those voiced at his last supper as he stood before his disciples at that faithful night so long ago.

Without any further delay he said, "Fear not the future or the uncertainty of whether there is a heaven or hell. Know today that I have appeared before you and I am not a figment of any fables or someone's wild imagination. Also know that my equal, in the state of pure evil, is also here among you. With each passing day you are getting closer to judgment day. Each of you will be involved in the final decision; a decision that will affect every men, woman, and child alive and dead. It is with my love for mankind that I return once more and I pray that I will make a difference or I will simply perish forever". With that he was gone, vanished as if he was never there.

The event was shown repeatedly throughout the world time and again. It was shown in slow motion; with extreme close ups centering on his face, his hands, and his body. It was the most watched video in news history as it was dissected more than the Kennedy Assassination film. Was it real, was it an image that was projected on to the stage, or just an illusion. The experts did everything possible to find some sort of a fault in the occurrence as if trying to find some way to explain what they had just witnessed before their eyes. From all the evidence gathered and the high technology analysis conducted the same conclusion rang out—this being, this person who spoke to the crowd was indeed standing there on the stage and was as real as that nose on their face.

The reaction around the world was spontaneous as millions openly prayed that a savior had returned to earth. Churches were filled to the rafters with people who had not gone to church in years. There was a temporary cease fire in the numerous armed conflicts against the world. People were truly beginning to believe that their hopes and dreams of again seeing that loved one who passed away is now within their grasp again. The cable networks were in overdrive in relaying story after story about how people are treating one another in an entirely different manner than ever before. The story that impressed everyone was the sudden but positive turn of events in Palestine where there was a calming influence in the battle of the holy land where Christ was born. It finally seemed as if the world had its share of violence and bloodshed all because of a short three minute speech by the man called Jesus.

Chapter twenty three

Satan reacts

Satan had sat in his dimly light strong hold and had watched the same CNN broadcast as so many others. Initially he thought to himself that this was going to be viewed as an absolute joke by the public and they would be laughed off stage. But immediately he had serious reservations that he was badly mistaken. As soon as those fools started talking about how Jesus touched them he knew things were not going his way. As the cameras panned the crowd he noticed their faces and the fact that they truly believed every single word being spoken. It wasn't bad enough when that idiot Nathan tried to tear their hearts out about their little boy who suffered so much at the hands of a maniac; but that old fool, Scotty, also was very convincing. Satan thought to himself he should have done that old fool in when he had the opportunity. He could easily have sent someone to convince him he was better off to be with his cancer stricken dead wife than to live another lonely day on this earth but he didn't want to waste his time. He could have someone do the old man in but again didn't think it was worth the effort as the majority had already questioned his sanity and story before. But this time the old fart was overly convincing and had won the hearts of everyone listening to his story. Satan thought that he could have been moved to feel sorry for him had he had any compassion in his soul. Instead he felt angry and despised the speakers for what they were doing to upset his apple cart.

Satan got more upset when he thought about that frigging Henry and his nitwit wife. Frigging cry babies he thought. Too frigging bad that they had some ups and downs in their lives—doesn't everyone. Yet they stood there like the other speakers as if they were the happiest people in the world because they had a chance to meet Jesus Christ. Give me a frigging break Satan thought. Jesus had given them nothing but an old metal cross. Did he make their lives better, give their more money than they could have ever imagined, give them a little more brains than their empty heads have now, or give them something that they desired in their most private and forbidding dreams. Shit, no, he did nothing but show up and convince them he was Mr. Goody Good Shoes and left nothing behind but hope. Give me a frigging break he thought to himself.

Satan was amazed that in a few short minutes his arch enemy had won over millions by uttering a few words and appearing on stage as if he was David Copperfield. He had miscalculated his opposition and was now paying the price. He had decided to let Jesus have his day in the sun without pulling anything that would disrupt the party in the park as he called it. Yet, as he saw things starting to get out of control he thought better of his decision. He sent a few of his goons into the park to cause a disturbance but they couldn't break through the crowd. It was too thick and it seemed like the people on the outside edge of the gathering somehow sense their intentions and would not let them through. He was royalty pissed at his failure to stem the tide and planned to take it all out on the thugs who reported back to him about their inability to penetrate the crowd.

When they returned he told them that he should have known better than to send some incompetents to do a man's job. How could you possibly screw up something as easy as causing a disturbance in a huge crowd; it was ridiculous. Satan waved his arms wildly as he spoke and the goons could sense that he was really pissed for screwing up. He stormed over to his desk and shoved all the papers to the floor, scattering them in every direction. He used the open area to rest his elbows; placing his head in his hands as he glared at the three failures standing in front of them. It didn't matter to him that their career paths took them from petty larceny right through to cold blooded murders; they did not frighten him.

Satan repeated one of his favorite sayings when he sputtered out I should rip your heads off and shit into the empty hole. That was when Clyde, the one with the quickest and most violent temper, stepped forward and told Satan that he made him want to vomit. You think you are such a big man yet you can't wave your frigging magic finger and cause a crowd disturbance by yourself rather than sending us out to do your dirty work? Fuck you; you frigging weirdo, I don't need this crap he said.

Without hesitation he reached for the forty four revolver stuck in the belt of his pants with the goal of unloading every slug into this demon's miserable body. As the gun was reaching the point where it was pointed directly at Satan, Clyde pulled the trigger and smiled. He expected to smell the burnt powder from the spent bullets and see the flash from the end of the gun as bullet after bullet sped forward into the demon's body.

Yet nothing happened—had the gun jammed or misfired? His first thought was, oh, shit, I'm screwed. The fact is he was. Satan's eyes glowed bright red and for a second the goons thought that they saw a long, serpent like tail swing angrily left to right behind his body. His face was so distorted in anger that it did not even look human as if transformed into some sort of a monster from one of those low budget horror films.

Clyde knew it was useless to try and apologize so he chucked Satan the universal sign of contempt by pointing his middle finger in an upward position directly at him. The other two thugs slowly stepped backwards realizing that they were witnessing the most brazen act of defiance since Clint Eastwood stood by himself in that movie, "The forgiven" when he single handedly wiped out a bar of men who killed his best friend.

What they witnessed sent a message to them that they were dealing with a source so powerful and evil they would not screw up on any other assignment if given a second chance.

Clyde's face was frozen in contempt with a snarl on his lips and drool running down his cheek—he had no idea what he had gotten himself into. Satan was going to use him as an example of what would happen to anyone who questioned or opposed him in the future. He would let the other two fools live to spread the word to the others that this dude is not someone that you mess with. If he says jump you jump, if he says the sky is pink, it is!

Clyde's defiance was gone in seconds. That middle finger posed in Satan's face was bent directly back as if some unknown force had grabbed it and wouldn't let go. Not only was it bending but it continued its downward path until it rested directly on the back of his hand. He screamed in pain and attempted to grab it with his other hand but it seemed as if his other arm was paralyzed on his right side. At that point the finger twisted in a three hundred and sixty degree rotation and was ripped off. Blood spurted everywhere as Clyde continued to scream in agony.

Satan just smiled and told Clyde that he didn't want him to lose track of the whereabouts of his finger so he had a place for him to store it. The finger bounced off the top of the desk and was aimed like a guided missile into his mouth. Clyde's eyes bulged and he realized that his finger was slowly descending down his throat blocking his ability to breathe. As much as he tried to cough it up it was useless and it lodged itself directly in his wind pipe. His face was turning blue and he was gagging uncontrollably yet his two buddies were frozen in their positions afraid to move or help him.

Satan let him suffer for a few more seconds and then told him that he would burn forever in the fires of hell but he would definitely stand out from the rest of the souls there. With a motion as if he was a surgeon operating on a patient with a scalpel he pointed his finger at Clyde's neck and swung it left to right. Blood shot everywhere as his head rolled to the floor and the body of Clyde stood there like some sort of strange red water foundation spurting the remainder of his blood until it dropped to the floor.

He turned to the other two men in the room and told them to clean the place up and get rid of Clyde's body. He also told them never to let him down again as he would not be so lenient with them next time. Satan looked at them and smiled as he said, "Good times are here again".

Things remained relatively quiet over the next several weeks as both Jesus and Satan allowed everyone the time to let everything sink in. There was a massive gathering of world philosophers, religious leaders, scholars, and country leaders on the validity of the events of the past several months. Although there were disagreements in the magnitude and scope of the meaning on the occurrences the bottom line was that we were experiencing phenomena like the world had never seen.

Through all the debates and sharing of ideas at these meetings one thing stood out to all and that was that this dormant state of inactivity would not last. The question was who would make the next appearance and where?

Chapter twenty four

Separate ways

Jesus "disciples" had appeared to go their separate ways after the event in the park or so it seemed to all the observers. Each party did not conduct any more interviews and told anyone who approached them that they had given their heart and soul in their speeches that day and they would let their words carry forth from that day on. Believe them or not was up to each individual person. They have done their best to present the facts as they experienced them. Each refused to answer any further questions and said that you all have seen it for yourself; Jesus appeared before you and yet you are still skeptical. What else can we say that would change anything?

So they traveled back to their homes where they returned to a normalcy in their day to day routines of putting their lives back together. Initially the news trucks and reporters staked out their homes as if they were Hollywood celebrities but soon grew tired of waiting around and getting nothing new to report. So they left Scotty, Nathan and his family and Henry and his wife alone and centered their attention again on the news of the day to fill the headlines.

It was at that point when each of the families got into their cars on a Sunday morning and traveled into the white mountains of New Hampshire to meet Jesus in a secluded cabin that was periodically used by hikers as a stopover point during the winter months. The road was hardened with dirt and small stones and it was barely passable due to some recent heavy thunder showers that bombarded the area for four straight days. They actually parked their cars in a clearing used for hunters and hiked the remaining three miles to the cabin.

Jesus was sitting on the small front porch in an old rocking chair which was the ideal spot to admire the beauty of the New England landscape. Wild flowers dotted the fields surrounded by maple and pine trees and in the distance was the White Mountains. As the couples approached Jesus stood up and waved to them as if they were long lost friends whom he hasn't seen for a while. He walked down the three wooden stairs and extended his hand to Nathan who was the first to reach him. Jesus shook his hand and patted him on the back and said he was glad to see them all. Little Will actually surprised him as he ran forward and in one leap jumped into his arms. Jesus managed to grab him and wrap his arms around him as if he was one of his grandchildren.

Jesus carried Will into the cabin and noticed that he still wore the cross that he had given Nathan to put around his neck. Will noticed Jesus looking at him and said, "I will wear this for the rest of my life and every time I look at it I will remember you. Jesus told him that was very nice and he took it as a real complement. Will smiled and offered him a stick of chewing gum while Jesus politely declined.

Jesus asked them all to sit down around the table and told Will that he could go play in the small room off the kitchen as there were some toys left in an old chest just waiting for him. Will called his puppy and scooted off. Jesus had placed a pitcher of lemonade on the table and poured each one a glass. As he handed it to each of them he thanked them individually for their bravery in standing in front of thousands of strangers and telling their stories. He told them that it was obvious that they spoke from the heart and so many people were touched by them on that day.

Jesus told them that he was closely monitoring the impact and results of the event in the park. He was determined to assure that his next actions further strengthened the necessary bounds of the believers while causing the non believers to think again and evaluate the side that they choose.

He, also, shared his concerns for their safety and well being during this turmoil. He told them that it was obvious that Satan initially didn't really care about them or telling others their stories. However, things had changed and Satan was extremely upset that he did not intervene earlier to disrupt the event. Satan had brushed them off and now was really perturbed with himself, but, especially with them for upsetting his apple cart. Given the opportunity he would try to rectify his mistake and make each one of them pay dearly for their acts.

Scotty piped up and said bring it on. He can't possibly do anything that could hurt me now. What kill me—I will then be with my beloved wife. Try to torture me—my faith will carry me through anything he can throw my way. Let him take his best shot as I am not afraid.

Jesus smiled at him and told him he was a tough old Irishman as Scotty just smiled back at him. The rest of the group had listened closely to what Jesus said and waited for him to further express his concerns and feelings.

Jesus told Scotty it was not that simple and Satan was not someone to take lightly or call out into the street at sun set for a gun fight. If he managed to get his hands on any of them he would make them pay dearly. He told them this not to frighten them but to make them aware that this struggle is imperative to win and Satan will do or say anything to come out on top. He told Nathan the reason he asked Will to go into the other room to play was because he had to warn him. He told them should Satan get his hands on Will he would put them through the same agony as before except that he would make them watch it. Satan would repeat the boy's torment time and again until they went stark raving mad. Autumn grabbed Nathan's hand and squeezed it tight looking for the strength to be able to go through such an ordeal again. It terrified her.

Jesus told them that Satan would try to manipulate them into telling everyone that they lied or it was some sort of a freak show that everyone saw that day. He would mane, torture, abuse or expose them to their worst nightmares to either destroy them or convince them to come to his side to stop the pain and suffering. At that point he told them why he called them together. They would be protected and safe as long as they remained close to him until the struggle is over. Satan did not have the power, at this time, to penetrate Jesus' forces of those close to him. Jesus told them that their simple speeches helped him to decide to appear on that stage that day. It was when they had completed their stories that Jesus realized that the overwhelming majority believed every word spoken is when he had decided to appear. It was then that he would show the world that he was real and had returned after thousands of years. He told them that they were remarkable individuals who set the examples to others that even a common everyday person can make a difference. He said he loved them very much.

With that he asked them if they were ok with staying together as a family until the crisis passed. The road was still going to be very difficult and dangerous but together they had a chance to get through it. He told them that he could not fully protect them if they were scattered and distant from him. He could only pray that they would be all right but against such an evil force and equal competitor he could not promise that they or a loved one would not suffer harm. He could not ever promise them a place in heaven because the struggle would determine if heaven will cease to exist.

It did not take them very long to come to a consensus that they would remain close to Jesus. They would do everything possible to win the battle with the evil one. Jesus was truly relieved in their decision and set forth with his plans to finalize the end of Satan and the beginning of eternal peace and tranquility for all mankind.

Chapter twenty five

Satan spreads fear

Equally busy was Satan who had plans of his own, big plans, plans that would win over the majority of people to his side and end this eternal struggle once and for all. As he and Jesus had kept everyone wondering what was going to happen next he was planning his strategy that would take everyone by surprise.

The months had passed as neither one was in a hurry to make a move that could possibly fail due to some unforeseen reason. It was like a chess match between the two best players in the world. Each move was being analyzed carefully to avoid being the one that was check mated. Far too much was riding on the success of the next step. Across the world the winter months were settling in and a lot of attention was being given to the massive changes in the weather. There were numerous blizzards and storms everywhere that were unparalleled in their violence and intensity. Nearly every European country had incurred at least one major storm that left them fully unprepared and in dire straits for help to dig their way out. Electrical failures, lack of heating fuel and people being isolated and unable to get help because of the extreme cold and mounting snow. Each day the news accounts reflected an increasing death toll because of the severe conditions. It left the authorities little recourse but to sit it out and hope that the situation did not worsen any further.

Even the United States where they possessed so much specialized equipment and technical knowledge to fight such conditions felt the impact of the severe weather problems. Not only did the storms hit the normal locations as the north east, mid west, upper New York, Nebraska, and Iowa, but major blizzards occurred in Florida, Alabama, Louisiana, and southern California. People in the southern states were ill prepared for the cold and driving conditions and it caused absolute havoc on them. Massive traffic accidents shut down highways for days and hospitals were packed with people who had suffered terrible injuries. Police and rescue workers could not reach many of the injured who just died in their cars before help could arrive. Other victims in rescue vehicles never made it to the hospitals as they got stuck in massive traffic jams and died on route. The blowing and drifting snow was making, not only driving, but walking conditions unbearable and it seemed that everything had come to a complete stand still because of the weather.

On top of the devastating impacts to traffic, power outages, heating fuel, medical attention, phone service and food supplies in the stricken communities; the people were being affected by "cabin fever". They were at their wits end due to their inability to do their normal routine and being cooped up for prolonged periods of time was showing its toll. Access to cable and the internet were limited, phone service spotty at best and people were held up in their apartments or homes as if they were actually prisoners. Some families with members with a violent temper were seeing them go off the deep end. Those living in apartment complexes heard the constant yelling and screaming from the next door apartment and then the sounds of things being thrown or broken. Then it was followed by the foul language and sounds of fists hitting flesh and someone crying out for help.

There were many reports of neighbors trying to intervene or getting pulled into the fracas and getting hurt or even shot. Others afraid to intervene tried to block their ears from the horrible things that were happening next store. What was amazing was that these combatants were normally good and decent people but the constant toll of the depressing situation brought the worse out of them.

It seemed as if each apartment complex was left to fend for itself as the local authorities were helpless to address every emergency call coming into the 911 alert systems. The phones rang constantly and the teams tried to identify which ones was a life or death situation. Many of the phone operators couldn't take the pitiful cries for help and actually broke down and cried. Some were so emotionally shaken that they couldn't deal with it and quit the position. Even with the National Guard Forces on full alert and assisting wherever they could the impacted states and cities were like a no man's land for disaster.

As the world scientists tried to sort through the historical weather patterns unforeseen for centuries, it was obvious that some other force beyond the changing world's environment due to global warming was a major contributor. The storms and events held no specific pattern. It was as if some of the locations were selected, in some strange way, to receive the majority of the terrible conditions because they did not know how to deal with them. As soon as just a small amount of ice and snow fell from the skies the amount of traffic accidents reached peak proportions. People unfamiliar on how to drive in such conditions were immediately caught off guard. Instead of braking slowly or leaving the proper spacing between cars to avoid a rear end collision they drove normally until it was too late to avoid it. Some took the other approach and drove so slow that when they came to a hill in the highway they couldn't get fully up the hill and caused massive traffic jams by sliding out of control.

If the events were planned all eyes pointed to only one possible choice. All fingers pointed at Satan and everyone knew that he was simply sending another message of his abilities to wreck havoc whenever he desired.

Yes he was watching and enjoying it all! In his evil and warped mind he thought it was comical that people were complaining about the cold and freezing weather. After all didn't they also scream and beg for mercy as he walked them through the gates of hell as their flesh burned from the bones of their body—again and again. He thought it amusing that they would be so ungrateful for the opportunity to experience the total opposite of what he would be dishing out to them. Satan thought—they are all whining little bitches. It just goes to show that basically you can't satisfy them no matter how hard you try he laughed to himself. They all will soon learn that they are just pawns in my game and would be for all of eternity. If they fear me now could you just imagine how they will be shitting their pants everyday knowing that I will control them for eternity? I have so much in store for them.

But first Satan could not let his guard down. He must convince each and every one of them that if they joined him that they would not be exposed to such awful and horrible things. He would protect them and they would be members of his flock. Others would suffer for their undying dedication to Jesus not them!

Satan knew his trump card was the fear factor. He had inflicted so much pain and suffering in such a short time on earth that many people were truly afraid of not coming to his side. Fear is a controlling factor and it will lead many people to do things that they would never ever think of doing. The cable networks were doing a fantastic job of tying all the devastating events together under the leadership of Satan. All he had to do was sit back and reap the benefits. People had already started to take sides and the latest ratings indicated that he was gaining momentum. It is human nature to react to an event, whether it is good or bad, and response with an action or reflex. Then people will listen to others discuss it and form an opinion. This would finally lead to a decision based on their interpretation of the information. One of the key factors in such a decision making process truly ends up with the one question—what is in this for me and my family? If the person believes that the outcome will be beneficial for their personal objectives than, low and behold, they will support it.

In Satan's mind he was doing just that. He had showed the world his tremendous powers and his ability to strike fear into everyone. His acts of rage, spread of disease, destruction of historical monuments, riots, and personal vendettas against anyone who crossed his path were well documented. He was deemed unstoppable and that was enough for many people to believe it was better to take his side before it was too late.

Besides what has the other one done to show that he could truly combat this evil force? Jesus had managed to develop a solid army of supporters himself when he appeared on stage at the Boston Commons. It was the most inspirational event in years. He left little doubt that he was also walking on earth but many questioned his ability to truly win the struggle between the two. They thought what has Jesus done since he returned? He simply touched a few unfortunate humans who had lived a basically sad and depressing life. Otherwise he has not demonstrated that he could stand in the same ring as Satan and expect to come out a winner.

True—Jesus had somehow managed to bring life into a dying boy but perhaps that boy was going to make it through the ordeal anyway. He had managed to hold off some thugs by standing there unafraid and questioning the guts of two of the three to carry forth with murder. Many of us may have done the same thing and perhaps placing that seed of doubt into their feeble minds may have worked for any of us. As far as that thug who died he basically stabbed himself and died. Sure Henry said his body disappeared to ashes but it was basically his word that he saw it. Perhaps his buddies returned to the scene afterwards, before the police arrived, and burned the body to try and keep them from also implementing them in the robbery. Jesus also touched the heart of an old man longing to be with his wife but did nothing but show him a gold angel bracelet that was buried with her. Heck, he could have seen a picture of his wife wearing it and purchased it at some jewelry store to try and win the old man over to thinking he had some supernatural powers. As far as knowing personal such just shared by loved ones in conversation so many physics could convince so many people that they have touched a dead loved one that these frauds made millions annually ripping off those who wanted to believe. Sure, Jesus had descended on that stage that day but what did he do except say a few words and warn everyone of the pending struggle. The sad thing considered by many was that he has done nothing that would demonstrate to the world that he could fight and defeat Satan. That saddened and frightened everyone enough to begin to realize that shifting course to support Satan may not be a bad thing to do at this time before the gates of hell closed and they were left out of his flock forever.

Satan was actually giggly and acting foolishly as he sat in his den watching news commentator after news commentator analysis the tremendous impact that he had on major earth shattering events. Without warning Satan had struck a devastating blow and had successfully escaped without a trace of his whereabouts. Could this evil one be even killed or destructed should he be found? How do they convince him to stop his destruction?

Satan bounced off his sofa and danced like a little child learning to do some sort of crazy dance to music for the first time. It appeared to be a mix of the twist, hula, and the chicken dance all in one. His bodyguards could not believe their eyes and started to laugh at his weird moves and stutter steps. Satan noticed them laughing and pointing at them to join in his little celebration. Before you knew it they had formed a dance train with Satan leading the way around the room performing a mixture of the various dance moves. It was truly a ridiculous scene and anyone entering the room would never had thought that they were watching the most evil man in the universe dancing his heart out over some stupid news report. As the programs were interrupted by commercials Satan stopped dancing and walked over to the bar and poured himself a large glass of Jack Daniels and swallowed it down. As he wiped his mouth he told his goons to help themselves things were coming up pretty rosy and he didn't mind if they joined in the celebration. Each eagerly grabbed a glass and starting downing the whiskey as they congratulated him on his noted celebrity status.

So the world finally understands that he is a force that may not have an equal and that he may be unstoppable. Even Jesus Christ was a weak opponent when it came to matching up with him. Time and again he had demonstrated his strength and destructive powers and had come out a winner. For some god forsaken reason Satan figured that he would now show the world that he is forgiving one as well. Hadn't the world seen enough of his ability to destroy, he would now let the world know that he can stop pain and suffering (if he so desired) by stopping something he had started in the first place. He would stop the massive violent storms and restore the normal weather patterns across the world. He would get life back to a normalcy even if it was just a temporary condition.

But this time Satan would definitely take credit for stopping it. He would not let some foolhardy religious jerk point to Jesus as the savior who stopped the storms. He would leave no doubt in anyone's mind that he was the one who started them and it was he who has taken the merciful step of ending them. He thought that it would be another factor in having more convert to his leadership and provide everlasting devotion to the evil one.

So it came to be that he interrupted worldwide satellite communication and spoke to the world at midnight on December 1.

Dressed in his best black suit, white shirt, sparkling gold cuff links, red silk tie and a bright red rose dangling from his coat pocket he spoke to the world. He told them that he had given them example upon example of his power and might and he laid them out in chronological order. He admitted the wave of violent storms and deaths were also his personal doing and they could have continued for months growing worse in intensity if he so desired. But he had a compassionate side as well and he realized that everyone had suffered enough. The storms would be ending followed by a normalcy that would allow everyone to get their lives back in order. He showed no remorse for those who died some horrible deaths during this period but only voiced that it was a "warning shot" that the world should unite under him. This could help avoid other such events in the coming months. He stressed that it was he and he alone who will stop the storms and provide the world with a recovery period to get their lives back together. He even took the liberty to call Jesus weak and pathetic and someone who will soon just fade away like some distance dream.

Without pulling any punches he stared directly into the camera so all could look into his eyes. His eyes the shape of a cobra's head and fire engine red reflected the evil inside. He warned the world that they better not under estimate him anymore. He didn't care that men, woman and children could be watching his speech, he simply told everyone that those who questioned him would soon be kissing his royal ass and sucking his royal cock for mercy and forgiveness. With that he swung the universal sign of contempt to the world by chucking his middle finger directly in front of the cameras as the broadcast ended. It was at that moment all the storms devastating the world ended. Satan had kept his word.

In one respect the world was thankful that the violent weather ended. They could start to dig out and help those in dire need of assistance. It was a monumental task that took the efforts of thousands of volunteers to get under control over the next several weeks. But as the weather cleared and the sun once again shined the people were extremely thankful for the pause in the onslaught. The sad part was that they were thankful to the one person that started it all and many found that very difficult to comprehend emotionally and physically. The biggest question in the world today was what was going to happen next and how would Jesus response to the challenge put forth to him from Satan?

Satan had decided that he had delivered his message loud and clear and he would give the world some time to mass under his leadership. How could they now doubt his power, abilities, strengths and perseverance to win this final conflict? He sensed he was unstoppable now and nothing in this world could interfere with his goal to be the ultimate supreme one . . . . forever!

Over the coming weeks the nations implemented a recovery plan that helped them get through the recent crisis. It also helped them contemplate the choices that they must surely make over the coming months. It is needless to say how frightened and intimidated everyone was of the power demonstrated by Satan. Yet there was still hope and faith that—somehow and in some way—Jesus would soon demonstrate that he was equal to Satan and will be the final victor.

Chapter twenty six

The Christmas holidays

With the recovery came the gradual relaxation that countries around the world settled into the holiday season. It was then that Nation upon nation realized that with the Christmas season comes a gathering together of families, friends, cities and countries in the belief that we share a common love and everlasting life through Jesus Christ.

The National Christmas tree was glowing in Washington, DC and throughout the nation massive Christmas displays lit the country. Homes sparkled with decorations and the city streets were a glow with lights and ornaments dangling everywhere. Tourists were flocking to Israel to visit the holiest of religious sites and churches were being filled with thousands joining together in prayer.

Yet the thing that motivated the world in this joyous occasion was that Jesus was here on earth and was among them. It was an overwhelming experience to all and gave them hope that something positive was going to happen to turn the tide on the evil one.

Of all the evil and destruction Satan had bestowed on the world he could not destruct the will power and faith of the millions that would rather go to their deaths than turn their backs on their Christian faith. On top of that they had living proof that Jesus was not some frictional character but real and that gave them unbelievable strength and endurance. It supported many in the determination to fight to the end in support of him.

The easy victory that Satan figured was going his way was actually far beyond his reach and he was truly in for a rude awakening. The major question was where was Jesus and when would he take his next step to end this conflict once and for all?

It had been snowing for several hours and the city streets and sidewalks were covered with a fine layer of white snow. The weather man predicted that the total accumulation could be easily six inches before the storm moved further north and into Maine and Vermont. Jesus had settled into the small town of Attleboro about thirty minutes from the city of Boston. He had a growing respect for the people who lived in New England for their strong beliefs and perseverance in toughing it out through difficult times. They had a certain will power and ability to understand that life is a series of events, both good and bad, and you need to tackle each one head on to come out a winner. Throughout the centuries it was obvious that New Englanders were not afraid of a challenge. He thought back to the Pilgrims landing at Plymouth nearly four hundred years ago and the tremendous losses they absorbed through that first cold winter. Through that first winter they suffered through hostile Indians, lack of food and illnesses that plagued their every move. He pictured the hardships and the struggles of the soldiers through the winter at Valley Forge and the eventual ringing of the bells of freedom. Throughout the years these people managed to stand for what they believed and instilled that same pride into others whether they were visiting from other countries or states.

On top of this New England was a beautiful place to enjoy the splendor of Christmas and the coming together of families and friends on an important religious holiday. As the snow fell Jesus walked through the city admiring the Christmas lights and displays set up in the various store windows and parks. It seemed as if everything glowed with red, green or white lights. Jesus even smiled as he passed numerous displays with Santa Claus as the center of attraction. He did not mind one bit that somewhere along the way Christmas had become commercialized as the gift giving started by the wise men to a small child in a manger are now game systems and electronic equipment. Although he had, in some respects, had taken a back seat in the true meaning of Christmas he still felt the spirit of the holiday all around him.

As he watched small children waiting in line to sit on Santa's lap and whisper into his ear what they wanted for Christmas he could not help but smile and enjoy the moment. Watching the kids then jump off Santa's lap and run into the arms of their parents telling them that Santa told them if they were good they would have some very nice surprises under the Christmas tree. The joy in their faces and the smiles on their parent's faces gave him a sense of calmness and security that the world and people are basically good and caring individuals.

He also thought back to the first Christmas when the wise men showed up at that small manger with gifts for him in a display of love and devotion. Although he did not remember his mother often told him the stories of her surprise and joy when they ambled up to the manger with their camels sticking their long necks into the shelter for a glance at the little baby lying next to his mother. She told him about the gifts and the kindness of the three men as they had tracked for miles that night in following that magical star that showed them the way. Jesus loved to listen to the story as it seemed to please his mother so much each time she told it to him. She told him he was very special and some day he would realize it. He just laughed and took it as something any mother would tell the son that she loved very much. Yet he also felt that he would not lead a normal life and it would be filled with situations that would try his very soul when all was said and done.

So the Santa thing didn't bother him as it reflected, in many ways, the importance of sharing gifts and coming together on a special day as family and friends to celebrate life and good will to all. As he walked through the city park he noticed a religious display and it brought back the memories. There was the manger with Mary and Joseph standing over him as he lay in the small wooden crib lined with straw and a small blanket to keep him warm. There standing off to the side were the three wise men carrying various gifts for the Christ child. As he approached he noticed some of the people looking at the scene were saying a short, silent, prayer and it warmed his heart that they were displaying their love to him as he watched silently from the side.

In the distance he could hear Christmas music and as he walked closer to the sound he observed that people were gathered around a small outdoor stage with some musicians leading them through a series of holiday songs. As he approached the crowd he heard them singing, "Santa Claus is coming to town". He noticed that the small children were clapping their hands and jumping up and down with the rhythm of the beat of the music. When the song ended the children started to cheer as a man dressed in a red suit trimmed with white fur and wearing black boots climbed up the stairs to the center of the stage. Over his back was a large canvas sack and as he slowly ambled forward he waved to everyone as he kept repeating ho, ho, ho. He then sat in a large wooden chair that was trimmed with bright colors and a red cushion seat as the parents scrambled to get their children into a waiting line to tell Santa how good they have been all year and what they wanted for Christmas. The Christmas music still continued to blare from the speakers and everyone seemed to be enjoying the sights and sounds of the season.

Just before Santa started to meet with the first child standing in line the band started to sing "Silent Night" and the meaning and beauty of the song seemed to grab the attention of everyone standing there. Initially the crowd grew silent but then two six year old girls holding their mother's hands began to sing the song along with the band members. It was immediately contagious as everyone joined in and sung the song that praised the night that Christ was born. Jesus was overcome with the reaction of the crowd and the fact that they all realized that Christmas had much more of a meaning than Santa Claus and exchanging commercially advertised electronic devices for gifts. Men removed their hats and woman grabbed the hands of their husband or boy friend. Children huddled around their parents and the general sharing of spiritual strength deeply moved Jesus.

Chapter twenty seven

Pastor John Lincoln

When the song ended a minister from a local church that was standing in the crowd asked everyone for a minute to say a few words. His name was Pastor John Lincoln, a very religious man who dedicated his entire life to helping others through their personal crisis time and time again. He used whatever donations he received from the congregation to support a soup kitchen for the homeless and was deeply respected by those who knew him. A pillar of the community who was respected for his honesty and integrity he earned the nick name of "Honest Abe" from the town folks. He possessed a deep, clear and booming voice that could easily be heard without the use of any electronic equipment.

He turned to the crowd and asked them to say a short prayer with him in support of Jesus in the existing struggle with Satan. With that everyone bowed their heads in prayer. Pastor Lincoln, never at a loss of words, said, "May we unite as one in support of almighty Christ in this epic battle that soon will be upon us. Let us remind ourselves that Jesus has already died once for us and is willing to do it again for the salvation of mankind. For the non believers who questioned his existence and followed that path of contempt to those who believed I tell you that you have a chance to redeem yourself. For those of us who have always believed it is your golden opportunity to demonstrate that you will back him until the very end regardless of the consequences! Based on all that we have witnessed through the horrific acts of Satan man's survival as we know it today is in serious jeopardy should the unimaginable happen?"

He slowly raised his arms to the sky and said, "Jesus, we know you are somewhere on earth right now, walking among us, trying to save us, once more gathering your strength from those who believe in you. We pray on the souls of our dead loved ones who reside with you in heaven that we believe you have the strength and ability to help us through this dark period. Without you we will be lost and will exist in nothing more than a black and murky maze that will sicken each and every one of us to the bone. May the strength and spiritual presence of this holiday season help all of us drive Satan back to his hell hole forever and bring us closer to Jesus Christ our lord"? For this we pray!

When he finished the crowd whispered amen and raised their heads. The true meaning of Christmas was felt in its entirety through that short prayer spoken by a man of the cloth. As the pastor worked his way through the crowd he was greeted with handshakes and pats on the back and thank yous. As he finally broke free of the crowd and walked slowly back to his small parish church a young man that was leaning against a pine tree stepped forward and extended his hand to him. The pastor grabbed it and shook it in friendship but then asked the man if he was new in town as he doesn't recall crossing paths with him before? The man smiled and said that he was new to the area, just passing through, when he heard the music and saw the Christmas displays and bright lights. He told him that he was caught up in the beauty and the holiday spirit of the crowd and couldn't pass up the opportunity to participate before moving on.

The pastor welcomed him and wished him a happy holiday and safe journey to his destination and started to turn and walk away when he glanced at the old metal cross hanging around the man's neck. The pastor had seen that same cross before and then it hit him like a ton of bricks. It was the same cross that was shown on newscast after newscast of those individuals who had claimed to have met Jesus in his travels. There was no mistaking it as it had a unique shape with each corner of the cross slightly rounded in a half moon design and imbedded in the cross bar were two small holes as if they represented the nails that were pounded into Christ's hands the day that he was hung on the cross.

The pastor stopped dead in his tracks and turned again to the man without saying a word. He grabbed the man's hand again and studied his face. It was the eyes, the eyes that told the story. They told the story of a man who had seen it all, the good and the bad, the torment and joy, the stress of leadership and, yet, the strength to face any situation without fear of the consequences. Yet as the pastor studied him the man was also studying the pastor. It was as if they were walking to a common ground that would create a long lasting bond between the two of them. The pastor broke the silence by telling the stranger that he had seen the cross before and there was no mistaking that those who wore it were touched by a significant event in their lives. It was an event so spectacular that only a handful of people have had the opportunity so far. Without any further hesitation he tightened his grip on the man's hands as tears welled in the corners of his eyes. The man standing before him simply knotted his head up and down and whispered that everything will be all right my son.

Pastor Lincoln knew without a doubt that the person that he worshipped and preached about every Sunday was, indeed, standing in front of him. Initially the pastor just stood there in admiration of the man standing before him but then he slowly reached for the metal cross hanging around Jesus' neck and ran his fingers gently over it as a blind man would do to try to visualize every detail with his touch. As he did he felt a calmness absorb his entire body. As he studied it the cross began to slowly change color and pulsate as if it had come to life. As he laid it against Christ's chest he looked up and saw that Jesus was smiling at him and he knew that he was one of the chosen few to be brought into his life. He wondered how a small town minister could be of any significant help to Jesus in his battle with Satan.

The pastor did not want to make a scene and draw more attention to the man standing there with him. Instead he released his hand and also let the cross dangle untouched from the chain around his neck. As some of the town folks walked by the two men with some saying good night and nice speech to the pastor, he tried to divert as much attention from Jesus as possible.

Once the passer byes were a safe distance away from him, he simply said that I have prayed since I was a little boy to meet you at the gates of heaven and settle into a congregation of souls that would live forever in harmony. Yet you are here standing in front of me and I and others now have the opportunity to realize that we do have a true meaning to life and death. It has provided each one of us the strength to truly believe and face our lives a whole lot differently than ever before. For that I truly thank you.

Jesus gently placed his hands on the shoulders of the pastor and expressed his gratitude for his short sermon to the townspeople. He told him it truly touched him and served as a reminder of the importance of his mission and the salvation of mankind forever. As he talked the pastor studied his face and listened carefully to every spoken word and came to realize why this one individual meant so much to the world. He was a symbol of the possibility of man's redemption and the very heart and soul of man's ability to have the strength and will power to deal with the pending conflict with Satan.

He asked the pastor if he could spend a few minutes in his church with him to get out of the cold but mainly to be able to mediate in prayer. As the snow started to fall more heavily they walked together back to the small chapel where they would have a chance to better prepare for the days ahead and pray for the salvation of man.

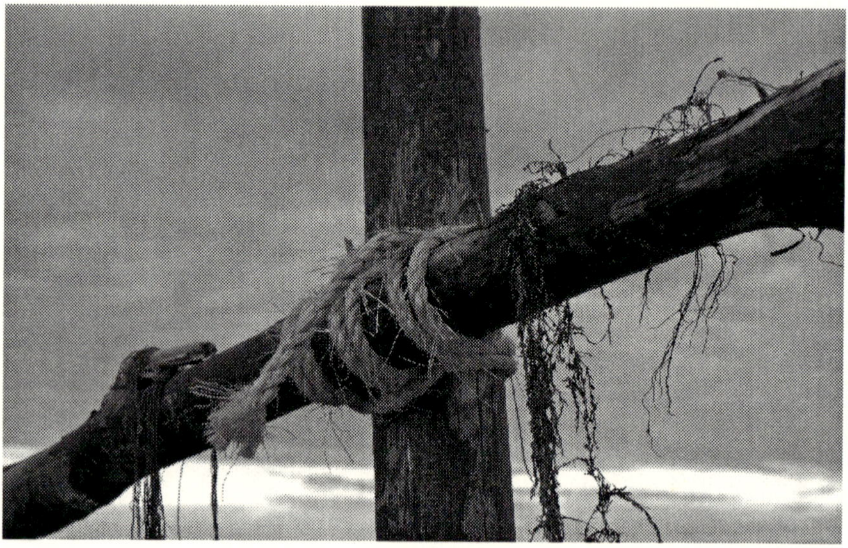

Chapter twenty eight

Satan meets the pope

Satan had grown tired of the United States and decided to a country much more suited for his next plan of attack. He had inflicted enough damage in the so called greatest country in the world without any fear of being stopped. The world is weak and it is ripe for the taking with only one obstacle in his way! But he had a plan, a plan that would show the world and Jesus Christ himself that he is unstoppable. He will instill so much fear into all those pathetic followers of Jesus that they will be begging him to join his flock. Now he would turn his attention to a small country that would allow him to show the world that no one is beyond his grasp. He, also, planned to demonstrate it in the most gruesome way possible.

It was nearing the Christmas holiday season and this pissed Satan off to no end. The joy and happiness felt worldwide in the celebration of Christ's born date was very disturbing to him. He realized that the Christmas holiday season had this hypnotizing effect that generated a feeling of harmony throughout the world. Hadn't armed conflicts in world wars actually been halted on Christmas? That is just plain bullshit he thought to himself. Then he remembered a short phase written in a novel about Christmas that made him chuckle. He smiled and said the words out loud, "Christmas, bah, humbug! Although there were small scatterings of people who worshipped him they paled in comparison to the respect provided to Jesus on "his day". He told himself that he would definitely remedy that when he destroyed Christ. After that the world will be spending eternity worshipping him and cursing Christ.

Screw them all he thought. They all would soon be his to do as he pleased anyway. Those followers of Christ would surely pay two fold for thinking that Jesus could possibly be their savior. He could even hear their screams for forgiveness now echoing in his ears and they brought tremendous satisfaction to his ears. Now he needed to concentrate on his plan. It was going to be a dozy he thought as he neared the city of Jerusalem—that special place where Jesus was born so many years ago.

Satan in Jerusalem is like a Boston red Sox player sitting in the New York Yankee Clubhouse prior to a big game. It seemed ridiculous to even think of such a thing but not if you were as crazy as Lucifer. His no holds barred approach is what terrified everyone including Jesus himself. Foremost in his mind was the fact that he was always curious about the place where the "saga" began. Interesting him further was that the city was considered such a sacred, religious location. People the world over traveled to visit it. As Satan studied his surroundings he thought to himself that you got to be frigging kidding me. The country was in the middle of nowhere, a desert community surrounded by Arabs that actually hated the very thought that it existed in their very midst. Even now the Jews and Arabs constantly fought for the basic control of the city. It was patrolled by hundreds of uniformed Israeli soldiers carrying automatic weapons as if it was some sort of prison camp. There were road blocks that resulted in searches of the vehicles and occupants. The two nationalities were equally separated in their religious beliefs—one believing in Christ almighty and the other to another god who was worshipped due to their specific culture and beliefs.

Regardless of the internal political and religious struggles present in the area it was the holiday season and the streets were bustling with tourists. Many of them were being escorted by tour guides as they were being shown the various religious sites that they had read so much about in the history books and biblical documents.

Satan felt like he wanted to vomit right there in the street. His contempt for Jesus was overwhelming and being in the city of his birth caused his emotions to run high. He had plans; plans that would again show that he would be the one that should be worshipped and respected by all. What better place to create a little "more" commotion on such a religious holiday he thought. As that sports announcer says before a world champion heavy weight championship fight—"let's get ready to rumble"; Satan was ready to send another message.

Satan did not simply choose Jerusalem out of curiosity or contempt for the other. He chose it because a very special religious figure was planning to lead the midnight mass services on Christmas Eve and Satan would not miss it for the world. He had as much contempt for this man as he did for Jesus because this man represented the Christian faith and was revered everywhere he went. He had decided to leave the Vatican where he normally resided over high mass and religious ceremonies on Christmas to instill everyone's faith in the return of Jesus Christ to the world. What better place than this holy city to support the struggle for Jesus. It was also believed by many sources that Jesus may decide to make another appearance here because of the significance of the day and the pope's presence. The pope was suffering from a severe cold and his physician strongly urged him not to take a chance and travel. He was nearing eighty two years old and was beginning to show the years of wear and tear on his small frail body but there was no way possible to convince him to alter his plans.

His travel drew worldwide attention and there seemed to be more reporters than tourist lingering around the city. His every move was being monitored and security was extremely tight to avoid any harm coming to the central figure of the Catholic Church.

The pope is protected by a combination of Swiss Guards, Vatican police and Italian police. When he moves around St. Peter's Square during his weekly Wednesday audience, he does so in an uncovered white jeep; when he travels overseas or outside the Vatican, he usually uses a vehicle outfitted with bullet proof glass.

The Rev. Federico Castillo who is a chief advisor and security administrator for the pope says that it is not realistic to think the Vatican can assure 100 percent security for the pope considering that he is regularly surrounded by tens of thousands of people in his weekly audiences and travels. Each attempt on the pope is reviewed and the episode is carefully studied to "try and learn" from the experience to avoid a re-encounter. The overall goal is to intervene at the earliest possible moment in which "zero risk" can be achieved.

There have been numerous attempts on the pope's life and the overall security measures to protect him. In the past there have been reported instances where the attacker has come in direct contact with the pope but unsuccessful in doing serious harm to him. In 2007 during an open-air audience in St. Peter's Square, a mentally unstable German man jumped a security barrier and grabbed the back of the pope's open car before being swarmed by security forces. There also was the assassination attempt against Pope John Paul II by a Turkish gunman in 1981. He suffered a severe abdominal wound as he rode in an open jeep at the start of his weekly audience in the Vatican piazza.

Satan did not plan to be as foolish as make an attempt on the pope's life in such an open and uncompromising location. He knew that security would be extremely high in every aspect of the pope's traveling to and from his various locations. No, Satan knew that he would plan his attack in the one location where security could be somewhat compromised—the place where all thought that he would be the safest—the very hotel where he would be staying while in Israel.

The entire top floor of the newly renovated Hilton Hotel located in the heart of the city was secured for the pope and his traveling companions. In addition to his team there were also dignitaries from various countries also placed on the same floor. They included the Prime Minister of Great Britain, President of France, and the Vice President of the United States, among others.

Each planned to attend the midnight mass celebration and then a special gathering at the Mount of Calgary where Christ was crucified on the cross. It would be telecast around the world and the goal was to draw everyone together, regardless of nationality or religion, into a spiritual event that would further unite everyone against Satan. A wooden cross was placed in the same location where Jesus hung so many years ago and alongside it were the two crosses where the two thieves hung beside of him. As biblical accounts recall one of the two asked for forgiveness from Jesus and was rewarded a place in heaven while the other is serving Satan well in the fires of hell. The historic location would again be a place of sorrow for the Christian world if Satan successfully implemented his plan.

Satan knew it would be a very special night; one that everyone would never, ever, forgets—it would be bigger than his first shocker with the return of the Black Plague after hundreds of years!

The pope would never make it to the midnight service and the only person who knew that was Satan. As he rode the elevator to the top floor he had a very special place reserved for the pope that night and he would assure that he would be on full display for the entire world to see. As the elevator door swung open Satan was approached immediately by three security guards and was asked for his identification card and security code number. He smiled at the guards and told them to relax as he reached into his coat pocket for the information. As one of the guards examined it the other two closely watched him for any sign of resistance or trouble that would drive them into action. One was immediately scanning his body for any hidden items while the other appeared ready to slit his throat with any sudden movement. Each of the guards were fully trained in every aspect of terrorist control and killing without remorse anyone threatening those that they are sworn to protect.

As the guard examined the documentation he compared the photo on the card to the man standing before him. Everything seemed to match perfectly. The guard motioned to the other two with a slight movement of his right hand that the man was an authorized visitor; actually a close friend of the pope himself. The documentation showed his name to be Alexander Gezense who worked at the Vatican as an interpreter for the pope. His name was on the authorized visitation list and he also had a room reserved for him on the floor adjacent to the pope's. The guards welcomed him, gave him back his identification and allowed him to gain access to the secured floor of worldwide leaders.

As Satan strolled down the corridor he chuckled to himself about how stupid and incompetent the guards were. Had they taken the time to further check his documentation they would have realized the real Alexander was sixty eight years old, a small man who walked with the assistance of a cane due to a serious hip injury several years ago. Poor old Alexander was in town but he would not be attending any more masses as he was buried up to his neck in the desert a few hundred miles in the middle of nowhere. As Satan left him there were a couple of scorpions making their way towards him as a welcoming committee. He was sure that other creatures would soon join their friends in making the man quite welcome to his new home.

There was an attaching door between rooms where Alexander could come and go as he pleased or when the pope needed his services for any visitors or preparation for the night's planned events.

The pope was still feeling the effects of the cold so his team decided to let him rest up for the night's activities. Access to his room was limited unless of extreme emergency. The restrictions would play right into Satan's plans. The pope would usually use his private time to pray and meditate while preparing his sermons. He watched very little television and enjoyed reading although his failing eyes made that more of a task than a personal item of enjoyment over the past several years.

The pope was sitting on the large Victoria sofa in the living room when Satan entered through the adjoining room door. At first the pope did not even look up as he was intent in finishing one of the scriptures that he would use during his speech later that night. The pope simply acknowledged Alexander's presence with a slight wave of his hand and a gesture to sit down on the chair directly across from him so they could talk in a few minutes.

Satan thought it was hilarious that he had gained access to one of the most powerful men in the Catholic Church and the old fool did not even think to look up to assure that it was truly his friend whom he had known for so many years. Satan decided to play along for a few minutes and sat down in the chair and studied the man sitting across from him.

Although the pope possessed a general aura of authority and righteousness he did not impose an intimidating figure in any stretch of the imagination. He wore wire rimmed glasses as he read, weighed no more than one hundred and twenty pounds and seemed to have a nagging cough that required him to constantly stop and blow his nose into a white handkerchief that he held in his left hand. Yet as he sat there intent in completing his reading of the passage his hands began to tremble as if sensing something was wrong. Satan realized at that moment that the pope knew that the man sitting across from him was not his friend. It was someone very different; someone who someway had successfully by passed all the security systems and get into his room. What emotionally affected the pope was the presence of evil in the room—evil so terrible that it chilled him to the bone. The pope knew that there was but one individual who could cause that sort of response from him. He realized who it was that was waiting across from him. There was no sense in delaying the formality of the meeting and the pope closed the book, placed it on the table next to the sofa and slowly looked up directly at Satan. The pope had already decided that he would not yell out for help as it would have been a useless exercise. Satan would simply leap from the chair and snap his neck like a twig from a tree. He was not afraid of Satan in any sense of the word. Yet he also knew that in some strange and perverse way that Satan had calculated him into his next plot to strike fear into the world's population again. What was difficult to comprehend was that he managed to maneuver past security without any difficulty showing his unrelenting ability to gain the upper hand in his conquest of Jesus.

Initially they each studied one another as if they were sizing each other up as their worthiness as an opponent. The pope remained composed and despised being in the same room with Lucifer. Satan was the first to speak and he left no doubt in what his intentions were as he said to the pope, "You are going to die tonight, you old fart, and your life will be drained from your feeble body so the whole world can see and I will be the one that will be remembered for all eternity for taking it from you." "You are just an old man who serves no useful purpose except as a figurehead for a religion that will no longer exist in a few short weeks". "With your death, the world will know I am unstoppable and if they don't join my flock they will soon join you and others who oppose me". "Welcome to my world, old man".

The pope did not hold back any punches either. He glared at Satan and told him that he was nothing but a fool if he thought that he could possibly strike fear into everyone's hearts with killing him. It would only further instill anger in the world against him and it would strengthen Jesus in his determination to destroy him forever. He ridiculed him by telling him that he dwelled in a fantasy world of despair and sorrow and he will never understand that evil does not have a chance of overcoming goodness in any sort of final conflict.

The pope continued his onslaught showing no fear of a reprisal from the most feared man in the world. He said it has been proven time and again throughout history that evil is the eventual loser in every known conflict! He told Satan that this time, however, he would be gone forever and the world would be a better place because of it. He said that he was a weak, pathetic individual who leeched off the blood of others and when the tide is turned he will simply melt away like a piece of chocolate candy dropped on a sidewalk on a hot summer day. The pope finalized his verbal attack by telling Satan that he was not afraid of him because when he killed him he will be residing in heaven.

As the pope talked he fiddled with a small bottle that he always kept in his pocket and loosened the cap. When he was done talking he reached into the pocket and recited the words, "In the name of the father, son and holy spirit" and tossed the liquid in the direction of Satan. The holy water struck Satan's pants and shirt while some splashed on the back of his hands and the right side of his face.

Satan leaped from the chair as smoke rose from the portions of his flesh that the holy water hit. Hi skin smoked and sizzled as if it was stir fry in a hot, oily frying pan. He went berserk and in one huge bound he stood in front of the pope and lifted him into the air by the front of his robe and with a powerful swing of his right hand punched him in the face breaking his nose and knocking three of his teeth out of his mouth. He dropped the pope on the floor and told him that he wasn't going to die yet it would be much too easy on him that way. He had other plans, much bigger that would show the world that he meant business.

With that he walked over to the window and carefully studied the surrounding area. Although there was a lot of activity in the streets below the upper portion of the building was cloaked in a semi-darkest that would allow him the opportunity to move follow with phase two of his plan. He unlatched the window and swung it open. He then walked over to where the pope was laying unconscious on the floor and picked him up. He swung him over his right shoulder and maneuvered himself through the opening and slowly climbed the fire escape to the roof of the building. As he reached the roof he looked up and stared into the moon lit sky and stuck his middle finger up to the heavens above. He, defiantly, stood there a few minutes in that same position as he said, "I am unstoppable, look at what I have just accomplished so easily. Soon this old fart will be dead and within days your son will also perish as well. With that he reached down for the pope and proceeded to his final destination on this Christmas Eve night.

Satan had researched the city and knew that many of the buildings were built so close together that he could simply jump from one to another until he reached the last building in the row. There he opened the door leading down the stairs and into a back alley where he had an old jeep parked waiting for him. He bundled the pope in some old blankets so his body was well hidden from view and drove off through the city to his final destination, Golgotha, the place where Christ was crucified so many years ago.

Satan knew that the area would be deserted at this time as everyone was preparing for the other events leading up to the midnight church service by the pope. This specific event was not planned for hours and he had plenty of time to take care of business. His plan was going perfectly and he could not wait until he could see the reaction of the world. He grabbed the bundle of blankets and tossed them on the ground and unrolled them, exposing the body of the pope. He, also, removed a black leather bag from the back of the jeep. He took a canteen of water and emptied the entire contents on his head causing the pope to regain semi consciousness. Grabbing the bag in one hand he reached down and simply grabbed one of the pope's arms with the other. Instead of carrying him up the hill he dragged him to the base of the center cross. He let him lie there while he used the pulley system to lower the cross to the ground. He then ripped off most of the pope's clothes with the exception of the white briefs he wore and placed his back against the front of the cross. He then opened the bag and pulled out a metal hammer and some six inch nails. Lucifer then took each one of the pope's hands and spreading them open. He then placed a large nail in the center of it and pounded the nail into the wooden cross. Satan repeated his action for his other hand. He then placed the pope's feet on the small piece of wood extending out from the bottom section of the cross and nailed both of his feet into the wood. Prior to rising the cross he broke both of the legs of the Pope with the hammer causing his body weight to hang from his nailed hands thus allowing death to come more quickly. Then raising the cross with the ropes he locked it into its upright standing position.

There hanging above him as Jesus did so many years ago was the supreme leader of the Catholic Church crucified just as Jesus with the world to see.

The pope was still conscious and he had tears streaming down his cheeks not from pain or fear but for the millions of people who will be intimidated by this act of cruelty. As he hung there he prayed that his death would unite the people not divide them and it would give Jesus the inner strength to realize that he must defeat this mad man before it is too late. With that he lowered his head on his chest and his soul winged its way to heaven.

It was shortly before seven o'clock on Christmas Eve when the cardinals knocked on the pope's hotel room door to help him prepare for the night's events. When they received no response they tapped louder thinking that he may have fallen asleep yet nothing. Cardinal Cardelli inserted the security card through the access slot in the door but it appeared to be wedged shut. With panic setting in each of the Cardinals started to rap on the door very loudly and yet nothing, the room seemed extremely quiet, too quiet. With the commotion they drew the immediate attention of the security guards who quickly ran to their assistance. The chief security agent inserting his master access card to unlock both the door and dead bolt but the door still did not open. With that the security guards used a metal door ram similar to those used by the police in drug raids and the door frame shattered. Leaning against the inside of the door was a chair that had been wedged under the door knob and it was now lying on the floor at the base of the entrance. With weapons drawn the guards stormed into the room praying that nothing had happened to the pope. Initially the fear was that he suffered a heart attack and required medical attention but the chair indicated an entirely different scenario. They spread out and quickly moved from room to room but the pope was nowhere to be found. As they entered the bedroom they noticed that the window curtains were pulled open and the window itself was unlocked. As the chief agent opened the window his attention was drawn to the fire escape and a man's slipper lying on the second stair leading upwards to the roof. It was the pope's. The reaction was spontaneously as they used their cell phones and internal communication devices to lock down the building and secure the immediate area sealing off any possible exit points of the kidnappers of the pope.

One of the agents returned from the living room area and said that there was a pool of blood on the floor next to the sofa and it was apparent the pope was attacked in that room. He was either knocked unconscious or deemed helpless against his attackers and taken from the room through the use of the fire escape. With guns drawn the security force climbed the fire escape and reached the roof in less than a minute. Each knew his job well and followed their directives to the letter. They spanned out in different directions looking for anywhere that could be utilized to hide the body or an exit point. As they circled the roof they quickly came to the conclusion that the closeness of the adjacent buildings allowed an easy access to carry such a small man without difficulty. As they jumped from roof to roof the search continued with no sight of the pope. He was gone and it was obvious from the blood in the room that he was definitely in harm's way. Who had him and why did they want to harm a man so admired by the world as a leader of the church and god himself?

As they expanded their search it did not take long before word spread to the press that the pope was missing. The big question was how this could have possibly happened under the very eyes of his security force and what mad man would risk the consequences of such a terrible crime?

Satan had returned from his short excursion and was at the restaurant located directly across from the hotel. Sitting at one of tables next to the windows he was overjoyed with the commotion and panic scenes playing out in front of his very eyes. While he sipped on a shot of Jack Daniels he thought to himself that they had not seen anything yet—wait until they find the old fool just hanging around while everyone was so worried about him. He actually couldn't hold back a chuckle at his little play on words.

Hey he thought—the pope got his final wish pertaining to his eternal resting place anyway. Sirens were blaring and more and more police cars filled the streets as road blocks were set/up. Police had started to go from building to building in search of the pope in the hopes that he was still secured in the immediate area. He was nowhere to be found.

It was shortly after eight o'clock when three young boys who were climbing the back slope came to the top of the hill of Mount Calgary. Soon it would be buzzing with people in anticipation of the pope's visit and the area overflowing with people witnessing the historical event. As the boys walked towards the crosses they noticed that there appeared to be something hanging from the center cross. It was dark and although spot lights were installed they were not yet illuminated for the religious ceremony. The area was dimly lit with a row of antique candles on six foot poles standing approximately ten feet apart. They formed, somewhat, a semi circle around the crosses to provide an atmosphere similar to what the town people would have seen at the time of the crucifixion of Jesus. As the boys slowly walked forward to the crosses they realized that whatever was hanging there had the shape of a man.

When they reached the base of the cross and looked up to study the figure they realized that a man hung there, a man who was stripped to nothing more than his underwear with his hands and feet nailed to the cross. On the ground in front of them were three separate pools of blood that had dropped from each of his hands and feet. One of the boys yelled up at the man and asked him if he was all right or could he speak. There was no response. This frightened the boys as they realized that he may be dead and whoever killed him may be still there watching them. They ran as fast as they could screaming at the top of their lungs for help as they followed the dirt path down the hill to the town below. They had no idea that within a few short minutes they would become worldwide celebrities and their names would, forever, be recorded in the history books as the three boys who discovered the dead pope hanging from a cross on Christmas Eve.

Coming up the path were three members of the preparation team. Their job was to arrive early and complete the final touches to the ceremony area. There was tremendous relief in the boys' eyes as they saw the three men. It was obvious that the boys were extremely frightened and in a panic state from something that they saw or happened to them. They were running for their dear lives.

The first boy grabbed the hand of one of the men and told him that there was a man hanging from one of the crosses and blood on the ground. The man was not moving; they think he is dead. It was obvious that each of the boys were extremely frightened so they left one of their team with the boys as the other two quickly ran up the hill. The one remaining with the boys used his cell phone to call for help and rescue assistance in the hope that the man could still be alive. He sat down with the boys on the grass alongside the path. There they waited for help to arrive and confirmation from the others on what they found at the top of the hill.

The first one to arrive at the crosses was Jacob Hyman a twenty six years old laborer who was hired for his carpentry experience in preparation for the historical event. The second man was Isaac Goosman who was a licensed electrician. As Isaac reached the base of the crosses Jacob was already looking up at the poor man hanging there. He immediately knew he was dead. There was no sense in trying to lower the cross or provide any sort of medical assistance based on the amount of blood on the ground and absolutely no movement from the body above. All they would accomplish was to screw up the crime scene and make it more difficult to apprehend the person who did this. They had not yet heard of the pope's disappearance so they had no idea that the body on the cross was his. They both kneeled down and said a prayer for the man as they waited for the authorities to arrive.

As they sat there they wondered what sort of a madman would commit such an atrocity as this on Christmas Eve. The person had to be a raving lunatic and the sooner the police caught him the better everyone would be.

Within ten minutes the area was swarming with police. It was curtained off quickly and only those personnel tied to the police or the pope's security force were allowed access to the crime scene. It was the pope's security chief who identified him first. As much as he tried to maintain his composure he found it too difficult and broke down in tears as he fell to his knees in front of the cross. He blamed himself for the death of the pope and he would eventually blow his brains out with his own gun a few weeks later as a lonely and broken man. The crime scene investigators arrived and as much evidence as possible was gathered in the immediate area before approval to lower the cross and remove the body was given. The sight of the pope hanging from the cross was tremendously emotional with grown men hardened through their exposure to death affected by the pope's death. Men were seen hugging to comfort each other and gain some understanding on who would commit such a terrible crime. As his body was carefully lowered to the ground they understood—branded into his forehead was the numbers "666".

The devastating news spread quickly and the world mourned. In one act of violence a worldwide religious celebration turned into a day of mourning and the joy shattered like a crystal glass falling to a hardwood floor.

As Satan sat back he continued to enjoy the bottle of Jack Daniels that rested on the café table. He couldn't help to think about the reaction of Jesus when he got the news. Would he cry? Would he become so overcome with emotion and sorrow that he would just give up and realize the uselessness of trying to win the struggle? Would he become fearful for the first time in his squeaky clean life that he would offer some sort of a compromise to weasel his way out of the conflict? Or perhaps he would become so overwhelmed with anger that he couldn't think straight and fall directly into Satan's hands for the final solution to his problem? Satan thought to himself—the final solution—yes, the final solution—that was what the burning of the millions of Jews during World War II was called. Satan will use the same principles again seventy years later when he will have Jesus and his followers march through the gates of hell to be burned to a crisp as well. Nothing could ruin this moment for him as his mind filled itself with how easily he was masterminding his plans one after the other. He again thought how ridiculously simple it was becoming to scare the living daylights out of everyone. He poured himself another drink, sat back in his chair and pondered his next move. Before drinking the shot down he raised it up in front of him and said loud enough for those around him to hear, "Merry Frigging Christmas to all of you".

Chapter twenty nine

Jesus hears the news

Jesus was sitting with Pastor Lincoln in Boston when he received the news. The pastor had gone into the kitchen where he was boiling some water for a couple of cups of tea. He had turned on the small television that rested on the counter to CNN to catch up on the various Christmas celebrations when the news hit him like a ton of bricks.

At first he couldn't believe his ears and then he saw the live video cams of Mount Calgary and the cross lying on the ground. The reports immediately switched from country to country with scenes of thousands and thousands of people gathered around churches and cathedrals holding candles and praying together. His legs almost buckled as he grabbed the edge of the counter top to keep from falling. The print at the bottom portion of the screen continued to roll forward with the words that the pope was murdered in Israel tonight as he was found by three young boys crucified on a cross on the top of Mount Calgary. All signs indicate that Satan had struck again in his announced struggle with Jesus Christ for the control and future of mankind. The pope is dead; the pope is dead as the message then repeating itself. Overcome with emotion Pastor Lincoln had to compose himself as best he could before going back into the other room where Jesus sat. As much as he tried to settle himself down he would break out in tears and uncontrollable crying. He moved to the small table and sat down in one of the chairs placing his face in his hands as he pondered how he could possibly control himself long enough to tell Jesus. As he sat there the water began to boil and the whistle on the pot started hissing to indicate the water had reached the boiling point but the pastor did not even hear it. His mind was absorbed with the pope's death and the fact that Jesus sat in the very next room unaware of the devastating news. With that he again broke down in an uncontrollable crying as his body trembled, his hands shook, and tears continued to flow from his eyes.

Jesus had heard the whistle of the kettle continued to hiss on the stove and decided to go into the kitchen to see if he could help or find out what was wrong. As he opened the door he saw the pastor sitting at the kitchen table with his head resting in his arms, body quivering and in extreme distress. As he walked over to him and laid his hand on his shoulder to let know that he was there he was startled at the pastor's immediate reaction. Jumping off the chair he turned to Jesus and said I am so sorry, I am so sorry; I prayed that I am able to be strong enough to tell you the terrible news being telecast at this moment worldwide.

But it wasn't necessary. As Jesus had placed his hands on the pastor's shoulders he had glanced at the television sitting on the counter and read the news flashing across the bottom of the screen. He then knew why the pastor was so emotionally drained and felt the sorrow in the man. Jesus realized that the pastor was the one that had to carry the news to him if he had not walked into the room. The sadness and sorrow that Jesus felt at that moment in time was unmatched by anything that he ever experienced. The news cameras flashed from country to country showing men, women and children crying, holding hands and praying for the dead pope. Country after country were displayed with the same scenes of people joining together to express their deep sorrow on the loss of this key religious leader.

Jesus sat down next to the pastor and placed his hands under the pastor's chin and gently lifted it. As the pastor looked directly into the eyes of a man, a spirit, a soul that seemed to be personally absorbing all the sadness into his own body to help others cope with the situation. Jesus said that everything will be all right and the world's loss is heaven's gain. He told him that the pope's death will not be taken in vain and that he would become a symbol of the importance to unite to rid the world completely of such evil acts in the future. He told the pastor do not cry for the pope but praise him and stand tall beside me to demonstrate to others the same faith.

Although Jesus spoke of kindness and forgiveness to the pastor, he was simmering with contempt and hatred to the one individual who he despised with all his heart and soul. Satan would pay for his deeds there would be no mistaking that fact. He sickened Jesus on his absolute ruthliness and total disregard for any living thing. Jesus pitied mankind should, for some unknown reason or event, he would lose this battle. With each act Satan seemed to re-energize and would eventually be totally unstoppable and the world would pay for all eternity.

The sadness shown repeatedly on the television screen seemed to strengthen Jesus as he was able to fully appreciate that so many people loved and cared about the man who represented him. Their tears of sorrow were actually droplets of love and they could have filled an ocean. The pastor saw the determination in Jesus and knew that Satan had underestimated his rival and would dearly pay for the pope's death. Without uttering a single word Jesus simply raised his head to the heavens and took the metal cross that hung from his neck in his right hand. As he raised the cross it glowed so brightly that the pastor had to look away from the light it generated. The light over the next few seconds changed from a bright white to a soft royal blue while pulsating for a few more seconds before returning to its normal state. Jesus turned to the pastor and said, "He is in heaven now and sits with God my father at this minute looking down at us. He has not died in vain and will be able to witness that his death only strengthened the resolution of our followers to cope through the unforeseen evil ahead of us.

With a silent "amen" Jesus walked over to the counter and grabbed the small television in his hands. Ripping the electrical cord from the wall he hurled the set across the room and smashed it against the far wall. He then turned to the pastor and said that we have work to do to show the world that we will meet every challenge and we will overcome as one. The pastor looked at him and smiled. He smiled because he was probably the only man alive to ever see Jesus Christ throw a television across a room but also because he knew that Jesus meant every word that he had just spoken.

Chapter thirty

Jesus attends mass

As the news spread across the world everyone wondered where Jesus was and how was he dealing with the loss of the religious leader of his faith? People were frightened that he may already be dead and they were already under the total control of Satan himself. If he wasn't dead how could he have let Satan get to the pope and do those awful things to him on the very night before he was born so many years ago? Perhaps he was much weaker than people wanted to believe and he was absolutely no match for the evil one? Was he, also, in hiding and fearing for his life and existence knowing it was impossible to win this battle? So many stories floated around that it was impossible to determine what was true or false. Yet the majority of the discussions centered on the powerful presence of Satan and his ability to cause havoc and destruction at his every command.

Although Christmas day was normally a joyful occasion the pope's death caused it to become a day of mourning throughout the world. In every mass service across the world the congregation held a moment of silence for his passing. In order to avoid Satan's cruelty from having a serious impact on the children, parents tried to maintain the Christmas tradition of exchanging gifts and sharing their precious family time together as they normally would. It made no sense to pull the children into this web of terror that was gradually encompassing the world in an ever tightening grip. So as the children laughed and expressed their happiness over the presents under the tree their parents' thoughts wandered to their safety and well being over the coming months. Would this actually be the very last Christmas that they would share together? If so they would try to make it a happy one; one that they will remember for the rest of their lives.

Jesus attended the Christmas services in Pastor Lincoln's chapel. As the church overflowed with parishioners on this solemn day, Jesus sat there among the congregation listening to the various discussions around him prior to the start of the service. Most of the talk centered on the death of the pope but many wondered where was Jesus and why hadn't anyone heard him, personally, mourn the pope's death? Again the gossip focused on whether he was also gone forever and his body soon to be displayed in some gruesome way for Satan to show the world that he was king. As the bells tolled celebrating the start of the mass, everyone stood up as the altar boys led the pastor down the center aisle to the altar. As the pastor walked he gestured left and right with his hands making the sign of the cross and sprinkling holy water on those within the immediate area.

As he neared the second row of pews he slowed to almost a crawl as he noticed Jesus standing next to the Ballister family. With a slight nod of his head and a smile he also made sure that the spray of holy water reached Jesus as well. Jesus appreciated the act of kindness and responded with a nod of his head and a whispered, "thank you".

As the pastor stood there and peered out at the crowd he noticed many sad faces; many already shredding tears on preparing for what the pastor was about to say. Satan had truly accomplished exactly what he wanted to do the night before and the pastor could sense it spreading like a virus throughout the room. The people were overwhelmed with a sense of helplessness and uncertainty caused by the constant bombardment of Satan's inhuman acts of cruelty. Before he could even start his sermon Mrs. O'Reily, a normally quiet and very religious widow who frequented mass regularly, shouted out to him, "Father, when is this going to stop we cannot take this much longer. We are all scared for our families, friends, our country and the world. What is to happen to us and when is it going to stop. We have all talked and we are afraid that Jesus, himself, is dead and we are waiting for the other shoe to drop. Soon, out of fear we will see people turning to the side of Satan out of fear of not joining his flock because of what he has already shown what he can do. When good people decide to take the path of evil you know that hope is lost and who the winner is. It is a very sad state we are in and we pray that Jesus will show us the way soon". With that she sat down and apologized for her outburst but knew someone had to speak up and say what everyone else was thinking.

The pastor thanked her for her honesty and told her that he was not offended by her taking a few minutes to voice what everyone else must be thinking as well. He told her he actually appreciated it because it was a perfect lead in to his short sermon today.

He started his conversation by quoting the famous words of Franklin D. Roosevelt at the start of World War Two when he stood in front of congress and said, "We have nothing to fear but fear itself". The pastor reminded everyone that once we allow ourselves to be controlled by fear, governed by fear, or live our lives in fear we have lost. He told them that we all have fears but they do not rule each waking moment. We cope with them because we have courage and faith that we will get through them when they do occur. Whether it is a fear of heights, snakes, bridges, an incurable disease, or death itself we all know that we will manage to deal with that fear because we have others who love us and will do everything possible to get us through that fear through faith, love and support. He asked everyone to take a minute and think about something that they deeply feared during their life time and yet when faced with it managed to overcome it with the help of others who cared. Then he reminded them that it was not as bad as they anticipated that it would be. As he spoke he noticed many of those in attendance shaking their heads up and down and grabbing the hands of a loved one as they remembered a specific example of what the pastor was saying. As they did he also observed smiles and people hugging one another as another thank you for getting them through that event that they were thinking of. He told them that today was Jesus' day not Satan's. It was a day of rejoicing the birth of Christ and the faith that he gave millions around the world century after century. We cannot and will not let Satan destroy this precious day. As we sit here together you can certainty bet your very soul that Satan is sitting back and enjoying his impact on the world? Please do not play into his hands warned the pastor.

He told them a short story about an old man that lived in the hills of St Juan that supposedly had some sort of magical powers that allowed him to look into the future and tell you what was going to happen. The old man lived by himself and did not seek or deserve this reputation. He was simply a wise man seasoned from all his years of dealing with life that he could pretty much surmise the end result of an event or issue that was thrown at him. One eventful day three teenagers were walking the path leading to the old man's house. The informal leader of the group was Jose who wanted to demonstrate to the others that the old man was simply a quack, a weird old man who needed to be put in his place. He told the others that he would prove it to them once and for all and then they can tell all the towns folks on what they witnessed that day. As they walked up the hill Jose spotted a small sparrow that had fallen from its nest and he quickly picked it up. As he did he told the other boys that he would use the bird to show what a fraud the old man really was. He took the small bird and placed it into his right hand and gently closed his fist around the bird. He told the boys that he would ask the old man three questions and they would see for themselves that he couldn't tell the future any more than they could. As he walked he planned his actions. He realized that he could not lose in the battle of wits with the old man.

Jose would first ask him what object did he hold in his hand and if he, somehow, got that right he would ask him which hand he held the object in. If from some wild luck he got that right too he would ask the old man whether the bird was alive or dead. If he said alive he would close his hand on the bird crushing it to death. If he said it was dead he would open his hand and show that it was alive. He had the old man either way and he knew it.

Little did Jose know that the old man was sitting on his porch watching the three boys come up the hill to his house. He also saw Jose pick up the small bird and place it into his right hand. As the boys approached the old man said good day to them and asked them why they came to visit him. Jose spoke up quickly and told him that they had heard about his ability to see into the future and that they did not believe he had such magical powers. He told the old man that he had a short quiz for him and asked him if he could do a little test of his skills in front of his friends. The old man knew that if he allowed Jose to make a fool of him in front of his friends Jose would use the display as a means to gain a reputation around town that he was the one that proved the tales about the old man was simply an old wives tale and he was nothing but an old fool. He would surely try to gain statue with the other kids and eventually lead them down the wrong path of life. So the old man simply turned to Jose and told him to fire away.

As the other boys intently watched Jose and the old man; Jose stepped forward and told the old man that he had three questions. The first was what he held in one of his hands. The old man rocked back on his chair, rubbed his chin, thought for a minute and said that he held a small bird. The boys were amazed that he got the first question right but Jose was really upset. The old man asked him if he was right and Jose responded with a yes you did old man, pure luck I would imagine. He then asked him what hand did he hold the bird and again the old man thought for a minute and said the right. Again the boys were amazed at how quickly the old man got the right answer. Jose was getting very upset because all his plans were quickly falling apart around him. If the old man got the next one right then he would look like the fool and the news would quickly spread through town about how the old man outsmarted him. As Jose stood there he peered into the eyes of the old man daring him to possibly get the final question right. He held out his right hand and asked the old man whether the bird was alive or dead knowing that he could not possibly get this one right no matter what he said.

As he stared at the old man he noticed that the old man was staring back. He was staring back with such a look that it frightened Jose a little. It almost appeared as if the old man knew his every move and was equally prepared for this question as well. Jose had to look away from the old man because he was intimidated by the old man's ability not to back down to him. The two other boys stepped forward and were now staring directly at the old man and the right hand of Jose in anticipation of the final answer. The old man rocked forward in his chair and looked directly at Jose and said, "Son, the faith of that small bird is resting in your hand, it is entirely up to you". What is your decision son?

As the pastor finished his story he turned to each section of the congregation and told them that like that little boy with each of you rest the faith of all of us. Will we have the courage and determination to maintain our faith and pull through the ordeal and do the right thing?

The Struggle by R. Cole

The pastor let the story sink into the minds and hearts of the gathering for a few seconds before he completed his sermon. As he spoke his voice gradually gained volume and strength as he stressed the most important words in the morning service. As his voice rose, his face turned a rosy red and his hands gripped the small wooden banister that separated the main altar from the rest of the church. In the Boston accent so familiar to anyone who ever held a conversation with a person from Massachusetts, he expressed his disappointment in anyone who was questioning the ability of Christ to be the ultimate salvation in this struggle. How could anyone sitting here today think that he is dead or not preparing to represent mankind one more time to save their souls? So lift up your hearts, regain your faith in the lord, and believe! Thou I walk through the shadow of death I will fear no evil because he will be there to guide me. So please take your children and join your family and friends in a day of rejoicing Christmas day. It will help to demonstrate that we have not given up and will remain on the side of goodness until we take our last dying breath. So help us god!

As he finished everyone stood up and applauded his courage and determination to motivate all of them to truly believe that everything will be ok. As Jesus stood there he also was touched by the sincerity of Pastor Lincoln. He knew it was not just a show that was put on because he was in the audience. It came from the heart and it was reflected in his every word, action and thought as he gave everyone new hope in that small New England church.

Jesus had no intention to take center stage and announce that he was there with them that morning. The pastor had done enough on his own to provide them the hope that he was going to battle for them and all is not lost. It also probably would have undermined, in some small way, the pastor's outstanding sermon by stepping forward. Instead he applauded with the rest of them and enjoyed the fact that he would not let them down. For that he was certain.

As everyone left the service the pastor stood by the chapel door and shook hands with each of them and wished them a Merry Christmas. The last to leave was Jesus and as he approached the pastor he smiled and extended his hand in gratitude. Jesus told him if he had a choice of listening to any minister or priest's sermon on a Sunday morning he would choose him hands down. Pastor Lincoln had to laugh at his comments and said he appreciated the kind words but he was not nearly that good each Sunday. Today the words flowed because he felt the need to console the people and to stress that they should not run and hide from evil but to face it.

Jesus told him that he needed to move on and he would be in contact with him again very soon. Before he turned to leave he reached out and grabbed the pastor's hand and placed a small metal cross into it. As he did the cross gradually changed color and began to pulsate in the pastor's hand. As the pastor watched he initially thought that the cross was beating to his heart but he immediately realized that it wasn't—the beat was far too slow and constant as if coming from someone who was at peace with himself and showing no sign of fear. Jesus looked at him and told him that the cross was a symbol of their friendship and unity in their faith. He also told him that the pulsating of the cross was the beating of Jesus' heart. Should it stop and the color fade to raw metal than the pastor will know that he is dead and Satan has won. Jesus said if the cross changes to an emerald green, as green as the maple trees on a crisp summer day than he will know that the struggle is over and Satan has been defeated. He asked the pastor to pray for him and mankind each day and continue to instill courage into those who will listen. He, also, told him that no harm would come to him as long as he is alive. With that he patted the pastor on his back, buttoned up the winter coat and strolled down the shoveled path of snow that led to the edge of town. As he turned the corner by the tall Christmas tree standing in the town common he was gone. His travels now will take him to that final location where he would deal with Satan and destroy him.

Chapter thirty one

Finding Jesus

Satan gloated at the havoc that he had generated with the killing of that old fool who had the audacity to try and stand his ground against him. He chuckled to himself that now the old fool is just hanging around like some outcast teenager with nothing but time on his hands. He thought to himself about how "high" he actually got as he pounded those nails into the pope's hands. It was a pure rush almost like a mixture of cocaine, heroin, speed, and Jack Daniels combined. He knew because he had actually tried the concoction himself since the dealers were members of his dedicated flock. What surprised him is that the old bastard didn't cry out in pain or beg for mercy. It pissed him off that he had the courage to know that he was going to die in such a horrible way yet seemed at peace with himself. Can't have everything thought Satan—at least not yet as he chuckled again at his improving sense of humor. Then he thought of Jesus and he thought of how "high" he would get when he inflicted the death blow to Mr. Righteous. Oh, he would suffer before he will be allowed to die, suffer like no one else has ever suffered at his hands. He had plans, big plans, plans that would make a mockery of Jesus and everything he stood for. Then he would deal with his followers and they will understand the power of the greatest show on earth, the one and only Satan the magnificent. Again he chuckled at his showmanship and of the things to come. Another high is on its way!

The pope was buried four days later and the solemn ceremony was held in the Vatican at Rome. Thousands paid their respects over a two day period as the great doors to the hall that his body lie in state was open twenty four hours per day for forty eight straight hours. And the line remained endless stretching for miles through the city of Rome. As planes and helicopters hovered overhead the aerial view was something to behold. The line of people appeared to be a very long snake curling through the city at a very slow pace. At nighttime the sight was more speculator as the mourners held candles and they lit the way to the final resting place for the pope. The outpouring of support was unmatched in the annuals of history. Even the deaths of US Presidents paled in comparison to the thousands who attended to show their dedication and love for this man. Periodically someone would start singing a hymn and others would join and soon it seemed as if it sweep through the crowd and echoed through the streets in peaceful harmony.

Standing waiting in line with the other mourners was Jesus. He had decided to also pay his respect to the man who died for him without any fear or remorse for doing so. Again the outpouring of support emotionally affected him and he was deeply touched by the endless line of people waiting patiently for that one moment when they can stand in front of the casket and say goodbye. When he finally reached the casket he had waited in line for nearly ten hours and the anticipation and anxiety of paying a final tribute had weighed heavily on him. Today it was different, much different from anything that he ever experienced.

He had witnessed the arrival of souls at heaven's gate and periodically participated in their welcoming. The pure enjoyment of actually seeing their reaction to truly realizing that they would reside in a world of tranquility with their loved ones was something to behold. The uncertainty of the unknown and the end of life as we know it haunts all of us. But it is just the beginning of the end and to see the joy of those arriving brought pleasure to him each time he witnessed it.

But today he was seeing the human side of death and it saddened him. As he stood beside the casket for those few short minutes allocated for each person he said a silent prayer. Although he already knew that the pope had arrived at his destination it did not help him to cope with the tremendous loss that he felt for the people around him. He had enough of the bloodshed and the terror that Satan has constantly bombarded the world with. Standing there he swore on his very own soul that there would be no more and he would meet his rival in a winner take all event. With that he followed the slow possession down the stairs of the Vatican and into the darkness of the night.

Satan had his goons searching everywhere for Jesus. The mystery man who moved silently through the people like he was some sort of petty thief waiting to be identified and thrown into jail. What sort of rival am I dealing with here anyway thought Satan? He was a real pussy, a loser who knew it, who was probably pissing his pants right now just thinking about what will happen to him when he finally meets the man! The mystery of where Jesus was haunted Satan to no end. He was sick of the little games and the relationships that Jesus was building up with these no bodies. "Where the hell is he", he screamed. I want him for my dessert and a little fun and games so the whole world can see how this pathetic soul is going to kiss my feet and beg for my mercy.

Through a pure coincidence a couple of his goons had stopped at a small service station in Attleboro, Massachusetts and were filling up their tank when they noticed a minister pull up to the gas pump next to them and get out of his beat up ford pickup truck. He wasn't much to look at an average looking guy, but what stood out were that white collar and that cross that hung around his neck. It was the cross that caused the one pumping gas to overfill his tank allowing the gasoline to seep all over the ground and on to his pants and shoes. While the other called his buddy a frigging idiot and retard, the one that had pumped the gas drew attention to the cross around the minister's neck. It was the same cross that Satan told them to watch out for and report back to him immediately if they came across anyone wearing one.

As the minister walked to the service station attendant to pay for his gas in cash, one of the men stepped in front of him and blocked his way. He told him that he was new to the area and whether he knew of a good place to stay for the night? The pastor said sure, check out Old Maggie's bed and breakfast just off of Main Street; she will put you up for the night at a reasonable cost with one of the best breakfasts in town. The man thanked him and said, "By the way, my name is Paul but my friends call me pappy. The pastor reached out his hand to shake it and said, "I am Pastor John Lincoln and my friends call me Abe". Pappy smiled and said it was nice to meet him. He then turned to his buddy who was still trying to wipe the gasoline from his clothes and said that his name is Razor but don't let the name scare you. He got it from always cutting his face while shaving and he would walk around with small pieces of toilet paper clinging to his face until he remembered to remove them. The pastor smiled and waved a hello to Razor who gave a quick wave of his hand and returned to his business of trying to stop smelling like a gas pump. Before he could walk away Pappy turned to him and asked him if he was the only minister in town. The pastor told him that he was the only Catholic minister and his chapel was at the edge of town on the road northbound to Boston. Pappy told him they might stop by to see him before they leave and thanked him for his hospitality.

Pappy immediately got on his cell phone and called Satan and informed him of the pastor that they happened across in Attleboro. When he mentioned the cross Satan was ecstatic. Jesus had been in the New England area and he told Pappy to spend a little social time with the pastor and find out where he is or where he went. He then told Pappy to use wherever persuasion necessary to get the information and then show your thanks by slitting his throat and throwing him on the altar at the church so the towns folk could get a bird's eye view of his dead, religious, body. With that he hung up the phone and waited for the return call so he could give Jesus an unexpected visit.

Pappy watched the pastor drive off towards the chapel and followed him down the road. As he pulled into the small driveway that led to a house behind the chapel, he turned to Razor and said "No time like the present". They waited until he opened the front door of the house and went inside. They pulled their car behind a clump of trees off the road and out of sight. They scurried quickly to get out of sight from anyone who could be passing by but Razor slipped on a small patch of ice and fell on his ass with a large thump. Holding his back he started to complain to Pappy and he was quickly told to shut his frigging mouth. Did he want to just use a bull horn and let the pastor know they were outside? He told him to get off his ass and get moving or he would be answering directly to Satan on how he screwed this up.

The pastor was in the kitchen preparing dinner and had not heard the commotion outside. As the two goons reached the front door Pappy slowly turned the door knob and was relieved that it was unlocked. These New Englanders are so trusting he thought to himself. Some day they will learn that everyone does not want to be their bosom buddies. As Pappy swung the door open and they both stepped inside they saw the kitchen light on and the shuffling of pots and pans as if he was preparing to make a meal. Razor turned to Pappy and told him that their timing was perfect as he was hungry and maybe they would be able to share the dinner table with the pastor. It was almost like a scene from the three stooges as Pappy simply slapped him across the face and called him an idiot—again.

As they walked across the room each reached for a gun that was kept in the waist line of their pants. They entered the kitchen and told the pastor that he had some guests for dinner and they hoped he didn't mind their unexpected visit on such a short notice? The pastor turned to face them and saw the guns in their hands and told them that it was really not necessary and they were welcome in his home.

Pappy just smiled at him and told him that he appreciated his kind words and hospitality but the guns were necessary and he would surely understand in a few minutes. Pappy told him to sit down at the table to have a short discussion and perhaps they could get through the problem fairly quickly and be on their way. The pastor sat down as Pappy pulled up a seat directly across from him. Without beating around the bush, Pappy told him that they were looking for a friend of his and all he had to tell them was where he was and they would simply go away. As Pappy talked the pastor noticed his eyes continue to wander down to the cross hanging around his neck and it was at that moment he knew who they were looking for. The good news is that he had no idea where Jesus had gone but the bad news was that he doubted that these two thugs would believe him.

As the pastor sat there in silence Pappy told him that he knew who he was asking about; the same guy who gave you that cross hanging around your frigging scrawny neck. Now before I take that chain and start choking the life of your measly body tell me where he is. The pastor just looked at Pappy sitting across from him and Razor standing next to the stove watching the small piece of steak simmer in the fry pan. The pastor told him he didn't know where he was and even if he did know he would never tell him.

Pappy reached across the table and with the butt end of the gun smashed it across the mouth of the pastor immediately drawing blood and knocking him to the floor. Then it struck him—what Jesus had told him just before he left. He told the pastor that no serious harm would come his way as long as Jesus was alive. As he wiped the blood from his mouth on to his shirt sleeve, he saw Pappy getting up from his chair and pointing the gun at his foot as if to send another message that he was not going to mess around with him for the information. But as he aimed the gun the pastor grabbed the leg of Razor who was standing next to the stove. Razor had just grabbed the handle of the frying pan and was preparing to remove it from the stove when the tugging on his pants leg caused him to lose his balance and the hot grease from the pan spilled on to his clothes. Some of the grease also spattered into the gas fired flame and created an immediate flash of fire and heat shooting forward. It was at that split second that both Razor and Pappy realized that Razor still was wearing his gasoline soaked pants and shirt and within seconds they burst into a fireball of flames.

Initially it looked like he was doing some sort of a crazy dance but his screams indicated a whole different problem. He cried out for help and looked in the direction of Pappy but all he did was to step further away from him and made no attempt to try to contain the growing fire. It was at that instant when it hit Razor; all the nasty comments about him being an idiot, a retard, a moron from Pappy that he knew no help was coming his way. He had reached the absolute breaking point. Without hesitation he reached for the gun still clinging in the belt line of his burning pants, aimed it at Pappy and unloaded six rounds into his body before he fell to the floor in flames.

The pastor turned to look in Pappy's direction and saw him sprawled on the floor against the far wall with blood oozing from various bullet holes in his body. The pastor quickly jumped to his feet and ran to the cabinet that was next to the stove and pulled out a small fire extinguisher, released the pin and sprayed Razor with the powdery substance. As the chemical settled on his body the flames were extinguished and the pastor leaned down next to him to access the damage. What was left of his shirt and pants were just pieces of burnt cloth imbedded into his charred flesh. His face was blistered with severe burns and already his chest, legs and arms were turning a charcoal black indicating third degree burns. He was in extreme pain and the pastor knew that he was well beyond any possibility of living much longer.

Razor was lying face up on the floor and managed to realize that the pastor had tried to help him by putting out the fire and with all the energy that he could possibly muster reached out his left hand and touched the pastor's knee. As he gashed for breathe he thanked the pastor for trying to help him and asked him to say a prayer for him. He told him that he was afraid of dying and didn't want to go to hell and begged the pastor to help him. His exposure to the pain and suffering that he just experienced was unbearable and to even think of that for all of eternity terrified him. Just as he was about to beg for forgiveness his eyes rolled over in his head and he was gone. It was at that point that the pastor knew that Jesus had no intention in allowing Razor the opportunity to repent for his years and years of sin and evil because he didn't want to suffer the consequences. It was far too late for that and he would not have an opportunity to reach out for salvation. He was on his way to his resting place and there would no stopping him until he arrived at the gates of hell.

The pastor sat back down on the floor trying to figure out what just happened in the last few minutes. It was a whirl wind of activity and terror and, yet, he was the only one alive of the three in the room. Sure his mouth was bloodied but he came through the ordeal just fine. Was it a series of events, almost comical when you think about it, something out of some class b crime drama? But the events were far too calculated to be a series of mishaps as they resulted with both men planning to take his life dead on the floor. It was then that he remembered the promise from Jesus. No major harm will come to you while I am alive. The two dead men on the floor paid dearly for their attempt to take his life. Although the pastor thought that the situation could have been handled a little differently; he, also, knew that Jesus was sending Satan a loud and strong message that it was time to fight back. If violence was necessary he was not afraid to use it and to send any of his rival's flock straight to their rightful place in hell. As the pastor rose to his feet, he squeezed the cross hanging around his neck and said thank you lord for watching over me. With that he reached for the phone hanging next to the door and called 911 to report the house invasion by two strangers. It was just a small sign of the things to come.

Chapter thirty two

Talking with Satan

Satan grew impatient with not hearing back from Pappy and he finally decided to call his cell phone to find out what the hell was going on. As the phone rang he waited for Pappy to answer so he could rip him a "new asshole" so to speak for not giving him any sort of feedback on the pastor's cooperation or lack thereof. He also wanted to know if the pastor was now resting on his chapel's altar bleeding like a stuffed pig.

Finally the ringing stopped and he heard someone on the other end of the line apparently trying to pick up the call. Satan shouted, "Where the hell have you been and who the hell do you think you are in keeping me waiting so long for an update?" "Did you forget who the fuck you are dealing with?"

The response on the other end of the phone was totally unexpected, as the person told him to go fuck himself. The voice wasn't Pappy's or Razor's; it was a voice that he did not recognize and the tone made him realize that he wasn't a favorite of the person talking with him. Satan thought about quickly hanging up but his curiosity got the better of him. He figured he would play along for a few minutes to get a better idea of what happened to the two clowns he sent to do a man's job.

The man said that he truly needed to improve his verbal skills and it was certainty apparent that he needed to brush up on his behavioral techniques when dealing with others when you want some help. Satan answered back by saying who the fuck are you to talk to me like that? I want to know where the man who owns this phone is and if he is there with you playing a fucking joke on me I don't think it is very funny. Now put him on this call now you fucking moron.

The voice continued to harass him by telling him he now knew how Pappy picked up his extremely poor choice of his vocabulary by using such words as moron, idiot, and retard. It was from you; you pathetic thing. Satan wanted to reach through that phone and let his hand come out the other side and rip the man's tongue right out of his head. He was so pissed that he couldn't think straight. Again he asked to speak to Pappy or tell him where he is. The voice on the other end of the phone said," Now that was much better, no cuss words this time, and I do know and I will tell you right now".

Needless to say it was the pastor who had found Pappy's phone in his pocket and "borrowed" it before the police arrived at his home. He knew it could potentially help Jesus locate where Satan was and to lead him to his arch enemy. Without further hesitation the pastor told him that Pappy was dead and he was shot by someone named Razor. Satan hearing the news went crazy. What the hell do you mean he was shot by Razor and how is that possible? The pastor told him that Razor had an accident, crazy as it may seem, as he caught himself on fire while standing next to a lit gas stove with clothes soaked in gasoline. A little spark and puff he turned into a toasty marshmallow and shot Pappy six times because he wouldn't help him. Both of them are dead and probably waiting at the gates of the place where you call home right now, why don't you go check?

Satan couldn't take it any longer and asked again who the fuck was on the phone. The pastor replied, "Why it is me, Pastor John Lincoln, my friends call me Abe, but since you certainty are not my friend you can call me Pastor Lincoln." There was dead silence at the other end of the phone as Satan tried to determine how the hell did everything go so wrong when the pastor asked him if the cat had his tongue? Before he could even reply the pastor told him that he did not have a chance, not even the tiniest, to overcome the power of Jesus so why don't you just crawl back to that slimy hole that you call home and melt away?

The pastor had managed to say and antagonize Satan more than any living person has done in centuries. Satan was going absolutely berserk on the other end of the phone as the pastor could hear him throwing things around the room, glass breaking and furniture being smashed to pieces. Satan actually started to stutter as he tried to response to the onslaught of the pastor.

Satan tried to regain his composure and tried to spit out a rapid reply. He said, "When when when I I get get my handssssssss on you youuuuuuuu won't be singing the sameeeeeeeeeee song you are now now now you little weasel." To further infuriate him the pastor just laughed again and told him he needed to calm down or he would have a stroke.

The pastor had accomplished his goals. Throughout the call he watched and wrote down the cell phone number and he was very close friends with a state police officer who could utilize his resources to locate where the call generated from. He was also extremely proud of himself for his verbal exchange with Satan. He would say a few Hail Mary's at the chapel tonight for his use of profanity during the call but it comforted him to know that he got under the skin of the man who tried to kill him. Jeez he thought he never even met me and he tried to kill me, now that just isn't right is it?

Before the pastor hung up on Satan he told him that Jesus sends his regards and he hopes to see him real soon. He told Satan next time why don't you come up here to do your own dirty work instead of sending your best enforcers—they were your best, weren't they—to kill me? Hey that is another problem for you, old boy, if they were your best you are really hurting aren't you? Come on up and we can have a last drink together before Jesus sends you back to hell forever you frigging nobody. The pastor was hoping that Satan would become so insane with rage that he would make some sort of comment to him that he would take him up on the challenge but he remained silent on the other end of the phone. At first the pastor thought that he had hung up but then he heard a little rustling as if he was moving around, as if pacing back and forth.

Finally a reply came through the receiver and the voice had changed. The tone, the wildness, the insanity of it became a voice of calmness, clearness and evil. Satan told him that the pastor had his fun and he, in some strange way, actually appreciated the fact that he managed to really piss him off. He told the pastor that he didn't have time to come see him personally right now to settle the score but he was certainty high on his priority list to deal with in the near future. He told him that you got your jollies off now but I will get them off later and you can take that to the bank. Satan ended the conversation by telling the pastor to inform his buddy that he is ready for him and has been for some time. By the way instead of screwing around with that cell number you have written down to trace me why don't you just tell him to meet me at the National Cathedral in Washington, DC on New Year's Eve. What better way to ring in the New Year than to brighten everyone's future knowing that I will be the sole master as the clock strikes twelve. He ended the conversation by telling the pastor to go fuck himself.

Pastor Lincoln had no idea where Jesus has gone and when he would contact him again. Yet he had this valuable information for him that could lead to an eventual end to the eternal struggle for mankind. How do I contact him, how do I let him prepare for a conflict only two days away? He sat there in the kitchen in the same chair that he sat in when Pappy struck him across the face with the gun and knocked him to the floor. He knew he was alive because of Jesus and his promise to keep him alive as long as he himself was. As he looked down at his hands that were clasped together as if in prayer he saw the cross dangling from his neck softly beating in sequence with Christ's heart. The thought struck him like a thunderbolt and he knew that Jesus was aware of the two goons breaking into his home because of the cross. It was serving not only as a constant reminder that Jesus was still alive but also a watching eye to protect him from any danger. He had to be right he thought to himself. Jesus not only was witness to everything that happened with Pappy and Razor but he also saw and heard everything discussed with Satan himself. It was not as if Jesus was watching his every move or invading his total privacy, it was when he was exposed to potential danger and harm when the mechanism kicked into full gear. When Satan called the cell number the cross automatically picked up the presence of evil and Jesus had seen and heard it all. There was no need to worry himself to death about contacting Jesus he heard every word. As he gently grabbed the cross in his right hand and stared at it, the cross immediately sparkled like a star in the night sky.

It was Jesus' sign to the pastor that he didn't have to worry he had got the news he needed. With that the pastor left his house and opened the door to the small chapel. He decided it was time to say those Hail Mary's that he promised that he would do to repent for his bout with Satan, but, also, more importantly—to pray for the safety of Jesus in his meeting with Satan on New Year's Eve.

Chapter thirty three

Jesus plans

Jesus had decisions, key decisions, that must be completed within the next few days. They had to be the right ones as the destiny of mankind rested on their outcome. He had grown weary from the endless chain of events and even his perseverance and stamina was being challenged. He had slept very little and those hours were filled with a continuous bombardment of thoughts that would not allow him a minute of peace. In addition his every waking thought centered on the upcoming conflict and whether he could defeat the master of disaster.

As he focused on the various plans that he had laid out in front of him as if he were an army general preparing for his unit's upcoming battle; he tried to determine if there was one way, one plan, one simple maneuver that he could take that would prevent a catastrophic incident that would cause thousands of innocent people to die.

He wanted this conflict to exist between just him and Satan, but he also realized that Satan wanted to demonstrate his power and abilities to everyone willing to watch or even participate. Satan had no desire to stand in a dusty street in the middle of town and try to outdraw the other before falling dead to the ground. His intentions were obvious and he would do everything possible to gather all his supporters in Washington to celebrate the victory in some wild orgy in the streets of the capital.

So all of Satan's followers would be there in one place to demonstrate their might and power as their leader would destroy the one person in their way. The mighty stand strong and in unity until they suddenly realize that things aren't exactly how they seem. When reality hits them in the face it can send up a wakeup call far beyond anyone's wildest imagination. The key result is that, sometimes, it is over before it can even start and that is where Jesus decided to place all his hopes and prayers. To personally deliver a message to all of the evil ones at the same time that it is over. There would be no mistaking the conclusion only that the victor was whom they did not expect and all is lost.

Jesus knew that Satan was contacting his goons; it was the way he operated. He not only wanted to be the victor but he wanted to bring in the New Year in style. He wanted all the do gooders to know what fear is really like and he would plan events and celebrations around using them as pawns in his games. The world would then know that it would never be the same and any hope was last forever in the true sense of the word.

Jesus called on his small, but effective, team to send out the word that judgment day was set for New Year's Eve. Spread the word and let the world know the location and time so that it would be remembered forever; etched in stone as the Ten Commandments so no one will ever forget!

Within hours of contacting his team the news spread as a wild fire on a dry and parched forest about New Year's Eve. It was called "The Day of reckoning" in the major newspapers and the outpouring of support for Jesus was overwhelming. Candle light services were being held around the clock across the globe in support of him. World leaders sent messages of support and stood in front of masses of people as they held hands and prayed for his victory against evil. In Washington, people were already staking out spots for them to sit and support him as the clocked ticked forward. With each passing hour he was gathering support faster than a presidential election for the front running candidate. Millions and millions of people were making plans to gather at holy sites to include churches, chapels, cathedrals, fields and arenas to show their dedication to the one man that could end evil forever. The demonstration of support was an uplifting experience; something that was never before been witnessed as far as worldwide belief in a single individual to make things better.

Chapter thirty four

The day of reckoning

Initially Satan was pleased that the news leaked as he wanted the world to see that poor, pathetic soul beg for mercy. He wanted the cameras focused on his own face to show the gratification he received with the destruction and humiliation of Jesus in front of the world! It would be at that very moment they would come to realize that every single one of their pathetic bodies and souls belong to him. He wanted to make them puke at the very sight of Jesus being slowly put to death in the most unimaginable ways possible. Yet, it, also, troubled him that he would be equally exposed to the world under the same scrutiny. It bothered him that—should the unimaginable happen—if he lost he would be on full exhibit to all in the final moments of his existence. The bottom line was that "To the victor goes the spoils" and he had to be the one standing at the end—then everything was his and he grew hard just thinking about it.

Jesus had not eaten for nearly two days, spending much of his time praying and meditating on the final conflict. He was not praying for himself but for mankind and the eventual end of evil forever. Jesus could just imagine the tranquility and positive impact on the world without the presence of evil. Man could center all their attention to helping others, finding cures for deadly diseases, and creating a worldwide culture that thrived on making it a better world for all living creatures.

As Jesus mediated he also realized that the outcome would not be one that everyone will understand or even expect. He wanted, so much, to be able to participate in the new world and to join hands and hearts with those who maintained their faith throughout their darkness moments. He knew the repercussions of his plan and the utter disbelief of those that it will affect. He had thoroughly analyzed every option available and knew of only one that had a chance of defeating Satan forever. He placed his head in his hands and cried. Here was a man who had already given his life once preparing to give it a final time and it was an overwhelming emotional roller coaster that he couldn't get off.

When he approached God and laid out the various scenarios he listened carefully to his son and was deeply moved with his preparation and determination to be the ultimate winner. Yet when Jesus presented the one option that he truly believed would be the one determining factor that would lead to Stan's destruction he rejected the idea. Just as a grieving father who has just summoned to a local hospital because his son had been critically injured in a horrific car accident; God listened to the soft and caring words of his son; knowing that his remaining time with him was too short to even imagine. The agony was too much to bear and that night the skies rained his tears around the world for a son that he may be losing forever.

So the day of reckoning arrived. The entire world centered their attention on the one city in the world that mattered this New Year's Eve—Washington, DC. The police had already blocked off any access to the Cathedral area. The streets were already overflowing with people who had been camped there for days awaiting his moment. Helicopters coned the skies as spot lights lit the building from every possible angle. News cameras were everywhere. The president, himself, was securely entrenched in the White House surrounded by federal agents swore to protect him to their dying breath. As he paced his office and peered out his Oval office window he also said a silent prayer that good will overcome evil tonight and he would help to be one of the world leaders to step forward and lead the change to a better world. As he stood there he reached out and took his wife's hand and pulled her close to him and gently kissed her on her cheek. She placed her arms around his shoulders and hugged him, hugged him as if it was the last time that she ever would see him again and told him how much she loved him. As Patrick Swayze in the movie "Ghost" said to Demi Moore, the president simply replied, "ditto" and lifted her off her feet as he drew her close to his body. The clock was inching closer to midnight and with that the first participant arrived on scene and it was not who the majority of the people wanted to see.

As if some sort of magical act Satan appeared on the concrete steps of the large cathedral with his arms raised to the sky. He was completely dressed in black—what else could you expect—and had some sort of a long pole in his right hand. At first the crowd was stunned with his sudden appearance and simply stared at the figure of pure evil standing in front of them. Then like a crowd at a professional wrestling match the majority of the crowd started to boo, loudly and nonstop. If you did not truly understand the potential devastating consequences of the conflict you would have laughed at the crowd's reaction. The bad guy arriving first on the scene to rile everyone up and then standing off to the side for the great entrance of the good guy strolling in to strike the killing blow for life, liberty and the pursue of happiness. But this was reality and the mass display of hatred portrayed by the people was as real as that nose on your face. The most surprising factor in all of this is that Satan stood there and seemed to enjoy every hiss and boo directed his way. The noise was deafening and nonstop.

It seemed as if it would be an impossible task to stop the demonstration when Satan took that long rod and raised it to the sky. Suddenly without warning a large flash of lightening shot from the end and bolted into the night sky again and again. With it the sound of rolling thunder could be heard generating in the distance and growing closer and closer with each passing minute. The display quickly silenced the crowd and Satan lowered his staff to his side and peered out at the thousands standing before him. The anger and rage that he felt at that moment created a storm of obscenities flowing from his mouth that frightened even the most fearless man standing there. His mouth spit out every foul word known to man and probably some that they didn't know existed. He called them all mother fuckers and motherless bastards and bitches deserving of their pending faith. He called them all sons and daughters of whores who would be willing to sell their souls for a second of relief from the pain and suffering that they would be enduring very shortly. He told each and every person that they would regret their pitiful display of disrespect and he wouldn't shred a drop of his piss to put out the burning fire that will engulf each and every one of them for all of eternity. He told them they would regret their fucking actions as they watch their children pay the price for every second that they booed him in their one opportunity to try to intimidate him. It was a fucking joke he told them and it demonstrated to him that the world deserved a true wakeup call. They had wasted so many opportunities in the past that he lost count; blew them like they were a common whore on the street. Now it was too late and they will surely understand that—right to their dying breathe.

The crowd remained silent as they listened to every word that he spilled out of his filthy mouth. It was at that moment that they realized that this truly was not a game and their fate truly lay in the balance of the pending struggle between Satan and Jesus.

As Satan stood there he looked around at the mass of people and smiled. He smiled because he knew that he struck fear into the hearts and souls of everyone standing there. He yelled out "What does the cat have your fucking tongues? I don't hear any more fucking noise; but that is ok because you will be making more than enough fucking noise while your soul burns in hell". He then asked the crowd where the fuck was Jesus anyway. Let's get this ball rolling; it's fucking New Year's Eve in a few minutes.

Chapter thirty five

Jesus appears

Just as Satan completed his gruesome display a bright light began to hover over the top of the stairs of the cathedral. Initially it stayed in a stationary position but slowly shined brighter and brighter as it lowered itself into position at the top landing. As people watched in wonder the light began to take the shape of a man; a man with his arms raised towards the night sky. As the glowing light faded away, there stood Jesus dressed in a white flowing cloth robe, wearing sandals and carrying nothing more than an old metal cross in his right hand.

What was strange was that the crowd did not react to his appearance. Initially it was eerie that so many people stood in silence as if they were in awe that they were actually witnessing the arrival of someone that they had just read about but never thought that they would actually see when they were still alive and breathing. There was no shouting or screaming in support of him. There neither was any screams or shouts from grown men and women to kick Satan's ass. It seemed as if Satan's short speech was a true wakeup call that this was no staged event that people could watch, enjoy, talk about over dinner and drinks later, and go to bed. This was something that would affect every living thing forever.

As Jesus stood there he, also, looked out at the masses of people standing before him and Satan. The thing that stood out most was the fear in their eyes and the hope that he would, in some way, defeat Satan on this night that would change the course of history forever. He thought back to an event centuries before when he saw that same look and despair. As he hung on that cross he saw the same defended look on the people who had hoped and prayed that some way he would break free of those nails embedded in his hands, jump down from that cross and show the world that a messiah would lead them to the promised land. But when he died on that cross many had lost faith in their belief that he was truly the son of God and openly voiced their bitterness over him being a fraud that got what he deserved. It wasn't until days later when the soldiers found the huge stone moved from the front of his cave that contained his body that they began to believe in him again. He was saddened with the recalling of the events. He was equally affected now by the overwhelming sense of despair and doom being projected by many in the crowd and this caused him tremendous sorrow.

What will it take for mankind to realize that change is an uncompromising necessary and destiny rested in their hands? Each and every day they are all witness to the struggle of good and evil around them. So much evil existed in today's world and yet in many ways it was tolerated as an element of society. So the news continued to be filled with reports about serial killers, child molesters, crooked bankers, politicians, lawyers and judges. These bloodsuckers were allowed to fester as an unstoppable cancer growth existing in today's society. There was still hope as for every one of the evil ones exist an opposite of goodness. There were the missionaries who help fight hunger and illness in third world countries, volunteers who reach out and touch those affected by natural disasters, nurses and doctors, mothers and fathers, and sons and daughters who could always be counted on to do the right things in helping others. The scales were evenly balanced thus creating this final struggle to determine the ultimate winner.

Jesus looked down at Satan and then scanned the crowd. Without wasting another moment he spoke to the crowd. In a memorizing voice he told them that he prayed that each and every person watching this understood their involvement. He told them that century after century he had watched hoping that eventually goodness would win out over evil and yet it never occurred. Jesus said that the key element that many people misunderstood was the fact that their life span on earth was but a brief second when compared to the amount of time that they would spend in eternity. It isn't until they take that last dying breath that they realize the massive mistake that they made in using their precious time on earth to build an eternity in heaven. The key message today is that one man, regardless of who he is, will not make a difference.

When he died on the cross thousands of years ago he knew that one man would not be able to make a difference. If he truly had make an impact he said, there would be no need to be standing there today trying to send the same message to those who could truly make a difference—each and every one of you! So, I stand here again and in me your hopes and prayers that I will come out the victor and make everything better again. Yet as much as I want to believe that I will truly make the difference this time I know in my heart that this will not be the case. My heart and soul break knowing that it is probably human nature to return to the same ways that existed before this night began. Each of you will wept and repent for your sins and promise to personally change those things wrong in your lives but it will probably be short lived. You will see my pain and suffering through this ordeal but you will not have felt it. Until that evil hits home and one is inflicted with such sorrow and grief do they realize that they must, somehow, stand up and be counted? It is not until the rich man suffers like a poor, or a healthy man suffers as an ill, or an intelligent man experiences the embarrassment of a dumb do we realize that things must change to help everyone. It is then when our eyes are opened and we can see things as they really are. So I stand before the masses one final time and ask you all whether this final stand will make the difference or do I die a second time for nothing? The only difference is that if Satan defeats me you will lose any opportunity to rectify all the wrongs in the world today. With one final warning Jesus turned to the crowd and said that each person around the world will truly understand that it takes personal loss and commitment to change things. This time each one of you must feel the same pain and suffering that I will feel in this struggle. Hopefully it will be the final wakeup call that evil cannot exist as a daily partner with good. With that he bowed his head in silent prayer.

The crowd listened intently; many were so emotionally drained with Jesus' words that they had fallen to their knees in prayer. As they listened around the world the reality of the situation struck the hearts of everyone. The true answer to the lingering question was whether they would finally cease this opportunity and do the right thing?

Chapter thirty six

Judgment Day

It was then that Satan shouted out, "Enough of this bull shit". Each and every one of you pathetic creatures made your bed and now you can sleep in the crap that you created. I have waited for centuries for this moment and your destiny will be held in my hands in a few short moments and you will not like it one fucking bit. I am the Supreme Being, I am king, and I am your fucking worse nightmare.

With that he looked up the stairs at Jesus who was standing approximately ten feet above him. As if sizing him up for the kill, he carefully studied him from his feet to his head. What amazed Satan was that he held nothing in his hand but that damn old metal cross. He was totally defenseless and Satan grew in confidence with each passing moment. Satan thought to himself what an easy mark standing there as if he is ready to give another frigging sermon to the crowd. Satan mumbled under his breath, "Words, nothing but words, and words would certainty not bring me to my knees". Satan knew that he would strike the first blow and bring this to a fast and satisfying climax in front of the entire world. What should I do to him first—bring him to his knees with a solid strike to his stomach or simply go for his juggler and allow his religious blood to spray over anyone standing near?

As Jesus lifted his head; Satan attacked. In one gigantic leap he was standing next to Jesus with his hands grasped around his neck. Satan had decided to show the world that he did not have to use any of his massive power to destroy him. A simple choke hold from the master of disaster would bring Mr. Goody Good Shoes to his knees he thought. As he squeezed Jesus' neck he couldn't help to imagine the future and how he actually felt a little pity for the millions watching him squeeze the life out of Jesus. They all would be his and each and every one of them would wallow in fear at his feet for eternity. He smiled at the very thought.

He then diverted his attention back to Jesus as he wanted to see his bulging eyes and red face as he tried to gather one final breath of fresh air into his deflating lungs. But as he looked into Jesus' eyes he did not see fear or any sign of a dying man. Instead he was immediately frightened with what he saw and he tried to release his hands from his throat but couldn't—it was like they were welded to Jesus' body. He panicked and tried to comprehend what the hell was going on. Jesus had not made any attempt to reach out and cause him bodily harm yet stood there peering into his eyes unafraid and at peace with himself.

Satan could do nothing but stare back at Jesus. As he studied his face he realized that he had made a tactical error in totally misjudging his opponent. There was no way possible that he could have defeated him in such a conflict and he realized it at that moment. But he also realized that Jesus may have underestimated him as well as he would not go down easily. Satan tried to figure out Jesus' next move and braced himself for any sudden action from his arch enemy. Jesus just stood there perfectly still studying the body of pure evil standing in front of him. He found it unimaginable that a person, spirit, soul could take so much pleasure in the suffering of others. As he looked into the red, glowing, eyes of Satan he knew that he was well beyond any possibility of redemption and needed to be destroyed.

From the crowd's reaction it appeared that Satan was choking Jesus to death and Jesus was standing there helplessly as his life slowly drained from his body. Women were crying and men holding their loved ones in their arms as they prepared themselves for their faith with Satan. As the cameras zoomed in things were not as they originally seemed. Jesus was standing there with his arms by his sides but he was not suffering or exhibiting any sign of pain. He was simply staring directly into Satan's eyes and sending a visual message that he would not be that easy to kill.

It was at that moment that Jesus looked to the heavens and said, "God, my father, I will miss you so and I thank you for allowing me to do what must be done". I realize the sadness that this brings to you and to everyone in the world at this time, but we cannot conquer evil unless all realize this will end only with everyone's support. Please pray for me in this moment of need. Amen".

With that Jesus lifted his right hand that held that old metal cross. It was not until that moment that the world understood its meaning or importance. As he slowly lifted it the cross started to glow an emerald green—a green so beautiful—that it resembled the majestic color of endless meadows stretching for miles on a quiet summer afternoon. Jesus held it high over his head and said, "For the salvation of mankind we give our lives and souls to end evil in this world today".

As he completed the words he took the cross and shoved it directly into the mouth of Satan who stood there hypnotized by what he was witnessing. At that instant the world knew what the cross represented and with it they knew the consequences of their selfish behavior century after century. Once the cross was inserted into Satan's mouth he disintegrated into thousands of small particles that briefly hung in the air and then slowly drifted away in the winter night. The world was cleansed of him and all of his demons but the price in accomplishing this feat was tremendous.

For a few brief seconds Jesus stood there peering out at the thousandths who had gathered to watch this spectacle unfold before their very eyes. Then in a flash, as brilliant as a thousand stars illuminating the night sky, he also disintegrated into thousands of bright sparkling small particles. They hung briefly in mid air before slowly growing dim and disappearing. They were to represent just a lasting memory of the overwhelming cost to give mankind one more chance.

As his body disappeared everyone understood how Jesus pulled off this miracle and eliminated evil from the world. Jesus had committed the souls of every person in heaven to destroy Satan; it took every one of them to create enough spiritual goodness to destroy him and his followers forever. Earth was purged and had one last opportunity to do the right things for all. But the price was high, much higher than anyone ever expected. Each person around the world saw flashes of their loved ones who had passed away before their eyes. Each face smiled at them and then disappeared only to be replaced by another. To some it seemed like the faces appeared to them over a period of fifteen minutes but, in reality, it was less than fifteen seconds. They managed to see vivid imagines of their close friends, brothers, sisters, mothers and fathers, sons and daughters disappear and leave their home in heaven forever. This was the cost that each person around the world paid for their final opportunity to start a new beginning in a world cleansed of evil.

As the reality hit home to the millions world wide the overall joy felt with the death of Satan was minuscule when compared to the sorrow experienced with the loss of Jesus and their loved ones forever. The sadness shook the very minds and souls of everyone and the impact of this night would be felt by all in the centuries to come.

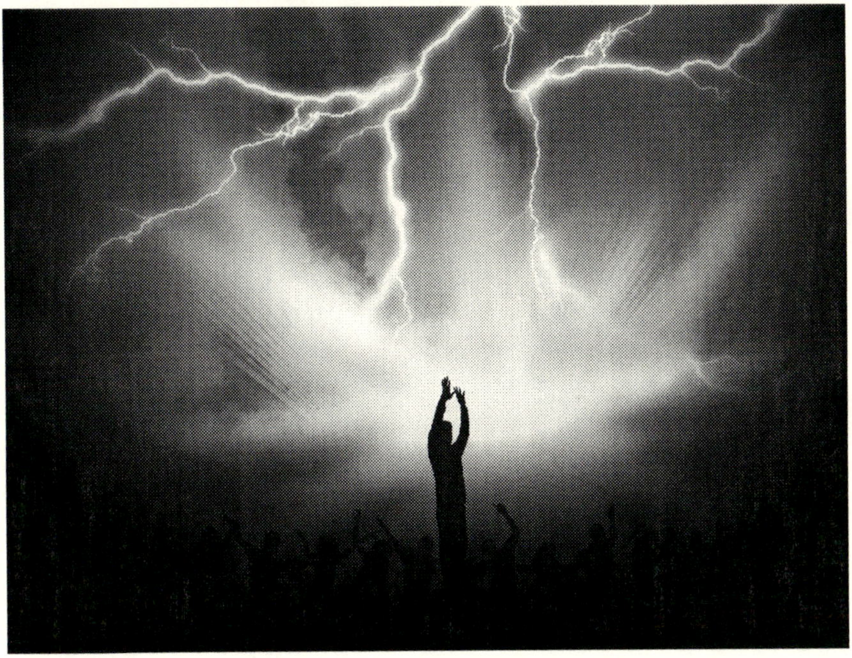

Chapter thirty seven

The cost of redemption

So it came to pass on that final judgment day that the price of redemption was high and the sadness overwhelming when everyone realized that they would never see their deceased loved ones again in heaven. Now they understood what Jesus had meant when he told them that they all needed to share in the pain and suffering to truly understand that they can be the only ones to end this eternal conflict forever. Each one of them had lost their ability to reach out and eventually touch those that they had shared so many by gone memories. For the true religious believers in the afterlife and existence of heaven and hell it was a devastating revelation and difficult to comprehend. All of those years believing that when it came their time they would be joining their loved ones was shattered. It torn the hearts out of those who anguished the loss of a loved one only to realize that they will only be a memory. For the fence sitters who were never swayed one way or the other the reality hit home even more. They now realized that they did have an opportunity to be in the presence of their deceased loved ones again but it was extinguished as one blowing out a candle. People around the world cried and prayed for forgiveness in their inability to take a united stand before it came to this.

High in the heavens God sat alone for the first time in his existence and wondered if the death of his son for a second time would make the difference. He had a difficult time agreeing with his son's plan to defeat evil and prayed many a nights to have the strength to support the loss of all those souls that were resting peacefully in heaven. It wasn't until the night where Jesus laid out his plan to heaven's residents did God understood that it was the right thing to do. Every man, women and child supported Jesus and stepped forward in his defense. It was then when God agreed and the end of evil was an uncompromising reality.

So God sat there, alone, in a place where only the righteous had earned a spot. He sat there and cried. He cried for all those who gave their souls on this final judgment day but he wept tears of sorrow for his innocent son who died a second time in the hope that man could finally learn from their past mistakes. His tears fell from the heavens as millions of white raindrops, as pure as a snowflake, but representing the purity of the souls of those who left their home in heaven to wipe out evil.

As God felt the utter loneliness of heaven with the sacrifice of all those souls he wiped the tears from his eyes and prayed that mankind would not blow another opportunity to make a better world.

With that he closed the gates of heaven and would wait for the true results of his son's loss to filter in before deciding whether he would ever open them again.